To Barbara,
for a mystery
addict and
the creative
fire before
bright Nil

A Deadly Draught

by

Lesley A. Diehl

Mainly Murder Press, LLC
PO Box 290586
Wethersfield, CT 06109-0586
www.mainlymurderpress.com

Mainly Murder Press

Copy Editor: Jennafer Sprankle
Executive Editor: Judith K. Ivie
Cover Designer: Patricia L. Foltz

All rights reserved

Names, characters and incidents depicted in this book are products of the author's imagination or are used fictitiously. Any resemblance to actual events, organizations, or persons, living or dead, is entirely coincidental and beyond the intent of the author or the publisher.

No part of this book may be reproduced or transmitted in any form or by any means, electronic or mechanical, including photocopying, recording, or by any information storage and retrieval system, without permission in writing from the publisher.

Mainly Murder Press
www.mainlymurderpress.com

Copyright © 2010 by Lesley A. Diehl
ISBN 978-0-9825899-2-2

Published in the United States of America

2010

Mainly Murder Press
PO Box 290586
Wethersfield, CT 06109-0586

For my cowboy

Acknowledgments

I am a beer drinker, not a beer brewer, so I want to recognize the people who contributed to the information on microbrewing that went into creating this book. Any mistakes are solely mine. My thanks to Ed Canty, Partner at Orlando Brewing and founder of the Florida Brewers Guild, who kindly and patiently answered every question I asked about making hand-crafted brews and never even hinted a question was stupid (although I truly believe many were); to Fran Andrewlevich, Brew Master at Brewzzi at City Place, West Palm, the first brewing guru who allowed me to pick his brain (and what a brain it was); to Randy Thiel, previously with Ommegang Brewery in Cooperstown, New York, now Director of Quality Control at New Glarus Brewing Company in Wisconsin, who taught me how special ales can be; and to Chuck Williamson, Owner/Operator of Butternuts Beer and Ale, a city boy now settled in upstate New York, growing hops on his land and enjoying life as a brewer right down the road from me (convenient when I want good beer!).

I cannot forget the support and input of several writers also: Jan Day, creator of children's books and my critique partner without whose eye my writing would suffer greatly; Deb Sharp, author of several humorous books set in what I consider my second home, rural Florida, whose unflagging energy inspires and exhausts me.

And of course, the person who first encouraged me to write, my partner, Glenn. He saw something in my work and said others would, too.

Lesley A. Diehl

One

The nutty smell of cracked barley and the warm milky aroma of yeast enveloped me as I walked through my brew barn. It was an illusion, I knew, but I could almost taste the bitterness of hops on my tongue. I paused next to a fermentation vat, wrapped my arms around the old vessel, and laid my cheek against its copper coolness. My heart seemed to beat in time with the gurgle of the developing brew within. Mr. Ramford would not take this away from me. This was mine. This was me.

"Get over here. Now." His midnight call had come unexpectedly, sending a surge of hope through my heart but setting my stomach somersaulting with fear. I could feel his hands reaching out for my business, twisting my product into his image of beer, mediocre beer, not the carefully crafted ales and lagers I envisioned. I'd meet with him, because he had the money, and I had nothing except my skill as a microbrewer. I needed to make that work to my advantage.

I gave a final look around my small barn, rushed out into the spring night, and jogged along the spruce-covered ridge separating our two properties. My approach led me to the back of his brewery, where I stopped for a minute to catch my breath, then pushed through the rusty gate.

The only light in the barn came from the gift shop. I

entered expecting to find him, impatient, waiting for me. The room was empty.

Leave, insisted a voice in my head, but I clamped my jaw tighter, determined to negotiate what I could.

"Mr. Ramford? It's Hera. Where are you?"

No answer.

Someone must have been restocking shelves. Half-emptied boxes of mustards, pretzels, and salamis littered the floor. I slipped through the rear door of the shop and hesitated. The smells of chaff and yeasty wort greeted my entry into the cavernous brewing room.

Through the dim light from the small, high windows, I could make out the fermenting tanks, looming over me like metal sentinels. I felt around on the wall to the right of the door for a light switch but could not locate one. A soft whooshing noise, as if someone was out of breath, came from the other side of the vats.

"Hello?" This time my voice reverberated off the tanks and walls. I was certain someone was in the room and playing hide-and-seek with me. *Why?*

I began to pick my way through the barn, over the hoses leading from tank to tank and from the water purifier, careful to avoid stepping into one of the sunken grates covering the drains. A shaft of light penetrated the dimness as the far door opened and then closed, enough light to warn me I was about to trip over someone lying on the floor.

"Mr. Ramford?" I knelt in the darkness and touched a body. It felt warm to my fingertips but didn't move. As I leaned in closer, my nose caught an unpleasant collection of odors, none of which had anything to do with brewing beer. *Oh, God. This must be what death smells like.*

I pulled back my hand and whirled around, my eyes searching the darkness of the barn. I thought I could sense a presence in the room.

"Someone there?" I called. "I need help."

Silence.

A hissing from behind startled me. I ran for the gift shop door and slammed it shut, then laughed at my fear. Silly me. That was only the sound of carbon dioxide escaping from an out-take valve in a fermenter. *But the body was real.*

I grabbed the phone on the counter and punched in the number eight. *Damn.* I hung up and tried again. This time, I got it right.

I wanted to run away, but I knew I had to wait for help to arrive. I needed something to keep my shaking hands occupied and a focus for my shocked mind. *Get a grip, Hera*, I told myself. I looked around the messy gift shop, desperate to seize on anything that might blot out the memory of the body.

By the time the ambulance arrived over ten minutes later, I had finished restocking the shelves and was stacking the boxes behind the counter. I was feeling calm again. *Sure I was.*

The first EMT to enter the barn shined his flashlight on the body but did not touch it. I stood close to the gift shop door to avoid looking at the figure on the cement.

"Put a call in to the sheriff's department," he called over his shoulder to his buddy. He then did a quick examination, and retreated.

"Is he … ?"

"Definitely dead," he said. "Now we wait for the sheriff. His head's bashed in."

"An accident? He tripped?" I took in a quick breath. "Suicide? It could be suicide."

"Not unless he bludgeoned himself to death. Do you know him?"

"No. I mean, I don't know if I know him. I didn't get a good look at his face."

"Lucky you, then. Not much of a face left."

I retreated into the gift shop and paced back and forth between the shelves. My stomach lurched, and I had difficulty getting my breath. Who would be in the brew barn at this hour other than Mr. Ramford? Perhaps one of the workers was doing a night check on the fermentation process. Unlikely. He never paid overtime, and no one would volunteer to work at this hour. It had to be Mr. Ramford's body, unless … unless he sent his son into the barn to check on something. I shook my head and continued pacing. *Of course not. It couldn't be Michael. Not Michael. Let it not be Michael.*

One of the EMTs interrupted my thoughts. "Cops are here. And the medical examiner."

A man dressed in the brown and tan uniform of the sheriff's department strode past me and into the barn.

"Jake?"

If he was surprised to see me, he hid it well, while I struggled to keep the shock of his appearance off my face.

"I hope I'm not here to arrest you," was all he said to acknowledge my presence. The medical examiner and the EMTs smiled at his words, whether out of embarrassment at the rudeness of the remark or at the absurdity of my being a murderer, I couldn't tell. I tried for a smile and failed. Jake turned his head before I could determine the expression on his face.

I said, "I haven't seen you since …"

"Since law school. What've we got here?" He stooped down to examine the body.

Since law school. Since Jake and I tumbled hot with passion in tangled sheets. Since Daddy died and I came home out of guilt toward a father I couldn't save from himself. The truth was, I came home to brew beer, my first love, and the hell with my lover and my father.

Since then, I had tried to tell myself I was happy.

Two

I suffered a sleepless night, much of it spent with my old lover, who interrogated me with a tenacity I remembered was his forte in our criminal law class. By the time Jake dropped me back at my place, I felt wrung dry. He, on the other hand, seemed pleased with the experience. With each question, his blue eyes shone with almost electric light.

"You'll need to come into the office and sign a statement, and I'll be in touch with more questions. Stay available," he said, then drove off in his cruiser.

I dragged myself up the back steps, turned on the kitchen light, and decided to brew some coffee. I knew I wouldn't sleep. Besides, I wanted to be up early so I could visit the Ramfords. I hoped my presence could do something to lessen the shock of having cops on their steps informing them a next-door neighbor had found their husband and father dead.

I looked into the bathroom mirror at the dark circles under my eyes. I didn't much like Ramford, Sr., but his son and I were good friends. Nothing more, just friends. I threw my hairbrush into the sink. Friends. I'd always wanted more.

Michael answered the door when I knocked early in the

morning. He looked no better than I felt. His eyes were bloodshot, and his hair lay flat on one side of his head as if he'd just gotten out of bed. I reached out to embrace him.

"You come to join the vultures circling the body? At least you haven't brought a dish to pass." He rejected my outstretched arms, turned his back, and stalked into the house, leaving me alone to search out his mother.

I found Claudia seated at the kitchen table, chewing on her nails. Several of her cuticles were bleeding. At my approach, she dropped her hands and hid them in her lap. Strands of silver hair stuck out from her usually helmet-like coiffure. She gazed without focus upon the large number of pies, cakes, casseroles, and salads neighbors had dropped by the house.

"I'm so sorry, Claudia," I said.

I heard a door slam. Claudia started and looked at me with despair in her eyes.

"He's been like that since last night when we found out about … I'm worried about him. Has he said anything to you?"

I shook my head no.

"I thought he might at least have talked with you. He's like another person now. I hate to say it, but more like his father. Please see if you can do something."

Claudia arose from her chair and swayed slightly, grabbing the corner of the table to steady herself. "Doctor gave me some pills to calm me." She swept her arm toward the food surrounding her. "There's not enough room for all of this in the fridge."

"I can take some over to my house."

"Never mind. I'll take care of it. Go see about Michael."

I knocked at his bedroom door, but he told me to go

away. When I tried the knob, I found the door locked.

"It's Hera. I want to talk to you."

"I don't want to talk to you. Get out of here." Something hard hit the door.

"You're being an ass, Michael."

The door opened. Only his head appeared. He swept his hand through his dark curls and leaned over to pick up a shoe lying in front of the opening.

"I am, aren't I? But could you let me be an ass for a little while? I'll be fine. Don't worry. I can't be around anyone right now." His anger had turned to pleading, and I didn't have the heart to deny him his solitude.

"Okay." He closed the door on me. "Okay, for now," I said.

Downstairs I heard the clattering of dishes in the kitchen. Through the doorway, I watched Claudia scrape untouched food from the platters and bowls into the disposal and turn it on. *No one in this house was right anymore.*

We were experiencing unusual May weather this year in upstate New York. Springs here were often rainy and cold, but today the temperature reached the high seventies, and a few wispy clouds blew by on a warm breeze. The grass in the cemetery smelled sweet, and the evergreens above our heads gave off the aroma of needles and pine cones. Only the newly turned dirt from the grave reminded me spring could bring death as well as new life.

It was *déjà vu* for me, standing at the gravesite, waiting for the coffin to take a final journey into the ground. It was a replay from five years prior, except it was Michael's father this time, not mine, and it was murder, not suicide, leaving Michael without him.

I held his hand as the coffin descended into the earth. Tears stood in my eyes, not for Mr. Ramford, who had met a bloody death at the hands of an unknown killer, but for Michael. His mother was right. He had turned into someone I didn't know. In the days between my discovering his father's body and now, he'd been unusually testy with everyone, including me.

But today he seemed happy to see me. I had sat behind him at the church, and at the cemetery he took my hand as we walked up the hill to the mourners gathered at the gravesite. I felt as if he had been angry at me, then forgiven me for something I had done. I was relieved, yet I had to ask the question preying on my mind for days.

"You don't think I had anything to do with your father's death, do you?" I guess it was the bluntness of my question that drew forth a dismissive guffaw.

"What? Oh, of course not, although I could understand your wanting to get rid of him."

I was shocked at his comment. "That's an awful thing to say. He wasn't my favorite person, but for someone to murder him ... It's barbaric."

"Unthinkable, perhaps? Maybe not. He was a horrible man, mean and cold to me and to Mom, who forgave him always. Who liked him? Aside from Mother, I mean."

"You loved him. You know you did. Why so callous about his death?"

"Hard to handle." Michael cleared his throat. "I guess I never thought he'd die."

I drew his arm closer, willing his pain and grief to flow from him to me. I wanted to protect him, to make him whole again. It was the same feeling I had when I was eleven and my mother died. I wanted to put my father back together, to re-form him into the man he used to be when she was alive. As I looked into Michael's face now, I was reminded of how I failed Dad. I wouldn't do the same to Michael.

"Who's that?" I whispered in his ear as the minister intoned the last words over the coffin.

"Where?"

"The scruffy-looking guy by the road."

"Oh, him. I'll tell you later at the house. It's a surprise." Michael's mouth broke into a smile. He seemed to catch the inappropriateness of this graveside grin, drew his lips into a scowl, and said, "I see our favorite law enforcement officer is in attendance. Maybe I should invite him back to the house. Yeah, I think I'll do that."

"Michael." I clutched his arm closer to my body to prevent him from leaving.

"You like him, don't you? I heard you had some hot stud when you were in law school. He was the one, right?"

"Why are you being so unkind? It's not like you. I told you about Jake years ago, and you thought it was fine. You and I never had anything going. Why so nasty now?" As quickly as he took on the look of a gladiator about to do battle with an adversary, his face changed again.

"I'm sorry. I'm out of sorts with Dad's death and all. The microbrewery is mine to run now, and I feel in over my head. You know Dad never would let me do much while he held the reins, and now I'm supposed to brew beer. I don't even like beer." A childish pout replaced the sorrow on his face.

"That's not true. I'll help you. We can lean on one

another like we did when we were kids."

"Like I did, you mean. You did all of my homework."

"Well, since you're all grown up, I'll make you do the work, with my support, of course." I pulled a punch to his arm and smiled up at him, hoping my words might help him look to the future with some enthusiasm. But he turned his attention to a Mercedes convertible pulling up alongside the other cars on the road.

"It's Cory. I'll grab a ride with her back to the house. See you there." He strode off, his black suit coat blowing behind him in the wind. Michael's abrupt departure made the minister look up from his prayer book and lose his place in the service. Michael was on his way to becoming as rude as his father was. I hoped this new and obnoxious persona wasn't permanent.

My gaze followed him to the car. His hand reached out to take hers as the woman emerged from the driver's seat, her long hair the same champagne color as the car's finish. Then he planted a passionate kiss on her lips, and they both leaned into the embrace as if hungry for more than each other's mouths. A dull pain worked its way through my heart.

I turned from the grave and followed the mourners toward their cars. Claudia caught up with me as we neared the road.

"I don't know what's gotten into Michael." She wore the requisite black for mourning, but today, unlike the morning after the murder, her hair was smoothed back in a shining, lacquered pageboy, and her nails looked newly polished. The red color on them caught my eye.

"Too much?" she asked. I shook my head no. "Good. I needed a bit of a lift." She smiled and waggled her fingers, the sunshine catching their cherry glint. "See you at the house." She got into the limo provided by the funeral service.

As I approached my beat-up truck, Jake stepped in front of me.

"I have some more questions for you."

"You heard all I had to say about the murder the other night." I reached out for the door handle. Jake's hand got there first and prevented me from opening it.

"You told me Ramford asked you to meet him at the barn that night. You didn't tell me about the fights you'd been having with him."

"Fights? More like business discussions where we agreed not to do business."

"I understand it was also personal. He wanted you and Michael to marry, but you couldn't get Michael interested in the proposition."

I could feel a flush working its way up my face. "Who told you that?"

"One of the workers at the brewery overheard your conversation when you and Ramford last tried to negotiate a deal."

"I'd never sell out to Ramford Beer. Never."

"My snooping tells me you need money to continue your operation, and you need it badly." His face was too near my own, making it difficult for me to avoid those probing eyes.

"Oh, yes, I do need money. So I would murder the one person who was offering it to me?"

"No, but you might remove the person who could threaten your loan with the local bank. Ramford played golf with the bank's president, and most of the men sitting on the board were his friends."

"There are other sources of money, you know," I said.

"Yes, but now, you can go ahead with your loan application."

This whole conversation was absurd. There was a hidden agenda at the heart of his interrogation, so I decided to call him on it.

"Look, I know you're pissed at me for the way I ran off and left you in law school, but you don't know what was happening then. My father …"

"You're wrong. I'm not harassing you about any personal issues we may have had in the past. I know about your father. I was real sorry about his death. Let's stick to the murder, shall we?"

How dare he invoke the past and then dismiss it as irrelevant? "Sorry, were you? I heard nothing from you. No condolence card, no phone call, nothing. Now we're years down the road, and here you are investigating the murder of the father of one of my dearest friends. I'm sure you're good at what you do, but do it to somebody else, will you? I found the body. I didn't make it dead."

I couldn't help myself. I behaved as I often did when I stepped into the log home Mr. Ramford had built for his family. I looked upward at the soaring beamed ceiling running the length of the downstairs. Skylights along the peaked roofline allowed brilliant sunshine to pour down on the heads of the mourners gathered in the great room below.

Claudia greeted me, and her gaze followed mine. "Michael wanted this house to make a powerful statement about the Ramford family, and it does," she said. "No one enters here without feeling like a tiny ant under these eaves, no one except for Michael Senior."

"Yes, it was surely his house."

"Reminds me of a barn, and it's a bitch to heat." Her words surprised me. They were the first betrayal of support for her husband I'd ever heard from the woman. She turned her back and waved me into the room, gesturing toward the food and drink. "Have something. It's on the house." I thought I caught a titter from her, but she turned away and approached two people entering the room.

It looked as if every important member of the local community and some from farther away were in attendance at the after-service get-together. I strolled the room, nodding to people I knew and stopping to chat with a few others. This felt more like evening cocktails at the manor rather than an ending for a funeral. Perhaps knowing her husband's taste and character, Claudia intended it as a tribute to him and the way he lived his life. Sally's Catering, a service run by my dear friend Sally Granger, provided the food. I caught her eye as she hurried to place another platter of sandwiches on the buffet table. She waved, then ducked her head and ran back into the kitchen. *Oh, Sally, too embarrassed to talk with me?* Or was she still mad at me for giving her unwelcome advice about Michael? I guess it was my move first, so I made a mental note to visit her soon.

A waiter offered me a choice of Ramford beer or champagne. I grabbed a tall flute off his tray. I spotted my brewing colleagues gathered in a corner sipping the champagne. Teddy Buser's voice carried across the room and drew my attention.

"I'm only saying what everyone is thinking. Good riddance to the man. He had the gall to ask if we could go into business together. I asked him, 'What business? I've got a brewery, and you've got shit.' The swill he's been making for years is so behind the times. Never was any good."

I joined the group.

"Swill, Teddy? I heard the recipe for your Twelve Gauge beer is oh-so-close to Ramford's Shining Moment Lager. You wouldn't call Twelve Gauge swill, would you?" asked Rafe Oxley.

For some reason, perhaps out of the boredom brought on by life in a small town, Rafe liked to stir the pot among the brewers. His observations about members of this brewing gang were astute, but, offered as they were in an English accent and by such an urbane man with dark good looks, most of us didn't see him as intentionally rude. We liked his dry wit and teasing humor.

As if to confirm my thought that he was angling for a good-natured rise out of Teddy, Rafe caught my eye and winked. No one else seemed to notice. Before Teddy could answer, Rafe continued, "Wasn't Ramford Beer giving you a run for your money? He wasn't introducing as much corn in his product as you do."

Teddy exploded. "Corn! I don't use corn." Everyone laughed, knowing hand-crafted beers such as those we made almost never used corn.

"Commercial brewers might add corn, but not you, huh, Teddy?' The voice belonged to Marsh Wilson, who had apprenticed under Teddy several years back.

Teddy shot Marsh a look of suspicion. I wondered if he

knew more about Teddy's business than Teddy wanted made public.

"What are you saying, Marsh?" asked Teddy. A flush worked its way up his throat and onto his already ruddy cheeks.

"Now, Teddy, don't get defensive. You know we like to rib you. It's our way of handling your success while we flounder around as smaller, second-best brewers," said Marsh and gave Teddy a good-natured slap on the back.

"First of all, I'd like to be thought of as a small, not a second-best, brewer," I said. "But, Marsh, I thought you were running the Highland House, not brewing beer."

"I sold it," said Marsh. Because I stood to his left and a little behind the group, I could see him place his hand on the back of the woman at his side. He moved his fingers in small circles, a caress signaling possession and intimacy. I was about to introduce myself to her when the sound of cutlery tapping the side of a champagne glass drew our regard.

"If I might have your attention." Michael strode to the center of the room. At his side stood the stranger from the cemetery, his brown polyester suit and mustard yellow tie shouting foot-long hotdog. "I'd like to introduce you to Stanley Frost. I've hired him as the new brew master of Ramford Brewery. I know Father would have wanted us to look to the future as he always did. Ramford will be introducing a number of new brews over the next few months. So let's welcome Stanley into our family of Butternut Valley brewers."

I could see shock on many people's faces. This hardly seemed like the right occasion for such an announcement, especially one promising to alter so dramatically the

Ramford business. I looked over at Claudia. For a moment, I thought her face registered the same note of surprise as did others'. If she knew nothing of her son's plans, she hid her astonishment by coughing quietly and sipping water from the glass she held in her hand. Then she nodded and smiled, set the glass on the buffet table and joined in the applause and the well wishes the room was offering the new brew master.

Michael wandered over to my side.

"I told you I had a little surprise."

"I thought you told your father this spring you had some new ideas for brews, and he rejected them. I don't understand why you need Stanley now when you have the freedom to put your ideas into operation."

"I have plenty of ideas, but when I thought about it, the ones I liked the most had nothing to do with brewing beer. Don't look so upset. Because you do it and do it well, doesn't mean I want to spend my days and nights smelling yeast and malt."

"Okay, so Stanley designs the brews. Then what do you do?"

"I provide the cash and the equipment. Oh, right. Then I collect the money."

Three

I pulled my truck into a parking space in front of the store, hoping it was just early enough in the morning for Sally to be at work, but before any customers came into her shop. She stood at the door and watched me slip a coin into the parking meter. I worried she'd reach for the "closed" sign and turn her back on me, but she waved me in. No hello, no smile. I followed her into the back room and watched as she extracted the last loaves of her bread from the oven. She gave them a quick tap and nodded. The aroma of hot bread filled my nose, and a sudden flood of saliva washed over my tongue.

"Coffee?" she asked. Without waiting for my reply, she picked up the pot, walked back out into the front of her shop, and poured me a cup. "Sit down. I'll get preserves and fresh bread."

"Yum," I said. She placed the bread and jam on the table, and I reached for them with both hands. She slapped my fingers.

"The bread needs to cool. You know that."

"Sorry," I said.

"No reason to be," she replied. We both knew neither of us was talking about bread and jam.

I nodded, drummed my nails on the table for several minutes, and inched my hand toward the loaf.

She gave in with a shake of her bright red curls and

sliced the bread, releasing more of that I-can't-wait-to-bite-into-it aroma as the knife cut through the crust and into the soft center. The two of us took one of the tables in the front of the bakery.

"How's business?" I gestured with my head at the four small tables positioned around the tiny room. Sunlight shone through the storefront windows. Along with the smells of ginger, cinnamon, and yeast bread and rolls from the ovens, the place was like being in grandma's kitchen, warm, welcoming, and certain to put five pounds on you if you didn't restrain yourself. This morning, I was the only patron.

Sally ran floury fingers through her curls. Her gaze swept the empty room. "It'll pick up soon."

"Bad, huh?"

"You warned me. Told me not to set up the tea room in the winter months. You were right. Happy?" Her tone sounded more depressed than snappish.

"No, of course not, but come June, your business will get a shot in the arm when we begin the tastings on Saturdays."

"You still want me at your Saturday festivals?"

"Don't be a ninny. Of course. I can't have people on the brewery tour swilling beer without the proper accompaniments. Because you had the bad taste to arrive at my Christmas Eve supper alone and leave drunk with Michael in tow doesn't mean I don't want you there to provide bread and rolls. Once they get a taste of your baking, you'll sell out every Saturday."

Her face turned red. "I have lousy taste in men, you know."

"Yeah, well then, so do I. How long have I had a thing

for Michael, and we're still nothing but friends?"

Sally grabbed my hand across the table with one of hers. I looked down at her chubby, freckled arms and hands. They were so tiny and fragile looking.

"Ouch."

"What?"

"For such small hands, you sure have a strong grip."

"It's all the kneading of bread I do. I still do it by hand. More authentic, you know."

I stuffed another piece of jam-covered bread into my mouth with my free hand. Neither of us spoke. A tear fell onto the table between us. Then another. Both of us were crying.

"I thought you were jealous when you told me to be careful of Michael. Now I know you were right." She picked up her apron and swiped at her face.

"Oh, honey, I'm so sorry he hurt you. And I'm sorry I tried to interfere," I said.

We hugged across the small table and then wiped away the wetness on our cheeks and gulped our coffee.

"Did you get a chance to talk with Michael at the funeral?" I asked. I uttered my words through a full mouth. Sally laughed at me.

"If I heard you right, no, I didn't talk to him, but I heard his announcement. Maybe what he's doing is a good idea. I mean, he'll be gone a lot promoting the business and stuff, and you won't have to deal with him at all. Neither will I. It could help both of us."

"I doubt it. You know what they say about absence and the heart, but I have to face the fact Michael and I are friends, only friends, and maybe not even that now. We used to talk a lot about business. That's changed since his father's death. We hardly talk at all." I blew my nose on a napkin. "No. That's not right. Michael started avoiding me before his father's murder. I thought he was uncomfortable about the two of you, but I guess he thought I might have a few words to say about his dumping you and taking up with Cory. I did, but I never got to confront him."

The taste of preserves on my tongue turned sour when I thought of Michael's recent behavior. "Since the announcement at the funeral, I don't know him anymore. Once, I might have solicited his opinion on what I was attempting in the way of new brews, but now, well, I don't know."

Sally opened the sugar bowl and began stirring the granules around with a spoon, patiently waiting for me to get to the point. She knew it was hard for me to ask her for anything. I was always the strong one from the time we first met in grade school, and I chased away all the bigger kids who taunted her with the name "midget."

"So you see, I didn't come here only to eat your bread and break down the wall we built between us. I need your help. I think there's something terribly wrong with Michael. His mother noticed the change in him, too."

Sally gave me a wry smile. "I think Michael would disagree with you. He thinks he's doing fine. Apparently, so does everyone else. His mother appears to be going along with his plans, and the rest of the community is applauding him for his business acumen. Oh, I'm not saying I agree with them. I find his behavior strange, too, but then, maybe it's merely jealously on my part. Of Cory, I mean." Her blue eyes again filled with tears.

"Jealous of her? What does she have that you don't? A Mercedes, you say? She has car payments. You don't."

"Right. My Ford pick-up is paid for except for the new transmission I need."

"Oh, forget Cory. No more boo-hooing," I said. "Despite the fact Michael hurt us, we both still care for him. The three of us grew up together, and we know him better than anyone. It must be grief. He told me he hated the brewery, and I know it's not true. Now he's turning the whole thing over to some stranger. I think he needs to get back to hand-crafting beer."

Sally laughed. "You always think the solution to any problem is hard work, especially if it entails brewing beer. Maybe his father's murder was an eye opener for him, and without his father hanging over him, he's found out he doesn't like beer making."

I thought about what she said. There was truth in her words.

"I guess I'm being insensitive. When Dad died, I converted my grief into taking over the brewery. I know he didn't want me to run it. He willed it to me, assuming I would find my calling in law school and, when he died, I would sell it to someone else, maybe Michael." I heard a noise at the door and jerked my head around to see who was there. *My nemesis.*

"Oh, oh. Here comes trouble," Sally said, looking through the bakery window. Assistant Deputy Sheriff Jake Ryan stood there with his hands cupped around his eyes, trying to peer in.

"The bakery's not open yet," I yelled through the door, then got up, flipped the Open sign to Closed, and shot the deadbolt.

"What is it with you two? Rumor in the village has it you circle each other like boxers in the ring," said Sally.

"Oh? What else does rumor say?"

Sally's eyes danced, and she clasped her tiny hands together like a child eager to open a birthday present. "He's the one, isn't he? He's the guy you told me about when you were in law school, the hunk."

"He's an insensitive jerk."

"Well, if you don't want him anymore, I kind of like his looks." Sally clapped her hand across her mouth. "Oh, God, here I go once more, trying to take your guy."

"You can have him with my blessing, but if you're curious about him, I could fill you in on some details any smart girl would want to know. Oh, shit. We're doing it again, letting a man interfere with our friendship." We held each other's gaze across the table, embarrassment and regret in our eyes.

Jake banged at the door. "I can see you in there. This is official business. Let me in."

"Get a search warrant, official sheriff person." *Me and my smart mouth.*

"He's kind of cute. He's only been on the job for a few weeks, so why not give him a break? Maybe he's different from when you knew him. Wasn't that years ago? People change."

"Not this one. This guy is the same as when we were in law school—a shark." Sally ignored me and leaped for the door to let him in.

"I'll get another cup and cut some more bread." She dashed into the back room.

"Your best friend, isn't she? Interesting person. Little, peppy," Jake said. His gaze followed her retreating back.

"You like little and peppy?" I asked. "I thought you liked tall and thin." *Now why did I have to make reference to our past relationship?*

He looked my slender, almost boyish, body up and down making me mentally squirm at the inspection. "Tastes change with experience," he said.

I was imagining the experiences that might alter his preferences in women.

"I need to talk with you."

"Not about this murder again, I hope. I told you at the cemetery, I don't know any more. Oh, and by the way, when it comes to Sally? If you're interested, go slowly. The woman had her heart broken by ..."

"By your boyfriend. Yeah, I know. The whole town knows. I'm not such an insensitive clod I'd use her that way." I was about to ask him how he'd use her or any woman, but he cut me off before I could speak.

"I want to talk with you about your father's death."

My father's ....

Jake turned down Sally's offer of bread and jam, so she packed him two slices in a baggie and sent us out the door, like mama sending two teenagers off on a picnic. As Jake and I left, I shot her a look of disgust, and she returned it with a wink.

"What's so important that I had to leave Sally's and come with you?"

"My SUV's across the street." He grabbed my arm and steered me toward the vehicle.

"I only put a quarter in the meter." I nodded at my truck.

"I already took care of it. C'mon."

Imperious S.O.B., I thought to myself. "Taking me down

to the station to sweat me again about Mr. Ramford?"

He ignored my testy tone. "This might be related to his murder or not, but when I first took the job here, I remembered the discussions we had about your father when we were in law school. I would have liked to have met him." He started the engine and pulled out into traffic.

"That was a long time ago." I hated remembering the day I got the call about Dad's death. "I prefer focusing on the present."

"Usually, I do, too, but this is unfinished business, business you should know about. Two brewers dying violent deaths in the short span of five years is too much coincidence for me, so I went back to the file on your father's suicide, and something struck me as strange. Most of the officers working on the case then didn't notice it, but I did, because you were his daughter and close to him. You knew his habits, and you knew the house. And what was in it." He turned the vehicle onto the highway that led over Jefferson Mountain.

"'He didn't own a gun,' you said. Now, Mr. Ramford, he said your father did own a pistol. The two of them used it for target practice. Some of the men working for Ramford told the officers they had seen your father and him shooting at a target set up on Ramford's property. They were using a pistol. But I think you were right. You would know if your father owned a gun. I thought the pistol had to be Ramford's. I checked the serial number on the weapon found in your father's hand and called gun shops in this area."

Halfway up the long grade, Jake pulled into a driveway leading to a ranch-style house that had been converted to a business. Mossie's Guns, the sign read.

"The guy who runs it now is the son of the man who was operating it back when your father died. He didn't remember selling the gun used in his death, but I asked him if he could find the sales receipt for it. He's been digging around in his father's old business papers and hit pay dirt last night. I got the call this morning."

"I don't understand. Mr. Ramford wasn't shot. He was hit over the head with something, right?"

Jake let me open my own door and catch up to him as he walked up the steps to the shop.

"Like I said, this isn't about Ramford's murder. It's about your father's."

Four

A fully stuffed black bear standing on its rear legs greeted our entry into the shop. It towered over me, its mouth open, teeth displayed with a ferocity I found frightening despite its departure long ago from the living. I reached out and touched the claws on its paw and thought of the power in them, now stayed for the purposes of decoration. I gave a short snort of disgust, which the owner caught. He hurled it back at me by spitting his chaw of tobacco into a spittoon located at the end of the counter. The place had atmosphere, I had to give it that.

I'd never been in a gun shop before, but it was pretty much what I expected. Lots of weapons—guns, pistols, revolvers, shotguns, and rifles displayed in locked cases. On the wall behind the counter, mounted animal heads joined the bear at the door in a state of infinite captivity. A beaver losing some of its pelt stood on the counter. I didn't like the place. It gave me the creeps, and that feeling emboldened me to speak before Jake had a chance.

"Where are the people?" I asked and nodded toward the wall.

The owner, who I assumed was the son of the Mr. Mossie after which the business was named, looked from Jake to me. He wore a red plaid shirt, trying, I thought, for the look of a sportsman, but his tiny black eyes set close together yelled predator to me. I wasn't crazy about either his dress or his love of tobacco.

"What?" He looked puzzled for a moment. Then he realized I was referring to the mounted kills. "Sportsman don't shoot people. We're very well trained in hunting safety."

"Right," I said, but I thought back to all those falls when hunters had better luck taking down their buddies than they did an eight-point buck. Jake turned his head and looked at me. His eyes said he had second thoughts about bringing me along on this run.

Jake introduced himself to the owner, whose name was indeed Mossie. The two men shook hands. The owner nodded at me. I pretended to take up a conversation with the bear. The owner cleared his throat and addressed Jake. "Dad kept good records, just didn't have a filing system that made much sense. Took me a lot of time, but business is slow this time of year. I found it. Here you go."

Jake looked at the transaction slip. His face revealed nothing of what he found there. "Take a look." He handed the paper to me.

From what Jake had said, I expected not to see my father's name there, and I didn't. I wasn't shocked to read the last name of Ramford on the signature line, but the first name surprised me. Not Michael Jr. or Sr., but another Ramford. Claudia.

"Claudia's pistol killed my father? I can't believe she would buy a gun. How did Dad get it?"

"What you can believe is I'll ask her about this."

Jake thanked the owner, and I gave the wall mountings and the bear a final glance of compassion as we left.

Neither of us spoke on the way back down the mountain. Finally, I repeated my question. "How did Dad get this gun?" I was half afraid to hear what he had to say, refusing to turn back to momentary suspicions I had buried along with my father.

"Your father never held that gun to his head, Hera. You must know that. We're talking about murder here."

"You're wrong. Dad took his own life because of how badly the brewery was doing. I was so grief stricken at his death, the gun issue didn't seem important, especially since others saw him with one." I dropped my head into my hands and ran my fingers through my hair in frustration. This was what I had believed for over five years. I needed it to be true.

Jake seemed to recognize a battle was going on inside me, and he said nothing as we pulled into town and he parked next to my truck.

"Whatever took you down this line of inquiry?" I asked.

"I always wondered about it. You talked about your father so often, I felt I knew him. It seemed impossible such a man would take his own life. I imagined him as the kind of person who would tough it out, find the money somewhere to make the brewery work. Suicide didn't fit him."

Jake's words made me want to grab him and shake him. "Why didn't you get in touch with me then? Instead, there was only silence from you. I needed you then."

"You had Michael. You told me about him, too. Remember? I had my own demons to defeat."

"You think someone killed Dad." It sounded so cold, so impossible to believe, yet now I wanted to know what Jake was thinking.

"Yes."

"You also believe there's a link between Ramford's murder and Dad's ... death?"

He nodded. "Hera." He reached out to take my hand lying on the seat between us. I lifted it as if to ward off his touch, his presence, his intrusion into a life I had put together. Imperfect though it now was, it was all I had.

"This doesn't make sense. My father and Mr. Ramford were friendly business competitors, and they also were friends. Why would Mr. Ramford do such a thing? I can't believe it."

Or could I? Something pricked my memory. In a phone call from Michael several weeks before Dad's death, he had mentioned Dad canceling a golf date with Rafe, Michael, and his father. *"Your dad said he wouldn't be joining us for golf anymore. He sounded unhappy, depressed, maybe sad. I asked Dad if he knew what was going on, and he said to leave it alone."*

Two weeks later, the cleaning woman found my father in his recliner with a bullet hole through his head. I thought he was depressed about business, but something was going on in Dad's life I knew nothing about. Whatever it was, it now looked as if it led to his murder.

I directed my attention back to the gun.

"There are other possibilities, you know." I wanted to bite my tongue the moment the words came out of my mouth.

"Like?" asked Jake. I knew he had already considered these and was letting me work out the names on my own. And say them out loud.

"All right, then. Others had access to the pistol, depending on where it was kept. Employees, maybe even friends, and anyone in the Ramford household could have used it on my father. Maybe even Claudia." *Surely not Claudia.* I thought back to the day after her husband had been found dead and the vacant, out-of-reality expression on her face. I dismissed her as a killer. "Claudia's too fragile for anything other than hostessing the best parties in this valley and stitching her quilts. But ..." Another possibility came to mind, but I rejected it. Let Jake say it, not me.

"Michael," he said, not taking his eyes off me.

"Michael? Michael would never ..."

"When I interviewed Michael about his father's death and asked him about your Dad, I got the feeling he didn't like either of the men much." Jake shifted around in his seat so that he was facing me. "Why didn't he like your father, Hera?"

"No. No. He liked Dad, but they had some problems because of Ronald, that's all." Before I could explain about Ronald, Jake interrupted me.

"I know who Ronald is. He was Ramford's youngest son. He left here over fifteen years ago. I believe he was somewhat of a pyromaniac, liked to set fires. His last fire was the old hop house to the north of your property. Now, what's this about Michael, and how is it linked to Ronald?"

"It's not as if Michael hated Dad. He thought Dad interfered too much between Ronald and his father. One night when Dad had a meeting over at Ramford's, he drove up to find Ronald locked out of the house, sitting on the front steps in the freezing rain. Ramford was punishing him for some misbehavior. Dad took him home. Mom warmed him up in a tub of hot water and tucked him into the bed in the spare bedroom." Jake interrupted my story.

"What was Claudia's role in all of this?"

"I never knew. I think she was terrified of her husband and didn't have the courage to stand up to him." I thought about what I had said for a moment. "No, that's not right. It was more like she couldn't connect with what was going on. Claudia's always been a little out of it." But that wasn't it either, so I finished by saying, "She was odd, I thought."

I rolled down the window of the SUV and leaned my head out as if fresh air could change the past.

"I know Mr. Ramford and Dad had words over the incident, and Michael told Dad he should stay out of their business, but I know he never would hurt anyone." Not physically hurt anyone, anyway, but thinking of Sally, I knew how thoughtless he could be emotionally without meaning to, of course.

"Don't you ever wonder what happened to Ronald?" asked Jake. "I do, and I'm making it my job to find out."

"None of this makes any sense." I grabbed the door handle and got out. Jake suspected everyone, all the people I'd grown up with and loved. I wouldn't listen to any more of his cop talk.

I walked around to his side of the vehicle to tell him to stop what he was doing. "What role can Ronald have in any of this? He's been gone for a long time, and I hope he has a better life than he had here. Why stir up things that aren't important?" I asked.

"I won't be the only one stirring things up. I'm sure the issue of inheritance and the will have already fanned fires of discord in the Ramford household."

"What do you mean?" I asked.

"If Ronald is still alive, don't you think Claudia's lawyer wants to find out where he is? Regardless of what's in the will, Ronald is still Ramford's son. If the old man left nothing to him, he could, and probably should, make a fuss and file suit. You had enough years of law school to know that."

Jake stared out the front windshield, and I could almost hear the click of puzzle pieces as he tried to fit them into a whole. "There's something about that family, secrets people are keeping," he said.

Secrets. Yes, there were secrets being kept and not only by members of the Ramford family. I ducked my head so Jake couldn't read my face.

"I've got to talk to Michael." I walked around my truck and got in.

Is there something you haven't told me about my father's death, I wanted to ask Michael. *Do you know more than you said?*

But I didn't get the opportunity to speak with Michael for several days. The state of my business took all my attention. I had introduced a brew last summer which I called Knightsbridge Ginseng Rush, a light, sunlit lager to which I added ginseng and elderberry. It flew out the doors during the beer tours and tastings I held at the brewery each Saturday during the summer months and into the early fall.

My plan was to continue this brew and add another summer beer, Hera's Honey. Its deep golden color and toffee-ish flavoring came from the use of Vienna malt with some Pilsner malt blended into it. Then cardamom and, of course, honey. The use of a number of different high quality malts meant a lager that would cost me more to produce, but I didn't care. I was excited at the prospect of making another beer with my unique signature on it.

I stood in my brew barn and looked at my wort kettles and the mash lauter tun. The vessels were solid copper and old. It took my hired hand Jeremiah and me most of a day to scrub them clean. I yearned for stainless steel wrapped in copper. Windex on the outside surface, chemical cleaning and a good hosing down of the inside, and they were ready for another batch of brew. I also longed for bigger kettles, so I could increase production, and steam coils rather than gas-fired ones, but that meant money, a lot of money.

Then there were ales. Change my yeast, and I knew I could produce distinctive ales—dark, hoppy, and bitter brews with the flavors of chocolate and cinnamon. A drink for a cold winter night in front of the fire or with dessert after comfort food like prime rib and roasted potatoes.

I walked back into my office. Well, I certainly had the ideas. What I didn't have was the capital. In the old days I would have talked over my ideas with Michael before I ever approached my other brewing colleagues. Now, I hesitated. I looked at the number of chewed pencils on my desk. *Don't be silly*, I told myself. *Call him. We were friends, right?*

"It's Hera. Can I drop by for a few minutes? I have some things I'd like to run by you." He sounded happy to hear from me, like the old Michael.

But when I entered his office, Stanley was there and settled in for a conversation. I thought Michael would get rid of him, but he signaled Stanley to keep his seat.

Stanley and I shook hands and eyed one another. From the look on his face, I would say this was not going to be a meeting of congenial business competitors. Nope. This was cut-throat stuff.

"Michael tells me you have some ideas you'd like to kick around?"

I felt trapped. I had called Michael. Now, I found I had little I wanted to say, but if I said nothing, I'd look like a fool. Oh, what the hell. Maybe I was misjudging Stanley's feral grin. Maybe he was a sweet puddy tat.

"I was going over the figures for my Knightsbridge Ginseng Rush. They look good."

"Yes, I imagine they do," said Stanley. "You were right on the money. People like to drink beer, and they think about health issues. So why not give them a great-tasting brew and one good for them? And that's what you did."

Everyone smiled. *This isn't so bad*, I thought. I plunged ahead.

"I thought I should increase production this year."

"Oh, definitely. I would," said Stanley.

"And add another health brew." Both of the men leaned forward in their chairs, their eyes on mine.

"What would that be?" asked Stanley.

I knew, but something kept me from saying. "Oh, I haven't decided yet. I'm working on it and an ale."

"You'll have to buy additional equipment," Stanley said. Michael seemed less interested in the conversation now. His eyes wandered away from Stanley and me as he gazed out the window and stifled a yawn.

"Oh, I know," I said.

"And money?"

"There's the problem. I don't have any. Yet. I'm going to the bank for a loan."

"Banks around here are funny about loaning money to breweries. Too much competition." Again, it was Stanley who spoke.

"Why would they think that? Each brewery has an individual niche here. Teddy's sportsman's brews, Rafe's ales, my health lagers, and you, well, I'm certain your expansion will produce some unique brews also. We all have different products. The beer-drinking public, at least those who go for microbrews, like to drink a number of different beers. We meet that demand."

"You know how conservative banks are."

"I know, Stanley, but this bank has loaned me money for the brewery before. I have a good record with them." I was feeling attacked by him, and I hoped it didn't register as defensiveness in my tone of voice.

"Well, Michael knows the members of the bank board pretty well. They're friends of yours. Right? You tell her. Has she a chance in hell of getting a loan?"

Michael turned his eyes away from the window and back onto me, but he looked uncomfortable at being called upon to speak.

"I can't say whether or not the bank will go for it, but I'll put in a good word."

"Maybe we can help her out," Stanley said.

"How?" I asked.

"We might loan you the sum of money you require to buy your equipment."

"At what rate of interest?"

"No interest. You would sign over fifty percent of the business to Ramford Brewery. You and Michael would finally be partners. Of course, you would retain creative management. We'd brew the beers you wanted." Both of them smiled in encouragement.

"I see, and if I wanted a brew you didn't, you wouldn't

be able to find the money to back it. Right?"

Stanley didn't reply. He tilted his chair back on its legs and continued to look at me with interest. *Like a puddy tat after a mouse,* I thought. Michael shifted around in his chair. He avoided my gaze.

"I'll give it some thought." I jumped from my chair and rushed out of the room. I was steaming as I headed down the hallway. Michael caught up with me at the door.

"You're not going for it, are you?"

I whirled around to face him. "Of course not. Do you think I'd allow anyone to take this brewery away from me after all I've done to put her back on her feet after Dad's death? I thought you hired Stanley as the brew master. You're letting him ride roughshod over you the same way your father did. C'mon. You're better than that."

Michael put his arms around me.

"You're my friend. I only want what's best for you."

This was more like it. *My old friend, my best buddy, my sweet childhood crush.*

"Tell me you don't want anything to do with this business. You can't mean it. Remember a few years ago when you and I were sitting on the hill above the old hop house, and we planned out the microbrews we would make if we had the money. Remember?"

"I do remember."

"If we can find who killed your father, you'll be your old self, the sweet and creative Michael I know. The beer king. I used to call you that, and you loved it."

Michael tugged my earlobe, as he did when we were kids, and he was trying to pull me out of a funk.

"Maybe you're right."

"I know I am." I hesitated, anger at Stanley loosening

my tongue and robbing me of caution. "This will be hard for you to take, but Jake, uh, Deputy Sheriff Ryan thinks someone in your family, probably your father or maybe ..." I couldn't tell Michael he was a suspect, too. "Uh, probably your father may have been involved in my dad's death." The minute the words left my mouth, I knew I shouldn't have said them.

Michael stepped back and looked down into my eyes. "What do you mean?" A hard edge of disbelief and caution replaced the softness on his face.

At that moment, we heard a rap on the outside door, and Jake walked in. "Well, well, if it isn't the love birds."

Michael dropped his hands from my waist.

"I think you'd better come into my office where we can talk, Deputy."

"I'd like that."

When we entered the office, Stanley was seated behind the desk in Michael's chair.

"Beat it, Stanley. Go do your job. Create a lager for me or an ale. Create several. I'm paying you enough money for a whole line of beers."

Stanley's head came up with a jerk, and he sprang out of the chair. I suspected Michael had never addressed him this way before. I was a little surprised at Michael's tone of voice.

"I think you should leave, too, Hera. This is between the deputy and me."

Stanley and I stood outside the office together. I'd held my dislike of this man in check long enough. Michael's implied reprimand of him gave me the license I needed to speak out. I smiled at him and chuckled.

"I guess you were the boss only briefly. Better savor

the moment. I don't think it's coming around again."
"Neither is yours," he said and walked out the door.

Five

I peeked through the window of Rafe's fermentation room to view the large vat of wort—a filtered blend of water, malted barley, and hops—being worked on by the yeast. His operation was as large as Teddy's, but Rafe brewed only Belgian-style ales.

"You can almost see the yeast gobbling away at the barley, eating up oxygen in the process. The room must be filled to the ceiling with carbon dioxide by now."

Rafe nodded. "Not someplace you want to visit for long, but you wouldn't need a fermentation chamber like this one. You can brew in your own vats." He stood beside me, proudly gesturing toward the carbon dioxide-filled room. "You do need better equipment than those old kettles you're using now."

I was right about Rafe. He expressed enthusiastic support for my ideas, and he offered me the names of others in the ale business who might also be of help.

"Just don't horn in on my cave-aged ales." He said this in a good-natured manner.

"As if I could afford to pay any of the caverns operating a tourist business around here the prices they ask you for storage." Rafe partnered with the cavern facility nearby to rent space from them in which to age his ales. The publicity was good for them and Rafe. "Cave-aged ales," and "Visit the aging grotto," read the ads.

"Someday you may. You're the best brewer around here. You read, you ask intelligent questions, you love the business, you just plain have a knack for beer. And you're damn pretty."

"If pretty were a prerequisite for brewing good beer, then most breweries would be run by women, and that's not the case."

Rafe hesitated a moment, then leaned back onto the fermenting room wall. "We may have more than one woman brewer around here, if what I hear is true."

"Really." I tried to hide my concern. I didn't think we needed another brewery in this valley, whether it was run by a man or a woman.

"Francine Ortega, the woman with Marsh Wilson at Ramford's funeral, hired him to brew for her."

"So that's why he sold his restaurant." I remembered the possessive way Marsh caressed her back at the funeral. "I thought she was planning to continue making wine at her winery on Kendall Lake."

"Wine, and she's going to try a brewpub at the same location." Rafe led me out of the barn toward the beer garden he'd created for his tastings. We strolled past the cedar trees and the grape arbor and into an area shaded by colorful umbrellas positioned in the center of round, wooden tables. He beckoned me over to one, and we sat.

"So Francine will only sell on premises." I wondered if Rafe heard the relief in my voice. *None of her beers sitting next to mine on grocer' shelves, thank goodness.*

"For now, at least."

"Didn't Marsh work for you as well as Teddy several years ago?" I asked.

Rafe chuckled and nodded. "Don't worry, Hera.

There's room enough for all of the breweries in this valley. Competition makes us brew well, better than if we were a monopoly," Rafe said, but then, he could be benevolent about competition. He had none in the area. His closest competitor for Belgian ales was in the Susquehanna River Valley near Cooperstown, at least thirty miles from here.

"Not all of us think as you do. Teddy hates competition. He'd like to be the single brewer in this valley, and I'm hanging on by my nails. Michael and Stanley would love to see me disappear, but maybe Michael will come to his senses."

Rafe reached across the table and took my hand. "I know you came to me for business advice, but let me give you a little personal advice too."

I screwed up my face at his words.

"Now don't run away, my dear. It's free, and personal issues aren't unrelated to your business. You're only as creative a brewer as your psyche allows you to be, and if all your psychic energy is tied up in knots over Michael Ramford, you're going nowhere."

"What do you suggest?"

"Get yourself some man who won't get in the way of what you want, someone who knows his own mind. Someone like the new deputy sheriff. He agrees with me."

"How so?"

"He thinks you're damn pretty too."

"You know it takes more than looks. He finds me a real pain in the patootie."

"Yes, he does and he's right. You are. That's why I like you."

As I signed for a shipment of malt and hops the next morning, Rafe's words came back to me. He was right. I could brew great ale. There was something else Rafe was right about. I had to get Michael off my mind. I rejected Rafe's suggestion that Jake was a better choice for me, but I couldn't seem to put Jake's lopsided smile and intense eyes out of my mind.

"This is the last load of product I can deliver and let your account ride," said the driver. "My boss says you're too far behind in your bill as it is." My head began to hurt when I saw the total on the receipt.

I needed a lot more malt and hops than I now had on hand to continue with my new brew. Business issues should be drawing my attention, but instead I was reviewing smiles on the face of a deputy sheriff who considered me past history. God, I hated his smugness. If I could find a way to wipe it off his handsome face, I'd ...

I did know how. Who was better acquainted with the brewers than I? Finding Mr. Ramford's killer and determining how Dad died would free all of us in this valley—free Michael to get on with his brewery work and release me from the years of guilt I carried not being able to help my father through my mother's death. Perhaps I could stop blaming myself for playing some unwitting part in his death, whether it was suicide or murder. Jake could have been right about one thing. Dad might have died at someone else's hands, maybe Ramford's.

How sweet it would be to defeat Jake at his own game. Whether he knew it or not, the old competition we embraced so warmly in law school was on again.

Oh, sure, Hera, take a few moments and solve the crime. You can wedge sleuthing in between brewing beers and finding a source of income for your business. I looked at my watch. Well, I did have a few hours before I was to meet with the bank president. Perhaps ...

I positioned the step ladder under the attic hatch and crawled up the rungs until I could shove the cover to one side. It was heavier than I remembered. I pushed at it with my right hand while I held the top of the ladder with the other. The doorbell chimed.

Shit. Who could that be? I heard the door open.

"Hey, where are you? It's Sally."

"Come on upstairs. I could use a hand or two."

She peered up at me from the bottom of the ladder. "What are you doing? Trying out for the circus?"

"Funny. Could you hold the ladder steady? I've almost got this." Assured it couldn't slip, I used both hands and moved the trapdoor to one side, stepped up a rung, and poked my head into the attic.

When was the last time I was up here? I pulled my torso through the opening and entered a world of ... cobwebs. *Uck.*

"Hey! Come back here. We've got a meeting, or did you forget?" Sally asked.

Oh, damn. I did forget. I'd cancelled a dinner with Sally last night so that I could organize the paperwork needed for my loan application. I assured Sally we could find time today before my meeting to talk about our business. The weight of worrying about the bank loan along with the issue of Dad's death made me forget Sally was dropping by. *Oh, be honest, Hera,* I said to myself. Most of your morning has been taken up with thoughts of men—Dad,

Michael, Jake — and the satisfaction of getting the better of Jake on this case.

Sally's head appeared over the edge of the trap door. "I left Homer in charge at the bakery, but you know how he is." I did know. Homer was Sally's five-by-five, part-time assistant, not a bad baker in his own right, but more likely to taste the product than to sell it.

"C'mon up." I reached back and helped pull her into the attic.

"Look at all this stuff. You haven't been up here since …"

"Since Dad's funeral. I never could face clearing this out."

"So you choose today for your cleaning spree?"

"I'm looking for something," I said. "We can talk and go through this stuff at the same time. Give me a hand." We moved some old cane-backed chairs and a small bureau out of the way to clear a path to the back of the attic.

"Looking for what?"

"A murderer," I replied.

Sally's eyebrows lifted in surprise. "Ramford's?"

"Jake thinks there may be some connection between Dad's death and Ramford's." I told her about the gun sale.

"I can't see Claudia as a pistol-packin' mama, can you?" she asked.

"Not likely. Let's take on this filing cabinet first." We left unspoken the names of the Ramford brothers, boys who, like all boys in the valley, had grown up with guns.

"What am I searching for?" asked Sally. She had extracted papers from the overstuffed cabinet, piled them on a broken rocker, and was sorting through them as she sat on the attic floor.

"I don't know, Anything that looks suspicious. Maybe a letter threatening to close an account for nonpayment or any kind of a personal threat. I don't know!"

"You don't have to yell. I'm just trying to help here. Hey, look at this bunch of personal letters to your dad. Looks like they're from old college buddies. 'Dear Stanton,' this one begins, 'Guess you won't make this year's reunion. We all heard you got shipped off to Korea.' I shouldn't be reading these."

"Go ahead. You have my blessing. That was a long time ago, and with Dad gone, I hardly think there are any dark secrets from his college mates. Here are some more letters." I handed them over to her. "You skim these while I examine his business correspondence."

"Didn't you look at any of this stuff when he died?"

"No, I did not. I shoved everything up here, figuring anything important in the way of business would come to my attention through his lawyer." I kicked a corner of the bottom drawer to align it so I could pull it out. "Now, about the tastings. I think we'd do well to include someone selling food other than your breads." I tugged more papers out of the filing cabinet. "I don't mean anything that would cut into your baked goods, but something like sausages, cheeses, savory items that might go well with my brews. What do you think?"

"How about some herbs, too?"

"Great idea." I stood up and stretched. "The only thing left to look through is the steamer trunk." I pointed to the trunk, then remembered.

"Damn, I've got to run. I almost forgot my appointment with the bank president about my loan."

"I can just take all these letters home with me and read them tonight, if that's okay." Sally looked at me and laughed.

"What's so funny?" I asked.

"I think I'd consider removing the cobwebs and the dust from your face and arms before I showed up at the bank."

"Oh, right. Just throw the stuff on the table when you leave. You've been a real trooper to help, but I'll finish the rest tonight in bed. I gotta jump in the shower."

"Okay, if you're sure. I'll leave the letters. What about the trap door?"

"Leave it open. I'll get it later." I ran for the upstairs bathroom, threw my clothes on the floor, and turned on the water.

This was hard, so hard, going through Dad's stuff. Memories came back with a forcefulness I did not anticipate. I should have done all this long ago instead of carrying my feelings so close to me. The hot spray felt good on my grimy skin, and it washed away the tears that coursed down my cheeks.

I stepped from the shower, wrapped a towel around me, and walked out into the hallway straight into Jake's arms.

"What the hell are you doing here?" I tugged the towel more tightly to me and backed away from him. There was the tiny, crooked smile on his full lips. "What's so damned funny? Would you give me a little privacy?"

"Okay. Sally let me in as she left. Told me I might find you up here. Nothing is funny. That's all."

"And the privacy? I'm in a big hurry for an appointment."

"Right. I'll be downstairs in the kitchen." He turned to leave, hesitated, and looked back at me. I could swear his lips curved in a smile. "I closed the attic trap door for you."

I threw on some clean clothes, rushed down the stairs, and looked at the kitchen clock.

"I'm a half hour late. I'd better call the bank."

Jake was seated at the table, gazing down at the letters which Sally had left there.

"You find anything interesting in your prying?" I asked. I snatched the sheets of paper from his hands and picked up the phone.

"Sally told me what the two of you were doing. I'm just filling in for her."

I held up my finger for silence when I connected with the bank president's secretary. "Oh, sorry, Hera. Mr. Claxton waited for fifteen minutes or so, but he had an eleven-thirty tee time with Michael Ramford and Stanley, what's-his-name, the new brew master there, and they were waiting in the outer office to pick him up. I can have him call you tomorrow. No, wait, next week. He's off for a short trip to the Bahamas."

I couldn't listen any longer. "I know, a short trip to the Bahamas for some golf," I said and hung up.

Someone rapped at the screen door. I recognized Manuel Diego, one of the workers at Rafe's. His face was sweaty, as if he'd run several miles in the heat. He looked worried, as well as exhausted. "Mr. Rafe says for you to come quick. He tried to call, but the phone was busy. He sent me through the woods to get you"

"What's wrong?" I asked. Jake's cell phone warbled. I opened the door for Manuel and pulled him into the kitchen. Jake listened for several minutes, then flipped the phone closed.

"I'll tell you what's wrong," Jake said. "Someone tried to kill the brew master at Rafe's. I've got to get over there." At the door he turned to confront me, his expression drawn in lines of anger. "I don't know what game you and your buddies are playing here, but next time there's an attempted murder, I expect the first call to go to my office, not to you and the rest of your beer-brewing gang."

"I'll give Rafe your message," I said, "when I have the opportunity, but right now, one of the beer-brewing gang, as you put it, needs me." I pushed past him, gesturing for Manuel to follow me to my truck. "Oh, and one more thing. Since you're pitching in for Sally, would you lock up when you leave?"

Something childish in me wanted my words to aggravate him, and I wasn't disappointed. My eye caught an old habit of his when he was angry—a barely noticeable facial tic, the result of grinding his teeth to keep from yelling. *Good. This round was mine.*

I roared off down my drive, in the lead for only several seconds. Jake's police cruiser, lights flashing and siren howling, blew past me on the straight-of-way, then veered into the road leading to Rafe's place. As he passed, he waved and smiled. *Damn. Now we were even.*

Several county sheriffs' cars, in addition to Jake's cruiser, stood outside the brewing barn. Two EMTs carried a stretcher with someone on it—I couldn't see who—to an ambulance idling at the barn door. They loaded the person into it and joined the stretcher. It raced down the drive, rocks and pebbles flying from its tires.

Workers from the brewery and locals, along with

Marsh, Teddy, and Stanley, clustered around the entrance to the barn. Jake was right. It looked as if Rafe called the brewers first, then the authorities. No wonder he was so mad.

I jumped from the truck and pushed my way through the crowd of onlookers until I got to Teddy, standing outside the barn arguing with a police officer.

"No one goes in there now. Back off, and we'll let you know soon enough what's happening," the officer said.

Just then, I caught sight of Rafe exiting the far end of the barn through the gift shop door.

"Rafe!" I waved my arms and broke free of the crowd. He signaled me to follow him to the house. Teddy didn't notice us until we were almost up the steps, then he propelled his rotund frame around the back of the group.

"Wait up. What's happening?" he asked.

"What did you do, Rafe, call all of us?" I asked.

"He didn't call me. I monitor the police band," said Teddy.

"Let's go inside, and I'll explain everything to you. Would you mind, Teddy? I'd like a word alone with Hera."

Teddy's round faced turned purple, and he appeared about to say something in retort, but he cleared his throat and backed off the steps.

"Sure. Fine. I'll be around if you need me."

Rafe showed me into his study and gestured to a leather chair. He moved toward a cabinet and opened it.
"It's a little early in the day for this, but I could use a brandy. Want one?" I shook my head no. "I wanted us to have some time alone before the authorities got to you."

"What happened? I heard from Jake someone tried to

kill your brew master? Is Henry okay?"

"He's going to be fine. I called the ambulance first, then had a quick look around the place. Tried your phone, but when I got the busy signal, I sent Manuel. I can't say how everyone else found out." Rafe poured a shot of brandy in a snifter and took a quick gulp of it.

"Someone locked Henry in the fermentation room. I found him there unconscious and pulled him out."

"Why would anyone want to hurt Henry?"

Rafe gave a short snort. "Henry? No. I think someone wanted to get to me. Maybe they thought without Henry I couldn't continue to brew, or, at the very least, finding another brew master would slow me down. But there's something else, something I haven't told the authorities. Not yet anyway."

He tossed down the rest of the contents of the snifter, then took a seat across from mine.

"I like you very much, my dear, but I have to ask you some painful questions before the authorities do. I need to know your answers now."

I'd never seen Rafe this way, his face dark with anger, his lips set in a grim line. I wiggled in my chair under his scrutiny. "I don't know what you're saying."

"I haven't been too forthcoming with the other brewers since I bought this operation. I know all of you think I'm a rich dilettante with little knowledge of the brewing process. That's not strictly true. I was brewing ales in England before you were born, but I had to leave there suddenly. A small problem with the owner's wife. So I wandered around the continent, taking brewing jobs here and there. In those years, I had a tendency to take short cuts. A competitor of the brewery I was working for called in the police and accused me of stealing his recipe for a winter ale." He looked across at the brandy bottle sitting on the sideboard, shrugged his shoulders, and got up. This time he poured the liquor halfway up the glass.

"Did you steal the recipe?"

"Well, yes, but the brew I was making for my boss wasn't that recipe. I kept the competitor's recipe in reserve. I was brewing another one I had lifted years before. I may have been a thief, but I wasn't altogether without intelligence."

I looked at the handsome and sophisticated man sitting across from me and found it difficult to believe he was anything but the gentleman he appeared to be. A thief? No. Then there was his present occupation and the money it required for him to purchase this brewery.

"But what about this brewery?"

"As I was dodging the authorities in Germany, the gods smiled upon me for no good reason. Gods can be whimsical, it appears. The lady I had had a friendship with years before in England? Her husband had died and left her quite a fortune. Then she died soon after and left it to me. I guess I made a lasting impression on her." He raised his glass and saluted the woman or the gods. "I decided to look at it as a sign of some kind and go straight. Changed my name, lost my criminal past, and looked around for a brewery. This one came up for sale, and here I am, a respectable English gentleman."

Throughout his speech, Rafe continued to sip from the snifter and smile as if he found his past life amusing. Maybe he did.

"Why are you telling me this?"

"To let you know I understand people, especially

people who have brewing beer in their blood. People like you. When you want something enough, you may take short cuts." He set the snifter on the desk and leaned toward me. "Not only has my brew master been harmed, but I'm missing some yeast, Hera, some very special yeast."

The confession about his past was over. I suddenly realized he was accusing me of theft. "Me? You think I would copy your ales and steal your yeast? I thought you liked me. How can you possibly think I would harm Henry and then steal something of yours? Those aren't short cuts, as you called them." I gripped the arms of the chair to prevent myself from flying out of it. I wanted to run from the room. No, I wanted to slap Rafe. How dare he suggest I might do harm to him or to Henry?

"No, they aren't. That's attempted murder." Jake stood in the doorway to the study. Neither Rafe nor I had heard him enter the house. "You said nothing about a theft to me, Mr. Oxley."

"How much did you hear?" Rafe asked. "The conversation was supposed to be private."

"Enough to know your criminal past could be related to what's going on around here, and that's my business, not some private matter between you and Hera."

"Hera and I share a passion for brewing beer. You might find our particular zeal odd. As I told her, passion can sometimes encourage people to do unusual things, especially when they don't have the means to carry out their plans. Nothing against you, my dear," Rafe continued, turning to me, "but we're too alike for me not to give you a chance to come clean about the yeast."

"I'd never take a thing from you. Maybe I can

understand how you could suspect me of theft, given my financial situation, but trying to do harm to Henry?" After what Rafe told me, I wondered how well I knew this man and how much I liked him or could trust him.

"I had hoped the two events were unrelated, if you were the one helping yourself to the yeast," Rafe said. "I can't think the deputy sheriff here would think you capable of murder."

"To cover a crime? People do all kinds of things when they feel threatened," said Jake.

There he goes again, thinking the worst of me. "I'm not just people here. I'm Henry's friend and his colleague. I don't go around shoving people into rooms where there's no oxygen."

"Well, you do have the perfect alibi, at least for some of the morning. There's Sally, and you and I were together part of it." Jake turned his attention from me to Rafe. "You say your yeast is missing? When did you last notice it?"

"I ordered yeast specially constructed for my summer gold ale. It arrived yesterday. Now it's gone."

"Who knew it was here? You, Hera?"

"Of course I knew it was here. I was discussing ales with Rafe when the truck delivered it."

"Discussing ales?"

"Yes, I told Rafe I was considering new ales, and he was giving me some pointers."

"Doesn't adding to your line of brews require money, new equipment and additional products? Didn't I hear you were a bit pressed for investment capital?" Jake was smiling again, probably delighted he had found I had a motive for taking the yeast. I was safe on this one. I had no motive for murder, but I should have known Jake wouldn't stop there.

"So earlier this morning, you sneaked over here, took the yeast, and got caught by Henry. You shoved him into the fermentation room and locked the door from the outside." Jake's green eyes looked as hard as arctic ice as they met my own.

I crossed my arms over my chest. "You're more than welcome to search my place for the yeast. You won't find it there."

"I intend to search all of the breweries around here. I'll find it. You can bet I will." The freeze in those eyes dropped another ten degrees.

After Jake left the two of us in the study, Rafe said, "He knows something is going on in the brewing community, and you and I know he's right. Murder, attempted murder, and theft in our ranks. Obviously the culprit or culprits must be one of us."

"He thinks he has good reason to suspect me. I hope now you don't."

"I don't, but I had to ask you the question, didn't I? Please don't think too badly of me, my dear, but over the years I've become the suspicious type, and sometimes I forget many people are just as they appear." He smiled at me. "Like you."

"He'll dog you because of what he overheard. He's smart. He'll begin looking into all our pasts, and some of us won't hold up well to his scrutiny."

"You know something about the others?" asked Rafe.

Some of the others, I thought as I left Rafe's place. I wondered if the prodigal son, Ronald Ramford, had turned up yet. Jake was certain the family would be looking for him, and so was Jake. I hoped he wouldn't be asking me any questions about Ronald. I wanted the past to stay buried. Or did I? I thought about the letters lying on the kitchen table at home. I wanted closure on my father's death. Maybe the letters would provide a clue to the past.

Six

Damn! I had so smugly asked Jake to lock up when we both took off for Rafe's place. Now I'd have to pay for that moment of arrogance. I forgot my house keys. No matter. I hid another key in the brew barn on the door sill leading into the bottling and storage area.

As I entered the barn, I heard the conveyer line start up, the bottles clacking against the metal sides guiding them down the belt and toward the hopper dispensing the brew. My employee, Jeremiah Standish, stuck his head out of the bottling area as I approached. When we were in grade school, the other kids gave him a hard time about his looks, calling him lab rat and giving him the nickname of "Whitey." Jeremiah accepted all of this with his usual calm, even embracing the nickname and often introducing himself by using it.

"Might as well," he once said to me. "It ain't gonna go away." I thought him very clever to confiscate the ammunition others would use and turn it to his advantage, and it worked. There was almost no one who didn't like Jeremiah with his easy-going nature.

What a worker he was. In the five years he had been with me, he never was late one minute, never took sick leave, and had some kind of mystical relationship with my aging machinery. Whatever demands I put on the kettles and hoses, burners and bottler, Jeremiah could meet them.

Where someone else would have turned his back on the ancient equipment, Jeremiah made it perform to perfection. But there was a limit, he reminded me, and I knew the old bottling line, purchased second-hand from the Ramford Brewery, would deliver a last gasp soon. I had Jeremiah's word on that.

"Didn't expect to see you here today. I thought you were going into town to meet with the bankers. Sure would be nice to get some new bottling equipment in here. This line is slow today, and it's under-filling bottles."

"Soon, soon," I said. I reached above my head, my hand searching for the spare key I placed on the door sill.

"Here. Let me get that for you," Jeremiah said. "Hey, it's gone."

"Looking for something?" I hadn't heard Jake's approach because of the noise. How many times had this guy sneaked up on me and heard something I preferred he not? Jeremiah seemed as surprised by his presence as I. The two men nodded hello to one another. Before I could say anything to Jake, the racket from the machine stopped.

"Line's jammed," said Jeremiah. He ran into the bottling room, leaving Jake and me to confront each other.

"You have a nasty habit of sneaking up on people, you know. That's very unpleasant, especially on private property and during personal conversations."

"Yeah, I know. I've been working on that. You hear interesting things when no one knows you're around. By the way, that's a dumb place to keep a key. How many people know it's there?"

"No one, just me," I said, but that wasn't true, and Jake had just seen why not. "Okay. So Jeremiah knows." There were others. Michael, Sally, others. "Nice of you to lock up as I asked you to, but I left my house key on the kitchen table."

"I know," he said. He was dangling the key by its chain between his fingers. "I picked this up on my way out of the house and thought you might need it."

"Anything else?" I heard the line start up again, then as quickly shudder to a stop.

Jeremiah called through the door, "Well, she's done for. I hope you were successful talking the bank into giving you a loan."

"Can't you persuade it to finish this batch?" I asked. Jake and I stepped through the door and surveyed the now silent machinery.

Jeremiah shook his head. "Maybe. This equipment was trash when Ramford palmed it off on you. The old man never kept his machinery in good repair. Lucky he found a customer in you and you found me." Odd. There was a note of bitterness in his voice, something I'd never heard from Jeremiah before. Jake was quick to pick up on his tone.

"Sounds like you didn't much like Ramford Senior," said Jake.

"Wasn't I didn't like him. Wasn't much to like. I just didn't respect the man. Didn't treat his family any better than he treated his machinery. Probably less well."

"Jake," I said, "just back off a little."

"Never mind. I know what he's doing. He's sniffing around, trying to find out who might have had a reason to do in the old man. You might as well count me in as a suspect. I went to him for a job before Ms. Knightsbridge hired me. Ramford said no way was he going to hire a freak."

"So you didn't like him," Jake said.

"He lied to me. It wasn't because I was a freak he wouldn't hire me. It was because of my sister. I knew about the two of them, and he didn't want me around, afraid I'd open my mouth to the wrong people."

"I didn't know Mr. Ramford and your sister were, uh, seeing one another," I said. Out of the corner of my eye, I caught a look on Jake's face saying he already knew the story Jeremiah was telling. *Returning my keys. Ha! Just more interrogation.*

"They weren't. She was sixteen at the time. She thought he was going to get a divorce and marry her. I took her into the clinic when she got the abortion. He was nowhere around. Sent her some money." Jeremiah paused and looked Jake in the eye with a gaze daring him to comment. "I gotta get back to this machinery." He approached the line and resumed his work.

Jake used my key to let me into the house.

"You locked up, but you didn't close the window. Now look at the mess," I said. The letters and other papers which had been on the table were blown around the room. We gathered them up, bumping heads once in the process and colliding with one another several other times. Each time we touched, the physical contact sent tingly waves through my chest, and I found it difficult to catch my breath. I was crawling under the table to retrieve the final envelope and happened to look around and up. Jake was standing behind me with his hands on his hips, staring at my rear.

"You wanted to say something?"

"Yep. Nice hardwood floors, and ..."

"And?"

"And the window was closed when I left. Take a close look at those papers. Anything missing?"

"How would I know? I haven't had a chance to read through them yet. First, the problem at Rafe's and now the lack of privacy. You had more opportunity to give them a glance than I did."

"I didn't see much when I did. You ran me off, remember? Accused me of snooping. I was ... "

"Being damned aggravating, a habit you had in law school, and I see you haven't changed much."

"Someone probably lifted the key from the barn, used it to get in here, then climbed back out by opening the window. Whoever it was wanted to shove the trespass in your face by making it obvious."

He turned and walked out the door. I could see his head through the open window.

"Some broken limbs on this bush," he said. "Ground's too hard for any footprints. We could probably get some fingerprints off the sill."

"Great," I said when he re-entered the room. "Someone broke in here using my key, or someone else stole my key. Regardless, it's gone, and whoever came in had sufficient time to go through my letters and take any that were interesting. What's going on here?"

Jake removed his hat and swept it against his thigh in a gesture of frustration. "I don't understand you. You almost finished your law degree. You were going to sit for the bar in six months. Why come back here and settle for operating this rundown brewery? Why the booze business at all?"

"That's not what I asked." I tossed the letters on the table and sat. Maybe it was time for a showdown between the two of us. "I guess you never knew me very well, or you wouldn't ask why I'm in the beer business."

"Guilt? Was it guilt making you take over after your father's death?" He was getting too close to what I had struggled with all these years. He sat down at the table, reached across it and enclosed my hands in his. "I need to know. We once loved each other. At least, I loved you. I still care for you."

I pulled my hands out of his grasp and placed them under the table. His physical touch still sent a shot of desire through me, even after all these years.

"The problem is, we're failures in each other's eyes. You can't imagine why I'm into making brewskis, and I can't see you as a cop. We were both on the fast track at one time. Didn't you tell me you wanted to do patent law? And here you are, handcuffs hanging off your belt, one hand on your gun, the other reaching out to grab me and arrest me just for being part of the brewing world. What have you got against beer?"

"Okay, okay. Here goes. I guess you deserve an explanation, but then it's your turn." He folded his hands on the table and focused on them.

"My family had a problem with booze. Both my parents drank a lot. I was always able to control my drinking until you left me in law school. Then I really hit the bottle. I let my grades go to hell, and I dropped out. I took some jobs working in the lumber industry up north for a while, then drifted back down this way and started working with juvenile offenders. Went back to school for the criminal justice program. And here I am."

I didn't say anything for a while. Jake kept his eyes on the table top, then raised them to mine. "So what do you think?"

I let out a long sigh. "I think you're a big baby. It sounds like you are blaming me for your problems. You could do with some AA meetings to get your head on straight. As for your hatred of my career as a brewer, you're off on that one, too. I make the beers. I don't make people drink them."

I held out my hand. "Keys, please."

I watched something happen to his eyes, something I knew I was responsible for. First, they took on a look of astonishment, then hurt, and finally, a wall came up, one I knew only I could tear down. I intended to leave that wall in place. It protected me as well as him. I took my keys, turned on my heel, and left the kitchen. I heard the door close and his car start up. Whatever we had in the past was a memory. Now we were just cop and suspect.

I watched the sun settle on the valley meadow signaling late afternoon. I'd been pacing the kitchen floor since Jake left and thinking too much, reliving my stern speech to him earlier and knowing what I said was true but also cruel.

I thought of reading Dad's letters but vetoed that in favor of going to the hospital to see how Henry was doing. I called first and got one of my friends, Tom Cavanaugh, the head nurse on the floor to which Henry was assigned. Tom assured me there were no police around.

Rafe was in the room when I arrived.

Henry looked pale, and his breathing sounded thin, although tubes to his nose delivered oxygen. He wasn't up to answering questions, and I wasn't there to make him feel any worse than he already did. I expect he had had enough of interrogation earlier by the police.

"Rafe will tell you whole story," Henry managed to whisper.

"Do you know who locked you in and how long you were there?" I turned to Rafe for an answer.

"I found him around eleven, the time I usually make the rounds of the operations. He told me he heard something or someone in the fermentation room, and when he checked, he was pushed from behind. He struggled to his feet, saw the door close, and heard someone wedge something under the outside handle. As near as we can figure, that had to be around ten or so, right?" Henry nodded in agreement.

"If it was someone who knew your schedule, then the person was trying to get away, not kill anyone," I said.

Henry and Rafe nodded in agreement.

"That's what Jake figured, but it's little comfort to poor Henry here. He thought he was going to die from carbon dioxide before anyone got him out of there. I think Jake's right on the money. Someone from among us is trying to make trouble, but I can't figure out why."

"Someone broke into my house while I was at your place this morning," I said.

"Did they get anything?"

I thought about the letters. "No, not that I can see. It just unnerves me, and the duplicate key to my house is missing."

"The yeast," Henry croaked.

"Don't worry about it, old man," Rafe said. "I just ordered more before I came here. It should arrive tomorrow, and we'll be back in business."

"Does someone intend to use the stolen yeast?" Henry

asked. He coughed and sat further up in bed. "Who? The other brewers have their own yeast for ale, unless Hera here is making a new ale by moonlight."

It was a joke, and we all knew it. Rafe and I laughed, and Henry gave forth a kind of snort, dislodged his tubes, and had to replace them. Still, I worried about the remark. With the break-in and my key gone, I wondered what other trouble was afoot. Jake's words returned to me. I was certain he would find the yeast. I just wasn't certain where, and I hoped it wouldn't be in my brew barn, planted there to make me look guilty.

Tom stuck his head into the room and said, "Visiting time's over, folks. This man needs his rest." I patted Henry's hand and gave him a kiss on the cheek, and Rafe and I left.

On the way down in the elevator, Rafe turned to me and asked, "What's worrying you?"

"Nothing. Nothing. I just think I should change the locks on my house and my barn."

"Good idea. Got someone to do it for you? I could send over one of my men."

"Thanks, but I'll have Jeremiah do it tomorrow."

"We're all getting edgy with the murder and now this. Who's behind this. Any ideas?"

"Why ask me?" I heard the tone in my voice. It was sharp. "Sorry. I am on edge." I touched Rafe's arm and gave him an apologetic smile.

"The reason I asked is you've been here for years, and you know all the people in this valley. They were your friends and acquaintances even before your dad went into the business."

True. Everyone was familiar to me with the exception

of Francine, whom none of us knew well. "I can't think who would do all this," I said.

"Come by for a drink?" Rafe asked.

"Thanks, but I've got to run. I need to catch up on some reading." Past and present had to be linked in some way. Perhaps I might find the connection in my father's letters. They might help me understand my father better, perhaps lead me to someone who hated him enough to want him dead.

After I turned out the light, my mind wouldn't let go. I'd spent several hours going through all of the letters, most from Dad's pals. Cheerful notes about the good old days in college sent to the man in Korea. A few were letters from girlfriends. I noted the signatures but wanted to avoid reading missives from his love life, no matter how ancient and removed from me it was. There couldn't be anything of importance there anyway. I'd burn those tomorrow. They were yellowed and falling to pieces.

Then I ran across a small packet held together with a rubber band. It looked much newer than the rest. The paper was whiter, not as discolored with age, and the postmarks on these envelopes were newer, some during the seventies. The handwriting was too flamboyant to be anything but a woman's. It reminded me of Mom's. Dad and Mom were married during those years. Why would Mom write to Dad, when they were living together in this house? Some romantic game the two of them played? I didn't want to know about it. I had set the idea and the letters aside, but now they were keeping me awake.

I tossed back my covers and went downstairs to the kitchen. The letters lay on the table waiting for me to discover their contents. *Oh, what the hell. Dad is gone now, so what can it matter about his love life with Mom?*

I plunged in. After an hour of reading, I knew tonight was a night I wouldn't sleep. I blushed as I read the scorching passion coming through the words in the letters. Did my father return this woman's lust for him? As I read on through them, it appeared the two of them met often. So I had my answer. My father had had an affair.

What were you thinking, Dad? Did Mom know? Who knew? Did he? Did Mr. Ramford know? If he did, he was a man who would kill you for messing around with his wife.

Seven

I should just go over there right now. So what if it's three in the morning. I'd tell her a thing or two, let Claudia know she ruined my life, that she was a slut. Or maybe I should demand she tell me there was no truth in those letters, that they were the product of a delusional mind, hers.

The sad truth was, it wasn't Claudia Ramford I had a need to confront. I wanted to yell at my father. Anger roared through my head like a summer tornado. My father, my own father. *How could you do this to me, to Mom?* I pounded my pillow and shrieked out my bedroom window into the darkness.

By the time the sun came up, emotional and physical exhaustion overwhelmed me. Anger, grief, blame, and disbelief had fled, leaving behind them the smallest grain of rational thought, but enough to take me down another road, one more reasonable. I would talk to Claudia. Yes, I would, but not until I knew exactly what I wanted from her.

I suspected the affair between my father and Claudia Ramford somehow figured into recent events, but I wasn't certain how. Until I knew more I had to be careful. Whoever the brewer was concocting this murderous recipe, he or she was deft at stirring in a deadly product at just the right moment. So for once in my life, I decided to rein in my impulsive nature and hold my stubbornness in check.

I grabbed cleaning supplies and headed for the small shed standing near the brew barn. Good, old-fashioned heavy labor might free up my overloaded brain and allow me to think my way through to some sensible action. If not, it would exhaust me enough that I could nap in the afternoon and count on a clear mind later.

Dad had used the shed to store supplies, but since his death, I'd been throwing anything I couldn't decide what to do with into it. There were old hoses, parts from brew kettles, gardening tools, buckets, and who knew what else. It had been years since I'd taken inventory of its contents.

Now I needed the space to rent to Marni Henley, who was joining our Saturday tasting sessions with her herbs and flowers. The shed would be the perfect place for her to sell, display, and store her merchandise. She wouldn't have to load everything in her van each Saturday and cart it to and from my place, and the area to the side and back of it would afford her room to grow some of her herbs.

It would look pretty, too, I thought. *She and I could share the responsibility for taking care of the small garden during the week. In fact,* I said to myself, as I threw another rusty bucket out of the shed into the dump pile, *maybe Marni would like to use a half-day on Wednesday to open the shed for business also.*

Ned Potter's homemade sausages, which he was going to sell out of the back of his truck, Sally's breads, Marni's herbs and flowers, and my brews would provide summer tourists with a fun Saturday afternoon adventure. The other breweries—Rafe's, Teddy's and the Ramford facility—scheduled brewery tours every day between the months of May and October. If anyone wandered into my place on a weekday, I was happy to give them a walk through my small facility.

What the Ramford brewery might do for tours under the new brew master's and Michael's direction remained a mystery. Francine was too new to the business to decide yet how she would manage her own marketing and publicity, but she'd better get something together, or she'd lose the summer tourist season. *I should help her*, I thought first, but then reminded myself, *I should mind my own business and help myself by pushing for another meeting with the bank president.*

Money, money, money was the refrain foremost in my mind as I worked. In the background, my father's relationship with Claudia Ramford provided dark undertones to a chorus of concerns about the financing with the bank. I closed out the noise by digging more deeply into the junk in the shed and pulled out a spade shoved into the pile of items at the back. It looked new, but I didn't remember buying it or putting it in here. Could Jeremiah have gotten it? He usually told me if he needed new equipment. I'd have to ask him. It was too good to thrown in the discard pile, so I carried it outside and leaned it against the building. The spade would come in handy digging Marni a small herb bed.

In the bright sunlight, I noticed something on its blade. Oh, damn. It wasn't as good as I thought. It was covered with rust … or was it blood? I threw it on the ground and backed away as if it were a rabid animal about to attack me.

"You just found it in the shed? No idea who put it there? Do you keep the shed door locked?" asked Jake. I had dialed him as soon as I suspected the shovel could be the missing murder weapon, not that I wanted to call him, especially after our unpleasant parting. I preferred not seeing him ever again, and from the awkwardness he evidenced when he arrived, he felt the same way about me.

"Could you not keep pacing around and around with your back turned while you fire questions at me?" We were standing at a distance from the shovel, which still lay on the ground near the shed.

"I'll check it for prints, of course," he said.

"You'll find my prints on it. And that's blood, isn't it?"

"Of course. Your prints. Could be blood. Probably is." He walked away from me and back to look at the shovel. He was doing his best to treat me civilly, like a witness. So I settled on returning the favor. I would behave like one and handle him like a cop. *He is a cop,* I reminded myself, *even if he is one who looks damned good in the uniform.* The short sleeves showed off the muscles in his forearms, and the scattering of hairs there glistened in the sunshine. *Oh, man. Would my hormones ever learn to behave?*

"What now?" I asked.

"Like I said, I'll check this for prints, take it to the lab. I'll have my men go over this area and see what else they uncover."

"I need the shed back by this Saturday, actually before. I'm going to use it."

"I don't know if you can have it by then. Make other plans."

"Fine. Anything else?" *Should I ask him?*

"How long since you went into the shed?"

"Years?"

"How'd all this stuff get in here then?"

"Jeremiah and I just tossed things in from time to time. It's like a storage area for stuff we had no use for but couldn't throw away. It's never locked. What for? It's filled with useless junk. Is that a problem?"

"I wouldn't call a possible murder weapon useless junk. Where can I find Jeremiah? Is he working today?"

"Jeremiah is off today. He's a part-time student at the college. He should be in classes this afternoon. You can't think he could be involved."

"Everyone in this brewing community is involved one way or the other. A murderer, a thief, and those who would cover up for these acts." He turned and met my eyes for the first time today. "What're you hiding, Hera?"

I thought of the letters. "Nothing. Nothing." Now was the time to ask him, to change the subject. "Uh, what about the yeast? Anything?"

"I've been doing some reading, very interesting stuff on brewing. Now I know bottom-feeding yeast produce lagers and top-fermenting yeast create ales. Oh, yeah, the bottom fermenters work at a lower temperature than the ale yeasts."

"Oh, good for you. I hope you didn't think learning this was beneath your finely honed cop mind."

"I also found out there's a way to determine the owner of a particular yeast."

"How would that be?" I knew the answer, but I was testing him.

"A DNA analysis of the yeast. Fortunate you called me today. I'm visiting all the brewers, asking for a sample of each of the yeasts they use. I'll need some from you. The stolen product possessed a specific profile, which Rafe gave me. Now we'll see if any of the yeasts in the brew barns have the same make-up."

"Except for Rafe, most of us make both ales and lagers. I make only one ale, but I'm planning to add another when I get the money for the malt and hops."

"Ah, yes. That nasty issue of money again. So you should be my top suspect, then."

I ignored him and continued with a line of reasoning that didn't point directly at my vulnerabilities. "I can't understand why any of us would take Rafe's yeast. And why would the thief be so stupid to store the yeast in a place where you could find it, in our barns?"

"That's a terrific point. You're thinking like a true criminal, Hera. Now, how about it?" He held out his hand.

Jake left with the shovel and my yeast sample. The same thought kept running through my mind: *someone could plant the stolen yeast in a brew barn just as an unknown party stowed the shovel in my shed. What about the missing key to my house? Was there a chance someone had a key to my barn or to another brew barn?*

I shoved everything associated with the chaos in the brewing community into the back of my head, including my concern over Claudia Ramford's relationship with my father. The first tasting of the season was this weekend, and I had to be certain there were adequate supplies of the beer I wanted to promote in the brew barn's tasting room and the gift shop. The bottling line was cranky again, and Jeremiah and I had the devil of a time rolling out the supply I needed for the tasting. I picked through the bottles by hand to make sure each was filled and not merely halfway to the top.

Jeremiah directed a pretend kick at the bottler and looked at me. "Yeah, yeah, I know," I said. "That's what we're reduced to now, kicking our equipment to make it respond."

"I hear Michael's brew master wants a new bottler. Maybe he would sell you their old assembly. It might hold us for a few months until we got a new one."

"This one came from Ramford's. It seems like I depend on their operation to provide me with my equipment."

"Yeah, and it's lousy stuff besides. Sorry. You already know that."

I hesitated, not wanting to ask Jeremiah to do what I knew I should do. Knowing me, he offered.

"I could drop by there and ask, when I get out of classes," he said. Not awaiting an answer, he pulled his dark glasses down over his pale eyes, clapped his Yankees' cap on his head, and stepped out into the sunshine. I didn't have to tell him what I would pay for the machinery. He knew. Nothing, if they would donate to me. Cheap, cheap, cheap, if they wanted a few bucks for it. Getting the bottling assembly would hold off the wolf at the door, if only for a few weeks.

I didn't have the time to complete renovating the shed. Jake released it to me the Friday before the tasting, but ever the inventor in times of need, I had a plan for Marni's herbs.

Early Saturday morning, Marni and I constructed tables out of plywood and saw horses, decked them out with colored cloths, and set her herbs and flowers in brick tiers on them. Neither she nor I wanted to lose the opportunity to promote her offerings, but the weather was against us. The skies brought up black towering clouds around ten in the morning.

"We sure can use the rain," Marni said, "but I hope it either pours down right now and gets it over with or holds off until late afternoon." She extracted basil and thyme out of the back of her van and placed the containers on the table, wiping her hands on the denim apron she wore. Both of us were hot and sweaty from the work. I had tied my blonde hair back into a ponytail. Marni's short, dark locks, usually so smooth and sleek, curled in disarray over her ears and down her neck.

"Looks good," I said. "You should just give up and let it curl."

"Oh, right. Why do I bother with all the gel? I don't know. I always wanted straight hair like yours."

I chuckled. "And what do we gals with straight hair usually say? 'We want curly hair!'" A clap of thunder beyond the ridge cut short our laughter.

"Here she comes. Let's get in the barn."

Ned closed up the cap of his truck, and he, Marni and I ran for shelter. I slammed the door of the gift shop against the sudden wind, and we watched from the windows as the rain came toward us in a solid wall.

"Your herbs are taking a beating. I hope they survive the downpour and the wind."

A gust took a corner of the red cloth and whipped it over the pots. "There. Now they're protected," Marni said. The next gust pulled at the cloth, lifted it off the plywood and took the pots with it.

"Oh, no," we said in chorus.

I looked at the hill to the south of us. "Look at that." The swirling black clouds rolled overhead, but beyond the tree line, I could see sunshine and blue sky.

"I think we're lucky. This is a short one," Ned said.

Lucky for our tasting, but not good fortune for the area. We had endured a long, cold winter with little snow. Spring passed with no significant rainfall, and folks were talking drought. I felt blessed because my well was one of the deepest around, over two hundred feet, so the water for my brews was cold, clear, and plentiful. The other breweries' wells ran only one hundred feet deep. Ramford's dried up in a drought several years ago, but then, he had the money to buy water from the Indian Springs Company in the next river valley.

Five minutes later, after the storm passed, the three of us were picking up the cloths and containers on the ground, and tucking fragrant basil, tarragon, and cilantro back into their pots as Sally drove up in her beat-up truck.

"I had to pull off the road at the top of the hill and detour over the lumber trail."

"Can cars get through now, do you think?"

"I don't know. I know there are limbs down. Listen to those sirens."

"We were so busy picking up we didn't notice. I guess you were fortunate to make it here," I said.

The four of us looked at one another.

"Well, we're all here. All we can do is wait and see what happens this afternoon. There's still time. Maybe the roads will be open by then," said Sally.

So we waited. On five or six separate occasions storm clouds rushed into the valley, dumped five minutes of rain, and dashed out again. Between the passing storms, we moved all the products into the gift shop. In the later afternoon, four German tourists straggled in, took the tour, and bought a liter of Knightsbridge Ginseng Rush and a loaf of Sally's artisan bread, but they kept their eyes glued to the sky for another storm. The older man in the group confessed he was looking for the Belgian brewery but found the road closed to Rafe's place because of some downed trees.

"The road crews hit the county roads first for clean-up. Since my place is on one of the main roads, and Rafe's is not, I get cleaned up early," I said. "Maybe his road is passable now."

The German looked at his watch and shook his head. "Too late now. We have to get back to our motel and get ready for this evening. We're going to have dinner and then drive over to Cooperstown to the opera. But we'll enjoy your summer lager," he added. "It's just not the Belgian ale I set my taste buds on. I prefer ales."

Indeed. I'd heard the comment before, especially from German and English tourists. The English seemed to favor ales. Since the area was attracting more travelers from other countries, I knew my new ale would be a hit.

After our German visitors left, we decided to call it quits.

"I nearly gave away more brew in the tasting room than the liter I sold," I said. I knew the day was a bust for the other three also. I promised Marni I would finish the shed for her by next Saturday, but I could tell her spirits were low after today's poor showing. She and Ned were new to the Saturday tastings and looking for additional funds. If Ramford or one of the others could convince them to leave me, especially if I had no way to bottle more product and therefore little to sell, they had every right to look elsewhere. Sally, on the other hand, would hang stubborn. I knew that.

Once Ned and Marni headed down the road, Sally and I sat on the back steps bemoaning the washout of our day but feeling guilty that we couldn't be more sympathetic to the area's need for rain.

"That wasn't enough today to end a possible drought. Just our luck it rains only on Saturdays, though," I said. I took a sip of my tea and chewed on some of her bread.

"We might as well eat this. I can't put it in the day-old bin tomorrow, because I'm not open on Sundays. I guess I could run it over to St. Joseph's soup kitchen for their Sunday lunch."

"That's a long haul. Can your truck make it without its new transmission? Why don't I drive you there? We could stop at the burger joint, grab a sandwich, and then see what's on at the movies."

"Well, it's not dinner and the opera, but it'll do."

As we were gathering up our tea things, I spied Jeremiah on his bicycle pedaling up my lane.

"What're you doing out here today?" I asked. "It's your day off."

"I've got news to deliver and work to do," he said.

"Why didn't you just call? And what work?" I asked. I was puzzled. We weren't bottling today, and I had taken care of the other chores including transferring the wort into the fermentation kettles yesterday. He knew that, so what was up?

"Got to see if I can coax another run out of the bottler, 'cause it looks like we're not getting another one."

Eight

Sally and I followed Jeremiah into the barn. "They wouldn't sell?" I asked.

"Oh, Stanley and Michael sold their old assembly, all right. To Francine." Jeremiah stood in the doorway to the bottling room and shook his head at the old assembly line, uttering oaths of disgust under his breath. I couldn't tell whether his words were aimed at the ancient machinery or Michael and Stanley.

"Francine? She has enough money to buy new, and I thought she was planning a brewpub where she would sell only on premises, not bottle at all." When I took a breath, Jeremiah held up his hand like a school crossing guard, signaling me to stop.

He shrugged his shoulders. "I don't know. I don't know about any of this, just what I was told. No bottler for you."

"What does she need a bottling assembly for? I don't understand. I'd better go talk to her."

"I already tried that. You'll have to give her a call if you want to get to her today. Her road's blocked with an old oak the road crews are having trouble getting out of the way."

"No. I want to talk with her in person. I'll take the path through the woods and down across Teddy's pasture. He won't mind my trespassing on his property." I gave Sally a wave goodbye and told her I'd see her tonight.

I was wrong. *Why am I always off base when it concerns Jake?* I wondered. Just as I was emerging from the trees bordering Teddy's property, Jake stepped out from behind some bushes and blocked my path. "You? Teddy told me someone was up here, but I never thought you'd be the one."

I put my hands on my hips and planted my feet. "Teddy doesn't care if I use his property as a short cut. We all do this, have done for years. What's the problem now?"

"Teddy claims he's had visitors snooping around his property for the last several nights. I was taking a look at how a person might manage to get to his brew house without being spotted. Coming through the woods and across this pasture works."

"Well, it wasn't me until just now. Has Teddy had some kind of trouble?"

"No, but he's feeling spooked with everything going on here."

I nodded and scuffed my foot in the dirt. Jake dropped his eyes and toed the grass also. It appeared we had nothing more to say to each other.

After a few moments, he cleared his throat and said "So where are you going?"

"Francine's."

Silence again.

"Uh, found out anything about the yeast yet?" I asked.

"Not yet."

More toe scuffing. No eye contact.

"Hera?"

"Yeah?"

"I've got to go. Got work to do. You'd better let Teddy know when you use his property for a short cut from now on. You don't want someone taking a shot at you."

"Teddy wouldn't shoot me."

"No, but if he didn't know it was you, he might. Like I said, he's on edge with everything that's been happening, and now with trespassers."

I nodded goodbye and walked on. When I looked back, Jake stood in profile to me, staring off across the pasture toward the ridgeline beyond the trees. This couldn't be easy for him, a murder, theft, attempted murder, questions about my father's death. A tangled mess of events and clues, and Jake just recently hired into the position. I felt a little bit sorry for him, not that I'd ever let him know that.

I thought about the case as I hurried across the pasture, topped the next hill, and headed down the well-worn trail into Francine's place. The storms had passed, leaving fallen trees, downed limbs, and debris in their wake, but the air felt fresh as if all the wind, rain, and fury had been a big washing machine cleansing the earth and now hanging it out to dry. I wished the recent events would sort themselves out as cleanly.

I could make no sense out of the yeast theft and Henry's being locked in the fermentation room. They seemed unrelated to the murder. Perhaps they were, or perhaps the murderer had another motive in mind — keeping us all distracted and on edge so no one could think clearly about the case, not even Jake, who was running his tail off checking on trespassers and yeast thieves. All the brewers were becoming suspicious of one another, perhaps another goal of our murderer.

"Who's there?" A figure stepped out from behind the

barn as I hiked into Francine's yard, my presence shadowed by the towering oaks surrounding the brewery buildings.

"Marsh? It's me, Hera Knightsbridge. Is Ms. Ortega around?"

A rifle lay in the crook of Marsh Wilson's arm.

"Hera. Francine, come on out here. It's okay."

The short, auburn-haired woman I'd seen standing beside Marsh at the funeral poked her head around the barn door. I held out my hand. "We've never been introduced, but I'm Hera Knightsbridge."

She took my hand and gave it a firm shake, but her mind appeared to be elsewhere. "Oh, yes. I know the name. Francine Ortega. I wish we could have met another time. Right now, we've got a problem here. Our phones are down, and my cell is giving me lousy reception. I tried to call the county sheriff's department, but the dispatcher said Deputy Jake was tied up at Teddy's, and the other officers were out in the county because of storm calls."

"What's up?" I asked.

"Come in the barn, and look for yourself."

As we entered, I could see sacks of grain, many open and strewn about the barn floor. Francine had stockpiled a lot of malt.

"Thank goodness it's just the storage barn and not the big barn where we're setting up our brewing equipment. Who knows what damage she could have done there," said Marsh.

"She?" I heard a low moan from the far side of the room. A black and white Holstein cow poked her head around a pile of grain sacks in the far corner. She looked at the three of us with anxiety in her huge black eyes, but spotting no danger, she returned to munching the grain spilling out of the bags.

"How did she get in here?" I asked.

"We don't know. She probably ran in when she heard the storm coming. It's nice and dry, and the grain was just an added bonus, I guess," Francine said.

"You lost some of your malt, but it's kind of funny, you know."

"Oh, the cow's funny. What's not is the malt. Take a look at those bags," Marsh said.

I walked over to one for a closer inspection. Someone had applied a sharp instrument to it, and the sack spilled its contents onto the floor.

"They've been cut open."

"Yep, intentional vandalism," he said.

"No wonder you're so upset." I nodded toward the rifle.

The three of us watched the cow's full, soft lips snuffle the grain out of an open bag. She must have been in the barn from early morning, given the number of cow pies she had left around the cement floor.

"When was the last time you were in here before you discovered your bovine visitor?"

"I checked it last night around ten. We were getting ready for a wine tour today, so I was busy with the gift shop, tasting room, and the winery. We don't take the folks through this storage area," Marsh said.

"Well, she's somebody's cow. I'll call around and see what I can find out. Meantime, let's get her out of here before she overdoses on that stuff or leaves you some more gifts. It can't be good for a cow to eat so much grain at one time. If she drank any water, she'd probably sprout it out her mouth and rear end," I said. Francine let forth a short "Ha," and Marsh a "humph." I gave them a half-smile. The thought of who came into the barn and cut open the sacks overwhelmed any mirth associated with Bossy's meal at Francine's expense.

It took us the best part of an hour to get her out into the yard, where she began to chew her cud and cast loving glances back at the barn. Several phone calls on my cell to neighboring farmers led to the cow's owner, who sent his son right over to pick up their prize milk-producing Sarah Jean. It turned out that Sarah Jean was terrified of thunder storms and ran off when she sensed one approaching.

"Keep your barn doors closed, or she'll be back," recommended the son after loading her into the cattle trailer.

After Sarah Jean's departure, Marsh, Francine and I sat at the kitchen table, sipping one of Francine's fine Rieslings.

"I hope she doesn't tell the rest of the herd about her find, or they'll break down the barn doors," I said.

"You didn't just wander over here to help us out with the cow," said Francine. "What's up?"

"Maybe there's a better time to do business than while waiting for the authorities to show up and examine those slit-open sacks."

"No, no. I'm fine. I'm sure it's just a prank played by some teenagers around here. Maybe they even led the cow into the barn."

I thought Francine was being naïve, and from the look of doubt on Marsh's face, I knew he agreed with me.

"Go ahead. Tell me what's on your mind," she said.

"That bottling assembly you bought from Stanley and

Michael? I sure would like to buy it from you. I don't have the money for a new one, so I thought maybe, since, uh, you're in a better cash flow situation, you might sell it to me."

"Bottling assembly? From Ramford's? I didn't buy a bottling assembly from them."

I was hot, so hot ... furious with Michael for jerking me around and lying to Jeremiah. I ran back the way I came, detouring before I entered the woods and almost stumbling down the hill behind Michael's brewery.

"Michael!" I jerked open the door to the brew barn and yelled. A worker checking the fermentation kettles pointed toward the house.

Claudia opened the front door, a glass of water in her hand. I hadn't thought I might run into her. Foolish of me. It was her house. I put aside my discomfort. Besides, I still wasn't ready to talk about Dad. Maybe I'd never be ready for that conversation.

"I came to see Michael. I need to see him. Now."

Claudia ignored the abruptness in my tone of voice. "Hera, dear. Come in. You look as if you've run a marathon. Would you like something? Iced tea, a glass of water?"

"Nothing, nothing." I repeated my request. "I need to see Michael."

"He's off somewhere with that girl of his."

"Today? He's off today? It's Saturday, the biggest brewery tour day of the week. He should be here overseeing the tours."

"I do that now," said Stanley, emerging from the office. "Besides, today we had to cancel the tour because of the weather. Don't tell me you had any takers today?"

I spun around to confront him. God, I hated that smug look of his. A long cut on his face ran from his ear to his chin, from shaving perhaps. It pleased me, that cut. It was another flaw in the man, along with dressing as if he had just picked his clothes off the floor.

"I didn't come to talk with you. I came to talk business with Michael."

"I make the business decisions here, don't I, Mrs. Ramford?"

Claudia sipped her water, then nodded in a manner that said she couldn't care less who did what in the place. She turned and headed toward the kitchen. "If you want anything, just help yourself. It's in the fridge."

"If you want anything other than a beverage, I think you'd better talk with me. How about in my office?" he said. He gestured toward the door on my right.

"Your office? Isn't that Michael's office now?"

"It's company headquarters. I don't have all day. Do you want to talk or not?"

I watched him walk to the other side of the desk and sink into the leather chair, moving as if he'd done this all his life. He placed his hands behind his head and pushed the chair back. "Get to the point."

"You told Jeremiah that you sold your old bottling line to Francine. That's not true. I need ... I mean, I want to buy it."

"Not for sale. It's junk. I was going to sell it to her, but I changed my mind. I wouldn't consider selling it as a bottler to anyone. I can get something for it as scrap metal."

"Jeremiah can get it to work, I know he can." I tried to

keep the sound of pleading out of my voice. I would not, would not, beg from this man.

"I'm sure he can, but I don't want to chance your suing me when something goes wrong with what I sold you."

"I won't sue you." I was begging. I could hear it in my voice, and I hated myself for it.

"I only have your word on that."

That did it. I leaned over his desk, my face only inches from his. "If I give you my word, I give you my word." I bunched my hand into a fist and held it in front of him.

"If you're threatening me …"

"She's not threatening you," said Michael. He stood in the open doorway. "If she wants the damn thing, sell it to her."

"She's our competition. She's got no money, and if she's got no bottler, she's out of business. Don't be stupid, Michael."

Suddenly, a smile broke out on Michael's face. "You're right. She is our competition. Let's see what you can do, Hera."

"I've already made arrangements to have it sent for scrap metal," Stanley said.

"Make other arrangements. Next time, clear these decisions with me first."

I was about to rush over to Michael and give him a hug, but a voice called to him from beyond the room. I recognized it as Cory's.

"Honey, come on."

"We just came back for something, and we're going to be late. I'll have the bottler delivered tomorrow." Michael gave a rueful smile as Cory entered the room, grabbed his hand, and tugged him toward the door.

I looked at Stanley's face, which was purple with rage, but my heart was singing. *I have my bottler, I have my bottler.*

"Michael left it to me to negotiate price," he said.

"Did he? I didn't hear that part. I'll give him a call soon on the price thing." I left Stanley standing behind the desk not looking quite so in control of the situation as when I had entered. I won one, with Michael's help, of course. I couldn't count on his generosity to get me through in all business matters. Now I had to tackle the bank, but I was glowing as I left the office.

I could use some water, I thought. I'd sweated more in the office with Stanley than I did dashing across the fields and up and down hills to get here.

"Claudia," I called. She wasn't in the kitchen, which was fine with me. I hardly knew what to say to the woman. When I opened the fridge, I spied a container of cold water on the bottom shelf. I grabbed a glass out of the cupboard and poured the liquid to the top. Here's to business, I said to myself, holding my glass aloft in a silent toast. I gulped and coughed. Not water at all but pure vodka. Was that what Claudia was drinking all during the funeral and today?

Nine

The next day the bottling assembly arrived, just as Michael promised. The best part was, he came along and helped Jeremiah set it up after we dismantled the old one.

"Remember when you bought this one from us?" asked Michael. "It was the year after your fa ... after you took over the business, and you were strapped for money, so Dad offered you our old bottler. I think he never bargained on your being such a good brewer. But I knew. I knew you'd do well. Okay, let's see if this baby works."

I flipped the switch, and the apparatus let out a loud screech followed by a rumbling noise. The line began to move. The clatter of the bottles traveling down its length and the howl of the grinding gears sounded like a concerto to me. Jeremiah looked shocked and ran for the wall switch. I headed him off as Michael and I broke into peals of laughter.

"That sounds about right," Michael said. I agreed.

"Yep, that's the chatter and bawl I remember from your place." I looked over at Jeremiah whose mouth had dropped open and remained so. "Well, Jeremiah will want to fine tune her a little."

Michael clapped him on the back and encouraged him to have a run at smoothing out the operation. With a nod of agreement from me, Jeremiah walked the line listening for the worst of the screaming and clunking, then returned to the switch and flipped it to the off position.

"I'll have her purring in no time," he said. Michael and I left him there with tools in hand. As we walked toward his car, Michael slipped his arm around my shoulders.

"Feels like we're back in high school, huh?"

I agreed. "It does." It felt like the days when we were teenage friends, and our interchanges and work together came with ease. There was no strain in our relationship, and the deaths of our fathers didn't somehow come between us.

Michael accompanied me into the kitchen. "Coffee?" I asked.

"No, thanks. I've got a few, uh, errands to run."

I wanted to ask him if he had a date with Cory, but I feared the answer would be yes. Instead, I said, "We never talked about a price for that piece of junk out there."

"As I understand it, that piece of junk is saving your life, brewing wise."

"Okay, so what do you want for it?"

"I don't suppose you'd give Stanley and me a chance as your partners, would you?"

"Stanley doesn't want to be my partner. He wants to eat me for dinner." That got a grin out of him.

"Okay. Look, I'm sorry that you don't like him, but he's a great brewer. You should talk to him sometime. The two of you have a lot in common." Michael arose from his chair at the table and approached me, laying his hand on my shoulder. Talking about Stanley set my teeth on edge and ruined the camaraderie I had experienced this morning with him. I resented his bringing up Stanley's name in our conversation.

"No way." I shrugged off his touch and walked across

to the sink, grabbing a glass and turning on the faucet. The water flowing into the glass reminded me of the pitcher in the Ramford fridge yesterday.

"How's your mother doing lately?" I asked.

"As well as you would expect, given the violence of my dad's death and her worry over Ronald."

"Ronald?"

"Yeah. We're trying to locate Ronald. The terms of Dad's will left the business to Mom, Ronald and me. We've hired a private investigator to find him, but so far, no luck. I have to tell you, I'm baffled that Ronald would get anything, considering the way Dad felt about him. I dedicated my life to that place and to Dad, and he goes and gives Ronald the same piece of the pie that I have."

Michael continued to babble on about his disappointment in the terms of his father's will, but my mind was miles and years away, back to the fire at the hop house and Ronald's last words to me:

"I know what you're thinking. Bad Ronald can't control himself. Another fire. So I'm going away. If I can get beyond Dad's reach, I'll be okay. I'm never coming back. Never! Tell your folks thanks from me. They've been great." Ronald turned his face toward the fire, his features outlined by the leaping flames, his eyes black with fear and disgust.

"Hmmm?" I said as Michael called my name, drawing me back to the present.

"You haven't heard from him, have you?"

"Me? Why would I be in touch with him?"

"Well, you know how your dad interfered with Ronald and our father."

"He didn't interfere. He was trying to help Ronald.

Someone had to. Your father was horrible to him. You know that."

"Well, he was horrible to me, too, and I didn't run off."

This was the first I heard that Michael's dad had treated him badly.

"He was strict with you, but did he hit you or humiliate you like he did your brother?"

"He didn't have to. I saw what he did to Ronald, and I towed the line, I guess. He was cruel in many ways, distant to both me and Mom. He ignored me until I was old enough to be of use in the brew barn." He gritted his teeth, working his jaw, then stopped. His next words indicated he had gathered himself together.

"But that's over now. I just thought maybe, since Ronald liked your mom and dad, he might have gotten in touch with them at some point."

"I'm sure Mom and Dad never heard from him after that awful night when he burned the old hop house down."

But I had heard from Ronald. It was a secret I'd kept for years, and I wasn't about to betray him now.

"If you heard anything, you'd let me know, wouldn't you?" I walked him to the door. On the stoop, he turned and put his hands on my arms, pulling me to him. "You'd let *me* know, wouldn't you?" He bent down as if to kiss me, but the sound of someone clearing his throat startled us, and we sprang apart. It was Jeremiah.

"That new guy you hired and wanted me to train? He's here."

"Just go ahead and get him started. Might as well bring him in from the beginning." I turned to Michael, glad of the interruption. "Sorry, but today I'm beginning more summer brew, and I'm training a new man, so I've got a lot to do. Now, about the price."

"Five hundred bucks, payable when you get that summer brew out and sold. No hurry. I'm almost as curious to see what you do as I am what Stanley can do for me. Good luck." He turned and headed toward his truck, then stopped and walked back up to me. In a low voice, he said, "About that deputy sheriff's suspicions ... "

"What do you mean?"

"You know, his wild speculations about my dad and your dad's death. You don't buy any of that, do you?"

"I don't know, but I have had second thoughts about Dad committing suicide. How about the gun? Your mother bought that gun, you know."

"So I was informed by the authorities, but I can't believe Mom would buy a gun. She's not the type. So, I'm thinking maybe ..."

"Maybe your dad forged her signature." If I thought voicing my suspicions to Michael would startle or offend him, he evidenced no surprise or anger in his reply.

"Come to think of it, Dad and your father seemed to have some kind of a falling out before the suicide."

I knew now it had to be murder, and I knew the motive. Mr. Ramford found out about his wife and Dad. Should I tell Michael what I knew? No, but I certainly should tell Jake about the contents of those letters.

"Hera? Boy, you sure are drifting off on me this morning. Are you okay?"

"I'm just fine. Now you'd better hurry, or you'll be late for whatever. Don't worry about Jake. I'll talk to him about all of this."

"You, but why? Oh, I get it. You still have a thing for

him." Michael gave me a thumbs up and retreated to his truck before I could deny his words.

I watched his truck turn onto the main road and started to contact the sheriff's department, then flipped my cell phone closed. A thing for Jake. That was absurd. I disliked the man. He was rude, insolent, officious—and damned sexy. In law school, our coming together oozed sex, but our competitive natures also colored the relationship. Jake and I vied for top honors in all our classes. Had it not been for the sexual attraction, I don't think we would have spoken to one another. So with all that lust in the past, what did we have now?

I knew something he didn't about Dad's death, information he ought to have, information I could use to find my father's killer. That would take the arrogant smile off his face. But there was more than defeating Jake at his own game. I fancied seeing him knocked down a peg for abandoning me when I needed him most after my father died.

As much as these meanderings gave me pleasure, there was something much more important at stake here. I wanted to find the truth about Dad's death, to be released from the load of guilt I continued to carry. I owed it to his memory to remove the stain suicide left on his reputation in this community. How could I not take action? I had been so remiss about the gun.

I threw the cell phone on the kitchen counter and headed for the brew barn to see how Jeremiah and my new hire were making out with Hera's Honey.

In the late afternoon, I fed the wort liquid from the heated malted barley put into the brew kettle. Sometime during the week, one of my neighbors who still had a milking herd would come to pick up the grain left in the bottom of the mash lauter tun. Cows loved the mash, and it was good for them. It would be my new hire Brian's job to remove it from the vessel and pile it behind the brew barn. Jeremiah and I boiled the wort for ninety minutes, adding the hops necessary for bitterness at the beginning of the boil. At the end, we would determine the amount of hops to add for aroma and flavor.

He and I drew the clear wort through the heat exchanger to reduce the temperature of the liquid. Now came the moment of truth when I added my new yeast, not repitched yeast used in my Ginseng Rush, but yeast I had sacrificed my last pennies to buy in order to produce Hera's Honey.

An hour later, nothing was happening. *Damn. What did I get for my money, a lousy batch of yeast?* I grabbed the liquid yeast bottle and examined the label. Yep. It was the yeast I ordered. I shook the bottle, then yelled at it.

"Why don't you run your errands in town," said Jeremiah. "I can look after things here." I hesitated. "I'll call you on your cell if I need you." He shoved me toward the barn door.

As I drove into town, I told myself I should feel on the top of the world. I had a bottler that worked, well, for now, at least, plus the addition of a new lager and a feeling I could get to the bottom of my father's death.

I had to talk with Claudia at some point, I knew, and when I considered that, my mood dropped into the cellar. Those damn letters. If the authority working this case was anyone other than Jake, I would turn them over to him and tell him what I knew about Ronald.

I swung down the street where Sally's shop was located. I could use a sounding board. I passed the bank on the corner and wondered if it had gotten around to considering my loan application yet. I'd drop by after I talked with Sally.

"You know where Ronald is?" asked Sally, her blue eyes wide with surprise. She plunked two mugs of tea on the table and sat down across from me. The bakery was empty. I had told Sally everything I knew.

"I don't know where he is, as in an address, but I can get in touch with him if I need to."

"As in, his father is dead, murdered, need to," Sally said.

"I know. I already took care of that. I put the message in the want ads of the Albany paper as he arranged for me to do if something important concerning him happened. If he wants to, he'll reply. I don't know how, but he'll get in touch. So far, nothing. It's been all over the papers around here, and if he's reading the want ads for any message, he'll know. I figure he couldn't care less about the death, murder or not. Ronald hated the man."

"Maybe hated him enough to come back here and kill him?" Sally asked.

That very question had been running through my mind along with a sense that Ronald didn't need a message from me to tell him of his father's death.

"Yeah, that's what I'm thinking too. Then again, I think it's understandable Ronald is laying low. As a preteen, he got blamed for almost everything bad happening around here, whether he was involved in it or not. What a mess. I have so many pieces of this puzzle, but none of them fit together to make sense."

"Isn't that what Jake is supposed to do, make sense out of this stuff?"

"That's not what I want to hear right now."

"You know I'm right about this. However much animosity you have for him, this is a police matter. You've got to tell him everything. Besides, from your odd behavior, I'm beginning to think you have some kind of a thing for him."

"I do not have a thing for him," I yelled. "Okay," I said, calming down, "maybe you're right. I'd better stop by the department and talk to him."

My cell phone rang. When I answered it, Jeremiah was on the line. Although his voice was calm, I could tell from the slow and determined way he strung together his words that he was worried, terribly worried about the fermentation.

"The yeast doesn't want to work. I thought maybe our thermostat was giving us trouble again, so I bumped up the temperature to the top of the fermentation range, around fifty degrees to see if the mercury moved. Nothing. She's not fermenting. It's like the yeast is dead," Jeremiah said.

Ten

That's all I needed, a bad batch of yeast. Was it incorrect storage on my part, or did the manufacturer send me a degraded product? *Damn, damn.* I pounded on the steering wheel as I raced home. I should slow down. These country roads were tricky. A patch of gravel, and my truck could fly off the road, and it wouldn't make any difference whether my yeast was dead or not. I would be.

I careened into my drive, floored it up the hill, and brought the truck to an abrupt halt in front of the barn. I jumped out, leaving the door open, and bolted into the brew house. The new man Brian, a slight, fair-haired college student, paused in his shoveling of the grain from the mash lauter and nodded to me as I entered.

"I told Brian this wasn't the way things usually went," said Jeremiah.

"No, it isn't." I climbed the metal steps to the top of the fermentation vessel, opened the hatch, and looked in. Nothing. The brew sat there still, not a bubble on the surface and no yeasty fermentation smell.

I checked the outlet valve and the temperature of the mash. "We're not pulling carbon dioxide from the outlet valve. Hand me the yeast bottle again," I said, holding out my hand. The bottle looked like our usual bottles. I smelled the residue left in the bottom and looked at the sludge still clinging to the inside. "It looks different somehow. Something's not right with this yeast." A growing suspicion began to work its way through my mind. I extracted my cell phone from my pocket and dialed Rafe's number.

"I'd be glad to drop by and see if I can help," Rafe said. "Be there in five."

When Rafe's tall frame entered my barn, I wasn't sure I was happy to see him. When he confirmed my hunch about the yeast, I was horrified.

We cranked up the temperature of the liquid as he suggested and waited. At around seventy degrees, we began to see bubbles, and I could bleed off carbon dioxide, one of the by-products of fermentation—alcohol being the other—from the chamber.

"You're making an ale," Rafe announced. He sounded proud of me.

"I didn't intend to make an ale and certainly not using your stolen yeast."

"You don't know that," he said.

"Don't be silly. You know it's true also. Now what?"

"Your call," he said, guessing what I would do.

I dialed the one number I'd been avoiding all day.

"Jake. You'd better get over here. I think I have the stolen yeast."

"I suppose you intend to arrest me now," I said. Rafe and I had explained about the yeast. "You could use that fancy DNA profiling to be sure, but I'll bet that yeast is Rafe's, and he thinks it is, too. A quick look at it under a microscope would confirm I have yeast made for ales."

"Don't be a boob, Hera. I know you didn't steal the yeast, but someone wanted to point a finger by planting it on you. They took a bit of trouble, too, dumping it into your yeast bottles. So who wants to get at you?" Jake asked.

I thought about the question and could come up with only one person, Michael's brew master, Stanley. I didn't mind mentioning the name to Jake.

"I'll take a run over there and see what both of them have to say about this. Meantime, let me urge you once again," he scowled at me, "to get those locks changed on both your house and your barn."

"More pranks, do you think?" asked Rafe.

"In the last few weeks, we've had one murder around here, an attempted murder, and a theft. These are more than pranks."

"Don't forget the cow," I said.

"The cow?" asked Jake.

"You know. The slit-open malt bags and the cow."

"I know about the bags, but what cow?" It appeared Francine had contacted Jake about the malt but hadn't let him in on the cow eating it. So I told them about Bossy. Brian, Jeremiah, and Rafe laughed, and I had a bit of a chuckle retelling the story. Jake continued to scowl.

"I didn't want to alarm Francine, but Marsh and I agreed. It looked like more than simple vandalism, especially when put together with the rest of these crimes. So you may not be safe, Hera. I hate to repeat myself, but get those locks changed. Today."

"I'm not a child, you know, so don't talk down to me."

Before Jake could reply, Rafe cut in.

"He's not treating you like a child. He's worried about your safety. Isn't that right, Jake?"

"I'm concerned for all the brewers around here. Some

person or persons has stirred things up. Everyone is getting paranoid. I had to remind Marsh a rifle wasn't a good thing to be carrying around. I just hope you two," he gestured at Rafe and me, "don't have some weapons you're wanting to reach for."

Rafe and I both shook our heads.

"As for those locks," I said, "you must think I'm rich or something. If I'm going to change those locks, then *I'm* going to change those locks, me, not some locksmith who's asking sixty or more dollars per lock labor plus the cost of the mechanism. In case you haven't heard, I'm strapped for cash." I didn't mean to be so testy with Jake, but I had more than locks on my mind. I should terminate the brew in my kettle, dump the mess, clean the tun, and pay Rafe for the expended yeast.

"I could help you with the locks," Rafe offered.

Jake looked Rafe up and down and seemed to come to some decision.

"Tell you what, Mr. Oxley, I'll give you a hand. I've got the afternoon off, so I can run into town and grab the locks. I'll meet you back here around three," Jake said.

My mouth fell open. "You're going to do what? Not on my building, you're not."

"It's all settled, my dear. Consider it a business comp from one brewer to the other. See you back here, then," he said to Jake. Rafe turned and left the barn.

"So what do you want to call this gesture? A comp from your friendly local cop?" I asked.

"How about an old friend comp?" Jake said. Before I could reply, he turned and left also.

Old friend. Ha! Up until now, he hadn't acted like an old friend. He was just all cop. I stood in the middle of my brew barn, clenching and unclenching my fists, my mouth opening and closing around cuss words like a big-mouthed bass on a worm. He stuck his head back into the barn.

"I'll bring you the receipts from the locks I buy. I'm not that good a friend. See you later."

Jeremiah cleared his throat, and Brian busied himself around the other side of the kettle, sweeping up nonexistent dirt from the floor.

"So what do you want to do about this brew here?" asked Jeremiah. He slapped his palm on the side of the kettle. "Toss it?"

I was about to answer yes, but my penurious nature got the better of me.

"Just one minute." I dialed Rafe's cell, swallowed with difficulty at the thought of what I was about to do, and asked Rafe my question.

"What do I care? The yeast is gone, and I'm covered by insurance. Why not put it to good use? Sure. Go ahead."

And so, my summer ale was born. I christened it Knightsbridge Summer Serendipity. Like any proud parent, I was curious to see how my offspring would develop and if others would find it as exciting as I did.

The locksmiths returned at three. I had my head beneath the bottler while Jeremiah turned the line on and off, and I fussed with the labeler. I didn't hear Rafe and Jake until they entered the bottling room to install a new lock on the door leading from there to the outside of the building.

In the short time they shared the labor of changing my locks, they seemed to be developing a friendship, a phenomenon I noted with much grinding of teeth. I liked

Rafe. He was my kind of person—charming, intelligent, complex. Now Jake, on the other hand, was charming, intelligent, complex, a pain in the butt, sexy, and a danger to my sense of sensual independence, clearly not a person with whom I should complicate my life. Well, maybe I could risk a quick look at his derriere, which appeared not to have changed much, unless it was more muscular, after five years. *Hmmmm.*

"All finished, except for the house," Jake said. I signaled Jeremiah to turn the bottler back on.

"I said …"

"I heard you."

"We need to attend to the house now," said Rafe.

"Fine, fine. This way. I'll make some coffee." I shimmied out from underneath the line and led the two of them toward my back door.

"Don't bother about the coffee," said Jake.

At the same moment, Rafe said, "Great. We could use a cup."

I smiled at Rafe and glared at Jake. "Coffee. Right." Jake appeared less than enthusiastic at spending any time in my house.

"Hera can fill us in on her plans for her new ale," said Rafe.

"I can't say I'm really interested in the brewing business," said Jake.

"Nonsense. Everyone who has a sense of history wants to hear about how beer is made, and you look like a man who respects the past."

Rafe and Jake worked on the locks on both the front and back doors while I brewed up a pot of coffee. Coffee alone seemed less than gracious, so I scrounged around in my cupboards and found a package of store-bought cookies, probably stale by now, and placed them on a plate. The three of us sat down at the table and sipped our coffees and munched on the cookies, for which I apologized.

"I've been too busy to do much cooking or anything."

"So I guess you and Jake knew each other in law school?" Rafe asked. "Where was that?"

Both of us began explaining at once, laughed at ourselves, and then shared the floor talking about our days in Albany. The more Jake and I talked, the more the old patterns of camaraderie and friendly academic competition took over. Out of the corner of my eye I watched Rafe's lips curve in a smile as if he had somehow planned for Jake and me to recapture the fun and excitement that defined those years together. *You old dog*, I thought to myself. *You're trying to play cupid.* I rose from the table, thinking I should put an end to all of this. I had no intention of getting entangled in Jake's life, and I was certain he would abhor the thought of recapturing romance with me.

"Never mind, my dear. I'll get it," Rafe said. He beat me to the counter and grabbed the coffee pot. Without asking, he refilled our cups and said, "And now you're making another ale, all of your own designing. Probably not the way you intended to begin, but nevertheless an ale. So where do you plan to go from here?"

"Well, as Jake said before, he's not interested in lager or ale," I said.

"I'll bet he's willing to get interested, especially if he's going to be living and working in this area. Right?" Rafe looked at Jake for confirmation and then continued,

"Brewing is a way of life here now." *Rafe Oxley, you're something,* I thought.

As I laid out my plans for the summer and the fall, I got more and more excited about the tastings and the new brews I might be creating. Soon, my ideas carried me away, and I was unaware of my audience, just of the images of golden lagers and brown, foamy ales filling my brain. When I paused for a breath, Jake's face drew my attention. There was an odd expression on it, something close to respect for what I was saying. Maybe I was wrong. He dropped the look when he shoved his chair back and got up.

"I've got to be getting back. Thanks for the coffee and the, uh, stories."

I approached him with my hand out. "No, no, thank you for doing those locks. Wait just a minute, and I'll write you out a check for the cost of the equipment."

He took my hand and shook it, then held on for just a moment too long for it to be a gentleman's handshake. I pretended not to notice, but I bet Rafe did.

"I'll get the check some other time," Jake said.

"It won't bounce." I snatched my hand out of his and put both hands behind my back where I curled them into fists. It was stupid, but I seemed to react to his approaches with pugnaciousness.

"If it did, I'd know where to find you. Good evening, Mr. Oxley. Nice talking to you." He closed the door behind him and left Rafe and me in the kitchen.

"I thought that went well, didn't you?" Rafe asked.

"Soooo, no problems installing those new locks, I gather."

"That's not what I meant, and you know it. That's one

smart man. Good looking too."

"Oh, leave it alone. It's water under the bridge. In fact, the stream is dry now," I insisted.

"Oh, I don't think so. The two of you had quite a thing going back then. Who's to say it can't start again?"

"Me, that's who. Sorry. I didn't mean to snap at you. I've got a lot on my mind. Money mostly. I mean to pay you for that yeast, you know."

Rafe flapped his hand at me in dismissal.

"He told me he'd checked out all of us," Rafe said.

"So he knows …"

"Pretty much everything. Not his fault. He's just doing his job." Rafe sighed. "I knew someday my past would catch up with me. It always does, you know."

I let him out the back door and watched as he walked toward his car, his shoulders slumped forward in an attitude of dejection. This case seemed to be exposing more of the past than many of us wanted revealed.

Back in the house, I flopped down in a kitchen chair and realized the cookies I'd had with coffee were the only food I'd eaten all day. There was nothing in the fridge. I was tired out from the adrenalin rush I'd had with the yeast issue and physically exhausted from the wrestling match the bottler had given me. Too weary to go into town and shop, I ate the remainder of the box of cookies. Filled with sugar and chocolate, I thought they were certain to keep me up well into the night.

But I fell into a deep sleep and dreamed of bubbles as they rose in a pilsner glass of amber colored lager. *No, no, that's not right. It's not a lager, it's an ale*, I was shouting to someone. *It's poisoned*, the voice replied. I woke up with a start, sweat covering my body. The clock blinked three in the morning. It was too early to get up, but I knew I'd never get back to sleep. *I'll check the ale,* I thought.

I grabbed the new keys off the hook in the kitchen and stepped out into the still night. Not quite still. I could hear frogs croaking from the pond on my property, and a night hawk flew across the fields on silent wings and into the woods beyond, offering his lonely cry. I turned my gaze skyward, looking for my favorite constellation, Orion, but clouds obscured most of the stars, forecasting a rainy day tomorrow. We needed rain, but I said a silent prayer to the thunder and lightening gods to put it off until Sunday.

The key slid into the new locks with hardly a catch or a sound. I turned on the lights and headed toward the fermentation kettle, but I never got there. A hand covered my mouth while another grabbed my arms. Garlic-infused breath whistled out of a mouth close to my ear, and I felt the scratch of an unshaven face on my cheek.

"Not a word, dearie. Not a word. It's time you and me had a little talk."

Eleven

My hand shook as I placed the teacup on the table in front of my unwelcome guest. For the second time in twenty-four hours, I was entertaining in my kitchen. This time tea, rather than coffee, was on the menu. A look of anger crossed his unshaven face when I said I had nothing to offer him with his drink.

"Not much for hospitality, are ya," he asked, "or are ya just stingy?" He looked in the fridge for himself and shook his head at my lack of supplies there and in the cupboards, which he also examined.

I was beginning to calm down after my initial shock that someone had broken into my newly secured barn. If he noticed my jitters, he didn't mention it, probably too intent upon guzzling his drink.

While he slurped his tea, spilling as much down his chin as he managed to swallow, I took in his appearance. A black, long-sleeved sweater and black pants clothed a stocky body. He wasn't much taller than I, but the sweater revealed the muscles of a weight lifter or fighter.

"Oh, sorry about that," he said as he pulled a black knit watch cap off his head. His scalp showed pink in patches, either the results of a bad haircut, baldness, or some skin disorder.

His accent was English, but working class, not the polished speech used by Rafe.

"What do you want?" I asked. I'd said little from the time he grabbed me in the barn until now.

"Oh, I see. You've got a tongue, have you? Good. Now use it. Tell me about this Rafe Oxley."

"Whatever you want to know about Rafe, you'll have to ask him."

His small, piggish eyes snapped in anger. He arose from the table, reached out, and grabbed me again. We headed out the door to the brew barn.

"I know enough about you, Missy, that I bet you don't want your nice, new brew being tampered with, do you? There are a lot of things I can do to make this batch a failure, and that would put you in a pretty mess." He looked around the brew barn as if searching for something.

"Let's see here. Should I throw all of your yeast into the kettle? Hmm? Or should I take this hose off here and dump the brew on the floor." He reached for the valve at the bottom of the vessel.

"Stop it!" *My precious brew.* I had to save it. Fearing less for myself than my brewery, I rushed at him when he grabbed for the hose. My sudden action took him by surprise. As he turned to ward off my attack, his foot slipped on a loose drain cover and down he went, hitting his elbow with a crack on the cement. I grabbed the pole I used for stirring wort and slammed it down on his head as hard as I could. He fell to the floor and lay there, not moving.

Oh, God, now I did it. I killed him. I didn't really feel bad that I'd done in someone who was threatening me and my property, but then again, I didn't know what a murderer felt like. Until now, that is. I felt relieved and a little guilty,

I guess.

Damn. Now I'll have to call Jake and tell him what I did. With trembling fingers, I picked up the phone in the barn and made the call.

"He's not dead, but he's still unconscious. He's going to have a hell of a headache when he wakes up. You really gave it to him. What did you hit him with?" asked Jake. He had arrived in a little over five minutes from the time I made the phone call. The body on the floor gave forth a moan.

"Looks like he's waking up. Maybe now we can get some answers." Jake propped him against the wall and stepped back. "What's your name?"

"Bernie Fisher. Who're you? I was attacked. By her," he said. He pointed a dirty finger in my direction.

"You were trespassing, and you threatened her and her property."

"I was attacked," Bernie repeated. "I want a doctor and a lawyer."

"You're going to need both, Bernie boy," Jake said. He cuffed the man and pulled him to his feet.

Early the next morning, I drove to the supermarket. It was humiliating having a common thief accuse me of being less than sociable. Having some food in my fridge and freezer gave me a sense of comfort and organization, a hedge against the financial insolvency about to overtake me. Pleased with my false feeling of satiety and with a stomach full of milk and Oreo cookies, I lay down for a short nap. *A night of nabbing thieves really exhausts a person,* I thought.

I awoke with a start, realizing my rescheduled

appointment with the bank was this afternoon. I had an hour to prepare myself. The truth was, I hated the idea of meeting with the bank president and asking for money. I knew I was procrastinating, but I decided to detour to Rafe's place to say hello. I wanted to ask Rafe some questions about my unwanted visitor. Bernie professed to want information from me about Rafe, but I wasn't buying that. Something told me Rafe knew this man. I pulled into the drive and wasn't surprised to spy Bernie Fisher leaving the brew barn with Rafe.

"Mr. Fisher. How's the head? And the breaking and entering business?" I asked. Sarcasm colored my voice.

"Sorry about that. I was in desperate straits, needed food bad. Kind of down on my luck, I was." Bernie removed his dirty cap from his head and kept his eyes on the ground as he talked to me.

"Rafe," I said, "could we talk?"

"I think you know the routine, Bernie. We'll leave you to it," Rafe said. He took my arm and walked me toward the house.

"Don't be so polite. Ask away," Rafe said.

"He's working for you? Why? I got the impression he was a real rounder."

"I'm sure he is, but he knows brewing, and I can use a hand until Henry gets back on his feet."

"There's something you're not telling me," I said. I was missing part of Bernie's story, but I could see Rafe was not.

"He's a hard worker, catches on fast," Rafe insisted.

"He's a common criminal who has something up his sleeve, I think."

"That's why I hired him. I want him close to keep an eye on him."

"He asked about you at my house last night. Why was that do you think?"

"I don't know."

I found this conversation frustrating, as well as confusing.

"What's going on here?" I asked.

"Just a voice from my past," said Rafe. "I know Bernie Fisher. He and I were good friends at one time, if you consider thieves can be buddies. Bernie's the kind of friend you can buy. So I bought him for a while. Maybe I can find out what he's up to. Don't worry yourself about him, my dear. He won't bother you again. That, I can promise you. Now, I must go. I've got a batch of ale I'm working on." He looked up at the cloudless sky. "I hope we get some rain soon." He walked off toward the barn with a smile and a wave. I was still puzzled at why he would hire such a man—a thief and scalawag.

"What's that guy up to?" Jake's hand curled around my arm as I hopped out of my truck. I brushed off his grasp and closed the door.

"Hey, let go. If I don't feed this thing, the local meter maid will ticket me." I slipped two quarters into the slot.

"Rafe. What's going on with him and Bernie?"

"I haven't any idea. I have an appointment with the bank president, and I'm late already. If you want to know what's going on, ask Rafe."

"I already did when he bailed out that piece of scum this morning. Then I saw the two of them drinking coffee at the diner, and they drove off together in Rafe's Mercedes. Very suspicious."

"It's Rafe's business." I opened the door to the bank,

hoping I would spy Mr. Culler, the president, and could get away from Jake's probing questions. I could tell Jake what Rafe told me, but it wasn't my place to do that. Anyway, none of it made any sense to me.

"The two of you are friends. You must know what's going on."

"I don't. Now leave me alone." I saw Mr. Culler's secretary Evelyn walking toward me, a scowl on her face.

"Mr. Culler is waiting for you. You're late."

"See? Gotta run." I rushed after her sling-back heels in my work boots, our footsteps making a clack, clack, clump, clump across the marble floor. She paused halfway to the office and looked down at my shoes. She said nothing but shook her head and continued on her journey with me in tow. I felt like the ugly duckling, but it was unlikely that I would turn into a swan, at least not today.

Mr. Culler may have been waiting for me, but it wasn't in his office. Evelyn showed me into what looked like the board room, empty except for a long table surrounded by chairs. She told me Culler would be right in. I wandered around the table, then chose a chair facing the door. Bankers must have an odd sense of time. Mr. Culler walked in the door fifteen minutes later, offered me the smallest of smiles, and sank into a chair with the deepest of sighs.

"You see, Miss Knightsbridge," he began, "this is a very conservative bank with limited funds for lending." I looked at him across the expanse of polished mahogany, bare except for a bottle of Maalox he'd set on the table when he sat. He caught me eyeing it and tucked it into his pocket. In all the years I'd interacted with him at the bank, I'd never seen the worry wrinkles on his forehead relax.

The man looked permanently distressed. Perhaps he was. His complexion had the pasty grey-green color that comes from too little sunlight. Maybe he only left the bank at night and came in before dawn. Unless he was golfing, that is. His voice drew me back to the matter of my loan.

"Also, the board is quite concerned about the recent death, er, murder, of Mr. Ramford. The county sheriff's office is on the case."

Oh, oh. I think I know where this is heading.

"So, given the status of the murder, we're not prepared to take a chance on you as a client."

"But I've borrowed money here before. My record is spotless. I make my payments and on time."

"Who knows how long this case may drag on with no resolution? Someone in the brewing community is responsible for the death, er murder, and, although we don't suspect you, we can't take the risk given the, uh, situation."

He started to rise from his chair, but I reached out my hand to him.

"I can assure you this will be wrapped up in no time. I know the officer in charge and he's ..." Words failed me. All I could see was Jake's scowl every time he approached me about the case. "The officer is very dedicated and serious about making headway, and he's relentless in his pursuit of the truth. We were in law school together."

I knew I had said the wrong thing by the look of skepticism that crossed Mr. Culler's face.

"In law school together. You're friends?"

"Uh, we were friends. Kind of lost touch since then. I just know the caliber of man he is, that's all. He's not the type to let friendship get in the way of examining evidence in a case." Well, that was all too true. If Jake could figure out a way to do it, he'd love to slap me in jail for any number of legal and personal infractions—dumping him in law school, my acerbic personality, suspicious connections to the deceased's family, and the yeast theft at Rafe's. So perhaps he wasn't entirely free from prejudice in his dealings with me. I decided to change the direction the conversation was going.

"If you're concerned about the future of my business, let's go over my business plan together. I expect to add to my offerings. Why, right now, as we speak, I'm brewing up what I hope to be a truly outstanding ..." *Oh, oh, better not mention the ale in my fermentation vat, the product of stolen yeast, even if I didn't steal it.* "...brew," I finished vaguely, "a great new brew."

"I'm sorry, but we cannot take a chance with our money where there is criminal activity involved. Once this murder and theft thing is cleared up by your outstanding friend, Officer Jake or whatever his name is, then come on back here and have a talk with me."

Now I was getting mad. How dare this little, rinky-dink bank with its balding, cowardly president deny me a loan.

"I can go elsewhere, you know, and I will," I said and arose from my chair.

"Please do, but I think you'll find all banks around here to be skittish when it comes to the brewing businesses in this valley. The story of the murder made local and state headlines. The banking industry knows about it. I doubt you'll find a bank will take you on, but give it a try." He seemed to look smug at the certainty I would be denied funds.

"I suppose that applies to all the brewers around here?" I asked before I turned toward the door.

"You're the only one who's applying for a loan that I know of," he said. "Good day, Miss Knightsbridge."

A rap on my truck window alerted me to the presence of Officer Williams, the most junior of the police on our local force. I lifted my head from my arms, which were draped across the steering wheel, and rolled down the window.

"I'm gonna have to give you a ticket, if you don't either move your truck or feed the meter," he said. His tone was friendly, but firm. Just doing his job, I knew.

I heard the knob on the meter twist with the insertion of a coin and raised my eyes to see Jake at the curb.

"Thanks, sir," said Officer Williams. He continued up the block, stopped at the next expired meter and looked back at us, a puzzled expression on his face.

Jake stepped up to the driver's side window.

"They said no, right?" he asked.

"I am so screwed," I said.

"How about a drink?" he asked.

"Booze?"

"I do drink from time to time. In moderation. I'm off duty. Come on. Follow me in your truck, and we'll go to my place."

"Nope."

"No?"

"No. This is not the time I want to drink in moderation. I want to get ugly drunk, just for a while, and I want to be home to do it. And I'd like to be alone. No, I take that back. It's not good to drink alone. I'd like to get stinking drunk with a friend."

"I'll be a friend tonight. We'll go to your place, and if I get too drunk to drive, I'll just sleep in your barn or something."

I looked at him carefully. He wasn't kidding. No lopsided grin on his face, no sarcasm in his voice. Why the hell not? I didn't feel like inflicting my poor old self on any of my friends. Jake would do.

I started up my truck, backed up, and floored it. In my rearview mirror I watched Jake run for his car.

No money, no money, no money. The reality of my financial jeopardy ran through my head as I drove. *Oh, damn.* I missed my turn. I looked in the rearview mirror to see Jake's car pull into my drive and then stop. It crossed my mind to just keep driving, but I braked at the next lane and made a U-turn.

What the hell. I might as well get drunk with an old lover and ... and what? What difference did it make? My life is a shambles anyway.

"So, are you ready for a little Rush?" I asked. I jumped from my truck and approached Jake. His face registered something like shock, and then he grinned his lopsided smile.

"It's the name of a lager, Dummy. This might be the last chance you get. I don't have much stock left." I grabbed his arm, and we headed for my fridge.

Twelve

"Hoppy, but not too hoppy." Jake sipped the golden lager with a look of pleasure on his face. He sat in Dad's old easy chair with his feet propped up on the ottoman.

"Oooh, I'm impressed. Where did you learn the lingo?"

"I've been reading a little about the beer business. It's pretty complicated, but interesting. Now I know there are several kinds of malt."

"More than several," I said, then shut up and let him go on.

"And hops give the brew bitterness, right?" His tone of voice reflected satisfaction at having mastered his homework. "Your hops come from the Pacific Northwest."

"You didn't get that from a book. You've been snooping around in my barn." There was no suspicion in my voice. I was feeling too mellow to be accusatory. I sat on the couch, feet up, slurping my second scotch. I could feel the liquor make its way into my stomach and produce a warm, curling glow there. Jake was on his first bottle of Ginseng Rush. If the small moans of delight emanating from his throat were any indication, he was enjoying it. I'd told him about my conversation with Mr. Culler.

"You can wipe that look of phony concern and sympathy off your face. Be honest. You could care less about my business. If it goes down the tubes, so be it. In fact, you think I should find a more legitimate way to earn a living. Right?"

With a slow, precise motion, he set his beer glass on the side table and leaned forward.

"I was wrong to go off on your craft the way I did the other day. You were right. You're a businesswoman, not the devil. My drinking, my problem. I'm sorry."

Jake offering an apology? This was a side of him I'd never seen before. Maybe I should re-evaluate my assessment of this man. I squinted at my drink. Or was that just the scotch muddling my judgment?

Thunder sounded in the distance. I turned to look out the window. Clouds were gathering over the ridge, and lightening split the sky. The rumble that followed sounded closer.

"Maybe we'll get that much-needed rain." He took up his glass again and sipped, turning it so the liquid caught the dim light through the window.

I settled back into the couch with my scotch. *I should go slow here*, I thought. *No sense in abusing good scotch or taking for granted the apology of a proud man. There's been a bell weather change in our relationship in the past few days. Are we both mellowing, getting used to one another's presence, leaving the past behind, what? Or does he want something from me?* I waited.

"So what are you going to do now? About the business, I mean?" he asked.

"I don't know. I've got enough product to last the early part of the summer. The ale I'm working on now will help my sales, but once the season is over, I think I'm done. I can't make enough money in the next few months to get through until the new year. I'm out of the brewing business unless I take up Michael and Stanley on their offer to go halfsies with me."

"Halfsies?"

"I'm the brewer. I brew here, but they own half this operation. I don't trust Stanley. I need that bank loan, no strings attached, and I'm my own boss. But the only way I'll get it is if Ramford's murderer is found." I took another small sip of my scotch, my courage for what I was about to say.

"Jake." I shifted my butt around on the couch in discomfort. Jake's face had the alert look of a feral cat being stalked by a coyote, convinced it could use its wits to outsmart its predator. "You know what I'm about to ask, I guess."

He leaned forward in the chair, his elbows on his knees, and studied me.

"It's fine with me. I wouldn't mind some inside scoop on this community of brewers. Your take on what's going on could only help, unless you decide to snoop on your own," Jake said.

"I'd never do that. I promise you. I need to find out who killed Ramford, especially since you think his murder is tied up in my father's death. It's not just a matter of financial survival for me. I can't carry around this load of guilt about Dad's death forever." *Whoa here. The scotch must be loosening my tongue.*

"What guilt?"

"I thought at first Dad killed himself because I didn't do enough to help him get through Mom's death, but now I know I was being selfish, focusing on my own feelings of inadequacy and not seeing the situation for what it was. You said it yourself. I knew my father didn't own a gun, and I knew he wasn't the kind of man who would take his own life. I was playing pitiful Hera and have been for these past five years. I need to pull myself together."

"You think scotch will help?" He accompanied his comment with a small smile, an obvious attempt to break through the tension of my confession.

"Oh, crap, no." I banged the glass down on the coffee table with a thunk.

"Okay, deal. You're my silent partner, but no attempts to go off like the Lone Ranger on me."

We both stood and solemnly shook hands. Lightning and the rattling of the windows from a thunderclap sealed our new partnership. We dropped our hands and laughed. The tension in the air wasn't just ozone.

"How about some cheese sticks?" I headed for the kitchen. As much as I wanted to get sloppy drunk, I didn't need to be sick drunk, not in front of an old lover, a man who was evidencing sensibilities I admired and my new partner. I pulled out some crackers, salami, and cheese sticks from my newly replenished larder and put them on a plate. As I turned, Jake walked up behind me.

"Let me help with that." I turned to hand the tray to Jake just as a crack of lightning hit in the yard, and the thunder shook the foundation a nanosecond behind. I jumped and dropped the tray before Jake could catch it.

"Clumsy," he said.

"I am not."

"I meant I'm clumsy, not you."

We both bent to pick up the scattered remains of our snack.

"There goes our snack. I'll make more."

"Never mind. Let's wait out this storm and drive into town for a real meal, my treat."

"I'm not so poor I can't pay my own way." *Bite my tongue.* I was back to surly while he remained nice.

"Fine. Pay your own way, but we need to get some food into you. Those two scotches can't be sitting well on your stomach."

"Then I'd better take a look at my ale before we leave." I left the remainder of my scotch in the bottom of the glass. "Want to come?"

The wind kicked up and hurled leaves and other small debris at us as we headed across the yard to the brew barn. The sky was turning dark. I flipped on the lights as we entered the barn, mounted the platform, and opened the hatch on the fermentation vessel. Yeasty. If I could define heaven in terms of smells, that was it. Then I held my breath, crossed my fingers for luck, and peered in. Everything looked great. I extracted some of the liquid and poured it across the refractometer to read the specific gravity of the brew. That would tell me the alcohol content, but before I could get a reading, the lights went out.

"You okay up there?"

"Yeah, I'm coming down."

As I was about to put my foot onto the first step, a crack of lightning startled me again. I grabbed for the railing but missed and fell down the steps and into Jake's arms. *Hmmmm. This feels pretty good.*

He held me close to him. I could make out the flecks of gold in his green eyes, and I remembered how they seemed to catch fire when we made love.

"You're not going to take advantage of a drunk, financially insolvent, clumsy old friend, are you?'

"Only if she wants me to." *Oh, my.* His lips touched

mine lightly, then began a firmer exploration of my mouth.

Someone cleared his throat behind us. We froze for a moment, then Jake set me back on my feet.

"I hope I'm not interrupting anything." Rafe Oxley stood in the door of the fermentation area, his expression lost behind the fingers playing with his mustache.

"Not at all." My face felt hot. "I was just showing Jake my operation, er, I was showing him how the refractometer works."

"There doesn't seem to be enough light in here to get a good reading." This time I could see a smile working at the corners of his mouth. "I'm glad to find both of you here. I need to talk to you, and I'm sure the deputy would like to ask me some questions, too."

"We were just about to go out and grab dinner someplace," said Jake. "Why don't you join us?"

As we prepared to leave the brew barn, the rain hit, a torrential downpour that got my hopes up. I could tell Rafe was silently cheering on the rain, too.

"I'd give my Mercedes if this rain would keep up the entire evening and the rest of the night."

Another heavy gust of wind, the dying sound of thunder, and the storm rushed over the far ridge, barely leaving the ground wet.

"The county board meets tomorrow night and will be presenting a plan for dealing with this drought. The word is, if we don't get rain soon, there'll have to be restrictions imposed on all water use, and it will extend to private wells. The brewers could be hit hard if that happens," Rafe said. His next words revealed his concern over our situation. "Then there's the danger that our wells will go dry. You've got the only deep well in this valley, Hera."

"Yeah, isn't it the way. I've got the water, but no money."

Rafe put his hand on my arm to stop me as we were hurrying for the cars. "I'd like to offer you a small loan to tide you over the summer."

"No, no, you've done enough."

"Let me finish. I'd like to make the offer, but I can't. With the cost of the hops I use on the rise and this issue of water coming up, I'm close to the edge myself."

I was shocked. *Rafe with no money?*

"It's only temporary until I can get payment from some of my larger customers." He looked uncomfortable at this confession, and his eyes wouldn't meet mine. Was he lying about something?

On the way into town in Jake's car, I shared my concerns over Rafe's comments with Jake, but Jake didn't see Rafe's financial condition as odd.

"This winter was a rough one. The ski resorts couldn't make snow because of the warm winter. We only got one substantial snowfall, and it melted in two days. Everyone's feeling the pinch around here. Why shouldn't Rafe?"

Maybe Jake was right. I guess most of us thought Rafe's pockets were bottomless. I leaned over to check the outside rear view mirror. The Mercedes followed us.

"I always thought of Rafe as wealthy. I mean, he inherited all that money, and I know he didn't come close to using all of it when he bought the brewery. I think it's strange, that's all."

"Okay. I'll check into it."

"No, don't. I didn't mean for you to get involved. I like Rafe."

"I do, too, but I have to check on everybody associated

with the Ramford murder. Rafe's financial situation may be relevant."

Dinner was not a success. Rafe was quiet, not mentioning whatever it was he wanted to talk to me or to Jake about. My head was off doing mental calculations of how long into the fall I could continue the Saturday tastings before I ran out of product. The pizza arrived, and we settled down to eat, but before Jake could slide a second bite into his mouth, his pager trilled.

"Sorry. Emergency. I'll get back to you." He threw a twenty onto the table and left. Rafe and I ate a slice each in silence, then had the waitress wrap the rest.

He dropped me off at my house, refusing an offer for coffee. "You look like you're about to fall asleep on your feet."

The earlier consumption of scotch caught up with me, and all I wanted was a pillow under my head. I was grateful Rafe turned down the coffee. One quick peek at my brew, a walk through the barn, and I locked up for the night. The scotch knocked me out, but not before I reviewed my earlier calculations as well as the kiss Jake and I had shared.

Thirteen

The convertible shot up my drive and slammed to an abrupt halt in front of the brew barn door, where I was standing. I watched as Michael got out of the driver's side and noticed that Cory occupied the passenger's seat. I waved at her. She flapped her hand at me and opened a mirror to check her face. She smiled at her image and flipped the compact shut. Then she looked back at me, her glance traveling from my wind-blown hair to my dirty flannel shirt and my torn jeans. Her sculpted nose wrinkled slightly when she reached my mud-covered boots.

"Coming to the county board meeting tonight?" asked Michael.

"Of course. All of the brewers should be there. We need to present a united front to the board and make our requirements for water known, or we'll all be out of business," I said.

"Except for you. You'll have all the water you need, although I can't say much for your financial future with no hops or barley in your barn." What he said reflected my own words last night to Rafe and Jake.

"I'm working on that," I said. I tried to put more confidence in my voice than I felt.

"Let me help you a little, then. Here's the deal. Our wells are low, and I'm sure the county is not going to worry about providing the breweries with public water. All of us except for you will be buying it from Indian Springs across the ridge. The cost of the water and of hauling it will eat up our profits. Tell you what. I'll pay you ten cents for every gallon of water you let me take from your well, up to a point, of course. I don't want you to go dry." He laughed.

"Is this little scheme yours or Stanley's" I asked.

"Well, of course Stanley knows about it," Michael said.

"Because it was his idea, right?"

"You're going to make me angry with your suspicious attitude. What other options do you have? This way, you get enough income to stay afloat for the summer."

"Barely enough, and my well isn't bottomless, you know. If the county board imposes mandatory restrictions on private wells, I wouldn't be able to sell you my water anyway."

"There are ways around that, you know," Michael said.

"That doesn't sound like you talking. It sounds like Stanley or … "

"My father. I sound like my father. He'd find a way around the law, and I will, too." Michael's face took on a look of stubborn determination.

"My well could go dry, too, you know."

"Until then, you might as well make a little easy money. Come on. It's a fair deal." Michael's usual pleasant and charming smile replaced the look of grim determination there just a minute ago. He reached out his hand and placed it on my shoulder and squeezed. I heard the car door open.

"We need to get going to make our tee time," Cory said. She swung her hip into Michael's while placing her hand on his. "Michael?" she purred. "Don't make us late."

I ignored her and gave Michael a friendly pat on the hand still resting on my shoulder.

"Let me offer a counter deal. You pay me the same amount for my water that you're paying Indian Springs."

"That's robbery," Michael said. He dropped his hand and moved away from Cory's embrace, shoving his face inches from mine. "I can't make any money that way."

"Of course you can. You save money on your hauling fees. It's only a short sprint for the trucks to carry the water from my well to your storage tanks. I think I'm being more than fair."

"Mickey?" Cory's voice was now more insistent, and she was using a nickname I'd never heard him called by before.

I looked at Cory's golf get-up, so new I was surprised tags weren't still attached to her white skirt and pink knit shirt. Michael's mouth opened to say something else, but I beat him to it.

"What's your handicap?" I asked Cory.

"What?" she asked.

"Your handicap, Dear. In golf."

"I don't have a handicap. Do you see one of those parking permits hanging off the mirror on my car?" She gestured toward the convertible.

"See you tonight." I turned back toward the doorway to the barn. "I'll give you until then to decide on my offer."

As I entered the barn, I heard Cory's voice, whining and angry now. "What's she saying about me? Do I look handicapped?"

"Just get in the car. We'll set you up with the course pro for some lessons." Michael sounded exasperated, whether at me or Cory or both, I couldn't tell, but I didn't really care.

Mickey, I thought to myself. *Who ever called Michael Mickey?* I chuckled and opened the fermentation hatch. *I'm making ale.* I sang a little brewing song to myself as I worked.

"This is bedlam," said Rafe. The two of us arrived early to the county board meeting and took the last two empty seats in the back. "All the golf course owners, farmers, the hospitals, colleges, and the brewers are here as well as other businesses and private landowners." The room was so packed with people fifteen minutes prior to the start of the meeting that the overflow was led off to another room to watch the proceedings on closed circuit television.

I turned to search out the other brewers. Francine had come early and sat beside Marsh in the front row, while Teddy, Michael, and Stanley, arriving minutes after Rafe and me, took up positions standing at the back wall.

The chairman of the board called for the meeting to come to order, and the room quieted.

"Some people don't believe we have a water crisis, but with the rate wells are going dry in this county and the lowered water level in the river and nearby lakes, we're in trouble."

"Maybe some of us got trouble," said an angry voice from the rear of the room. "You can't tell me not to draw water from my own well."

"Let's calm down here. We're not at the point of mandatory restrictions, but we may have to phase them in if we don't get rain soon. We'll lay out what we think is a good plan and then get comments from the floor. Until then, let's not interrupt," said the chairman. He wiped perspiration from his shiny forehead with a handkerchief. By the look on his face, I suspected he knew this would not be an easy meeting.

"Fine, but it's my damn water," retorted the voice. I turned to see Hank Johnson, one of the area dairy farmers, put his arm on the speaker and pull him back into his chair.

"There won't be any water in your well either if you don't take some conservation measures," said Hank. His friend shrugged Hank's hand off his shoulder, sat back with his arms crossed, and scowled.

"Let's move on here, and we'll get to everyone's comments soon," said the chairman.

Rafe and I both thought the county presented a reasonable plan calling for voluntary conservation for now, but I knew if we didn't get substantial rainfall in the next few weeks, the county would be forced to go to the second phase of their plan—mandatory restrictions for water usage.

Teddy voiced the concerns of all of the brewers as we stood together outside the county office building after the meeting: "This isn't going to be one of those years where any of us makes money."

"No expansion for you this year," said Stanley to Michael. He wandered off to his car and left. Michael's gaze followed the car out of the lot and then turned to me, putting his hand in the small of my back and steering me away from the others. He looked troubled, and his next words reflected his concern.

"So, how about it?" he asked.

"How about what?" I asked. I knew I was being mean

to him by acting as if I didn't know what he wanted, but the presence of Stanley and the realization he was the one running the Ramford brewery put me in a bad mood.

"Our well is about played out, and we'll have to begin buying our water. I need water, and I need it at a reasonable price."

"Or?"

Michael's shoulders slumped, and he jammed his hands in his pants' pockets. He looked down at his feet.

"Or Stanley will quit."

"So what? Then you do the brewing. You've been doing it for years anyway."

"I sold him all of Ramford's recipes. If he walks, he takes our brews with him."

His words shocked and angered me. "That's the stupidest thing you've ever done. Does your mother know? What were you thinking to give away your formulas?" My heart felt for him, but my brewer's instinct told me what he did was both short-sighted and unnecessary. No one bought a brewer by giving him the rights to the brewery's recipes. He'd gotten himself into a pickle, and he needed to get himself out.

"Make up new recipes then. You can do it. Unless you sold him more than the recipes."

Michael said nothing, merely shook his head and walked away from me. As much as I might have wanted to help him, it was clear anyone getting in bed with the Ramford enterprise just now was in for trouble. Ronald, one of the heirs, couldn't be located, and Michael was signing off on deals with little authority to do so. I wondered what else Stanley had control over at the brewery.

Michael was wrong about Stanley. The man had too much under his thumb to walk off at this point. Meantime, Stanley would let Michael worry about the water while he continued to collect his salary and sit in Mr. Ramford's big office chair.

"I couldn't help but overhear your conversation with Michael," said Rafe. We were standing by our vehicles and saying our goodbyes to Teddy, Francine, and Marsh. Rafe and I watched as the others left in their cars. I thought Rafe had something on his mind, so I leaned my hip against my truck and waited for him to speak.

"I had an idea, and I understand if you feel you must remain loyal to Michael, but … Well, I'll just say it. Would you be willing to let me have some of your water? I can't pay for it straight out, but I could trade you some of my hops, yeast, and barley for it."

I never expected such an offer from Rafe, and it left me almost speechless.

"Your well showing signs of drying up?" I asked.

"I'm still pumping water, but the silt in it is causing my filters to slow down. It doesn't look good. I know you'd rather have money for the water, but I can't offer that just now."

I waited.

"I'm not going to tell you why I'm short either. It's something you don't need to know, and it'll just get you into trouble if you do know."

"I'll sell you water. Sure I will. I'd rather you get the benefit of my well than anyone else. Teddy may grumble, but he can pay to have his water shipped in, and Francine's on a city water line. She's okay for now."

"And Michael?"

"I don't want to talk about Michael, because if I do, I'll have to talk about Stanley, and that'll raise my blood pressure." I held out my hand to Rafe.

"It's a deal," I said. We shook hands, two old business people happy to barter their way to financial solvency—at least until the rains came.

Fourteen

I had meant to do this days ago, soon after I found those letters. I rang the bell and heard its tone reverberate throughout the Ramford house. No one came to the door, yet all the cars except for Michael's were parked in the drive. I turned the knob and stuck my head in.

"Hello. Anyone home?" No answer. *Everyone must be out at the brew barn.*

I entered the barn by the gift shop door. Claudia might be there restocking books, snacks, mustard, and beer. It was empty, so I turned toward the door to the brewing area. The last time I'd been here was the night I'd found Mr. Ramford. I shivered and stopped. Silly of me to be so spooked. It was daytime. There could be no murderers hiding in the shadows now.

The door stood ajar, and I could hear someone talking. Stanley. Oh, no. Not the person I wanted to see today or ever. I turned to go back to the gift shop but heard the name "Teddy" mentioned. Was Teddy here? I returned to the door and leaned toward the opening. I could see Stanley with his cell phone to his ear. I had to eavesdrop. After all, I was serving as Jake's snitch on the murder, and who knew whether Stanley might be important in some way.

"Teddy, Teddy. I assure you it's perfectly legal. I didn't mean to insult you, but your brews are pretty old stuff, you know, and I have just the thing to ramp up your sales. I own Ramford's recipes. No, I own them. They belong to me and I can do anything I want to do with them. Right now, I'm using them here, but I might be interested in moving them to you, if the price is right. This is a one-time offering, so get back to me with your answer soon."

Stanley flipped his phone closed but immediately opened it again.

"Francine? Hi, Stanley Frost here. I have something you might be interested in. We should talk. I can make your business."

A hand squeezed my shoulder. Caught. I whirled around expecting to see Claudia, or perhaps Michael had returned. Ah, no, it was Jake. He placed his finger in front of his lips to signal me to be quiet, but Stanley appeared to be finished with his conversation. He dropped the phone into his pants pocket and walked past the fermenting vats and into the bottling room. He whistled as he left.

"What did you hear?" asked Jake.

"Uh, nothing much."

"You're lying. You're supposed to be helping me find who murdered Mr. Ramford, and you're holding back, probably protecting that one-time boyfriend of yours."

"Stanley was ordering some more hops from Washington or Oregon or somewhere out there."

"I can always tell when you're lying. Your upper lip sweats. Here," he said, handing me his handkerchief, "wipe it off."

I batted his hand away. "Leave me alone, and don't treat me like a servant or a child." I moved toward the outside door.

"Oh," I said, startled. Claudia stood near the door. Was

it possible she could have been here all along, that I didn't see her? Did she see me spying and hear Stanley?

Before I could say anything, Jake stepped in front of me. "Claudia. Good, I'm glad someone is home. Could I have a word with you? Some more questions have come up in your husband's death," Jake said. Jake had to have entered through the gift shop also, but it was clear he hadn't seen her when he came in.

Claudia said nothing but arched one eyebrow and looked at me inquisitively.

"What are you doing here, my dear?" she asked. She spoke as if Jake were not present and hadn't addressed her.

"I was looking for you," I said.

"Not spying on us, were you? Trying to steal away the Ramford secrets to brewing beer?" She laughed, but I couldn't tell if she was joking or serious about my snooping. She turned to face Jake.

"I've known Hera since she was five or so. She was a curious child even then, got my Michael into trouble. He wasn't very daring as a boy. Too scared of his father to take chances. I thought Hera was good for him, gave him some sense of adventure. The girl had backbone. Still does. Come up to the house, and we'll have tea." Claudia turned her back and left the barn.

"I don't have time for tea," Jake whispered to me.

"If you want to get answers from this woman, trust me, you have time for tea. That's the way she does things." I grabbed his shirt and pulled him after me.

Instead of the great room, Claudia drew us to the back of the house into her sewing room. The walls were hung with her quilts, award-winning designs. They were pieces of art, actually.

She poured strong tea from an earthenware pot into large mugs. There was no inquiry as to milk or lemon, only the offer of sugar in a matching bowl. It appeared that Claudia was being rustic, leaving the bone china in her dining room cupboard in order to make Jake feel more comfortable. If that was her plan, it appeared to be working. He sat back in an overstuffed green-and-red-plaid chair sipping his tea and munching an oatmeal cookie. He looked as if he belonged in the house. I smiled to myself. Odd as it might seem, Jake had found a worthy opponent in Claudia. If he planned to take her off guard, she might be outmaneuvering him.

Claudia had always been an enigma to me. She presented a picture to the public of the long-suffering wife with a passion only for quilting, but I always picked up an undercurrent of keen intellect in her. In social settings, Claudia was quiet, always the perfect hostess. Something told me that behind that passive exterior, she observed, judged, and acted in her own time. And since the funeral, well, Claudia was different. Maybe the alcohol gave her hidden side the courage to emerge.

Jake stuffed another cookie in his mouth and followed it with a swallow of tea.

"About that gun," he said.

"The one you claim I bought, the one Hera's father took his life with," she said.

"Explain again why you purchased it."

Claudia leaned forward and scrutinized Jake's face carefully, then leaned back in her chair, obviously satisfied with what she saw on his features.

"Fine. You believe I bought the gun. Maybe I did."

His next words told me he wouldn't be satisfied by the vague confession of a grieving widow, no matter how sweet her tea or buttery her cookies.

"Mrs. Ramford, you lied to me about that gun. You told me someone forged your signature to the license and that you knew nothing about the gun. It's time you told me the truth."

"The truth? It was so long ago. I don't think the truth matters now."

"Murder always matters."

"Hera knows part of the truth," Claudia said.

"I do?"

"Why yes, dear. That's why you're here today, isn't it, to talk to your father's mistress?"

My mouth dropped open, and Jake coughed.

"Tea go down the wrong way, Mr. Ryan?" Claudia asked. She arose from her chair and thumped Jake on his back. "There, that should do it."

Two pairs of eyes met mine. Their owners waited for me to speak. I didn't know who was running this show, Jake or Claudia, but I knew I was the one who should be asking her the questions, not the other way around. I tried to regain my composure.

"I think I'll let you tell the story. You were there, and I wasn't even born yet."

"Why are people so concerned about the past, I wonder? We live in the present, and that's all we have. Like your father. So sentimental of him to save those letters. It happened a long time ago and really doesn't make any difference now."

Now that freaked me out. "How do you know I found those letters?" I asked. Had Sally told her about them? Not likely. Or did someone go through my house when I wasn't there?

"That's not important. I have my ways of finding out what happens around here. Oh, I know. People think I spend all my time quilting or gardening or serving tea." She gestured with her hand in a dismissive manner. "But I'm a good listener, much like you, Hera, and I learn things, lots of things." My breathing stopped. Did this mean she knew I was eavesdropping on Stanley in the barn?

"So. The letters. I wrote them to your father when both of us were newly married, and our marriages were less than what we expected. I thought he was what I needed, so attractive, gentle, sensitive. Not like my husband, who quickly left our marriage bed for others. I pursued your father relentlessly, but he never wavered from his marriage vows, although I know he was tempted."

"That's all very interesting, Mrs. Ramford," interrupted Jake, "but I hardly see what this has to do with that pistol."

"I confided in your father that I was sometimes afraid for my life. Michael Senior had a temper, and when he drank, he lost control." She turned toward me. "You know what happened to poor Ronald. He bore the brunt of Michael's temper. Your father told me I should get a gun for my own protection, so I did."

"My dad suggested that?"

"As it turned out, the gun was unnecessary. Michael turned his attention to other things, mostly other women, gold, fancy cars, all the material things that success in brewing brings. Those diversions took the edge off his temper. He used Ronald as his outlet. My life was no longer in danger."

"What about Ronald's life?" I asked. I was horrified at the calm with which this woman was describing her situation and her disregard for her son.

"Ronald? I knew he'd leave when things got too bad. We were all safe then." Cold. The woman was cold or lying or drunk.

"What happened to the gun then?" asked Jake.

"I gave it to Hera's father, told him I didn't know what to do with it. He said he'd take care of it for me. I guess he did. I didn't know he would shoot himself in the head with it, did I?" I watched her closely as she said all of this. It fit with what had happened in the past, but it was her attitude as she spoke, as if she was reciting something she'd memorized. It was a story she was telling, just a story.

"Why would my dad save your letters?"

She shrugged her thin shoulders. "I don't know. Embarrassing for all of us, isn't it?"

"No, it's not embarrassing for all of us. It was a shock for me to read those letters and think Dad had a mistress. It shattered my image of him." A tear worked its way down my cheek.

Claudia reached over and patted my knee. I jumped at her touch.

"Oh, of course it was a shock. I'm so sorry you thought badly of your father. You should have come to me sooner, and I could have cleared all this up." She touched her head and pinched the ridge of her nose. "Those pills the doctor gave me when Michael died, I guess I've taken a few too many of them. I'm just not myself." I looked into her eyes and saw some of the old, self-contained Claudia there.

"Who do you think killed your husband?" asked Jake. His tone was affable, and he was still drinking his tea and chomping on yet another cookie, but his eyes said cop.

"As I told you when you were here before, my husband wasn't liked. He was feared and respected. Anyone could have killed him, but as you've discovered, everyone in this family has an alibi. I don't know what to say."

"Not everyone in the family has an alibi," said Jake. *Who could he mean?* "Besides, alibis can be set up and broken," he continued. "That's not the question. I'd like to know who you think might have killed him."

"Have you considered the wife?" Claudia said, then laughed.

I knew it. She was drunk or drugged, as she'd mentioned. Or playing with us.

"We're looking at all family members," Jake said.

"Even Ronald?" Claudia asked.

"We're looking for Ronald, as are you, I understand," Jake said.

"He's dead," said Claudia.

Fifteen

"I don't believe her," I said. Jake and I stood talking in front of our vehicles after tea.

"I think part of it was the truth, and part was a lie. I just can't separate out the one from the other."

"I guess you're going to fire me from my position as amateur snoop, huh? I mean, because of those letters I didn't tell you about."

"That wasn't very smart of you."

"Go ahead. Yell at me."

"I'm not going to yell at you. I understand why you didn't want anyone to know about those letters. You read them, I didn't, but they obviously led you to believe that your dad and Claudia were having an affair. That's pretty awful for you, especially after how your dad died."

"You understand?" I asked. I was stunned.

He nodded. "Just so there aren't other things you aren't sharing with me, things that might make it easier for me to break this case. There aren't, are there?"

"Nope." I hoped my lip wasn't sweating. Just in case, I put my hand to my mouth to cover a feigned cough.

"Maybe Claudia's drive isn't the place for this conversation. Someplace more private?" Jake asked.

I was so wrapped up in thinking about those letters that I ignored his suggestion. "I was out of my mind with anger, sorrow, grief, whatever, when I read those letters but as I remember them, she was pretty explicit. I'm sure the letters indicated much more than a lonely, lovesick woman pursuing a man she couldn't have."

"Why would she deny an affair if there was one?" Jake asked. The words barely out of his mouth, he uttered a long, "Ohhhh."

"A motive for murder? She killed my father so he couldn't tell anyone about them?"

"Maybe, but two decades after the affair? Why wait so long?"

"I'm going to take a look at those letters again, and this time, you're going to read them, too." I said. "Oh damn! I have to get back home and begin filtering." I jumped into the truck. Jake just stood there. "C'mon, then. I'll teach you something about the beer business, then we can talk murder." He looked confused. "The letters, you dummy. You need to read those letters. Hustle." I shifted into gear and sped out the driveway. Jake followed as soon as he jumped into his truck. He was talking to himself, or so it seemed to me when I glanced in the rearview mirror.

"Do you think Ronald is dead? Are we chasing ghosts?" Jake asked.

"Why ask me? How would I know anything about Ronald? He left soon after the hop house fire, and no one has heard from him since." A drop of sweat rolled onto my upper lip. I stuck out my tongue and licked its salty wetness from my mouth. Jake was pacing back and forth in the kitchen and didn't notice.

"Didn't anyone search for him? He was, what, thirteen or fourteen at the time? Weren't his parents concerned about him disappearing like that?" Jake asked.

I moved the curved cover of Dad's old roll-top desk back, pulled open one of the small drawers to one side of the writing surface, and reached into the space.

"I think Claudia called the police and filed a missing persons report," I said. My fingers searched around the top of the drawer until they found a lever there. I moved it to the right. The back panel of the desk, which looked solid, slid to one side, revealing a hiding space the size of a shoe box.

"I checked the records in the office. I didn't find any report, just an account of the hop barn fire, arson as the probable cause," Jake said.

I reached in for the letters but found nothing.

"They're not here!" I jammed my hand farther into the space but withdrew only a bit of paper dust. "They've got to be here."

"Maybe you put them someplace else."

"No, I read them late one night. When I was finished, I wanted a hiding place, so I put them here."

"And you had on every light in the kitchen, right?"

"Well, of course, I did. It was dark. You can't read in the dark." My voice was taking on an edge of anger. Then I caught his meaning. "Oh. You mean someone saw me through the window, saw me hide them, and then took the letters later sometime."

"Saw you hide something. Maybe your peeping Tom thought you were hiding jewels or money, but when he retraced your actions at his convenience, he found only those letters. Why would the person want to take your letters? Who knew you found them anyway? Only Sally, right?"

"She wouldn't tell a soul." A thought occurred to me.

"I know! Claudia had them stolen. Remember, she said she had ways of finding out things."

"How did she find out your Dad kept those letters? And she wouldn't know where they were. She did know about them, though, didn't she?" Jake paused a moment, then snapped his fingers. "The peeper took them, read them, and then offered them to Claudia for a price. The Mata Hari persona she was giving us was probably the booze and the pills throwing her alter ego into warp drive."

"You know, I just remembered something about Claudia I thought odd at the time it happened. Years ago, it must have been when I was in high school, Claudia sent a quilt to the state fair. Everyone was certain it would win first place, but it didn't. A bunch of us teenagers attended the fair, and Michael and I decided to find his mother and see how her quilt had done in the competition. No one was in the judging barn when we arrived except for Claudia, who was wielding a knife and slashing the winning quilt. She merely turned, looked at us, and walked out. Michael said, "You didn't see that," and neither he nor Claudia ever mentioned the incident."

"The lady is wrapped a little tight, you're saying."

"I think she wanted us to believe it was widowhood and drugs making her behave the way she did. Well, okay, it might have been partly due to drugs, but there's more to her than I ever suspected, more than anyone thought." I rifled through all the drawers in the desk in case the thief, not finding what he wanted, stashed the letters in another place. I found old tax returns, past issues of *Brewing Monthly* magazine, and faded family photos. No letters.

"So let me see if I've got this straight. You think your

father had an affair, but you think a befuddled middle-aged woman is lying about it and employs spies who steal for her and snoop? Correct?"

I thought for a minute. "Yes," I said. Now it was Jake's turn to reflect on what I said. His answer surprised me.

"I think much of what you're saying is right. Claudia is not what she seems."

I watched the truck from Rafe's place lumbering out my drive, its belly filled with water. Before I visited Claudia, I had driven over to Rafe's for a load of barley and hops. Now Rafe was getting his part of our deal—water. We both knew this exchange couldn't go on too long. The day after the county board meeting, people began reporting their wells were going dry. I raced to produce as much brew as I could, knowing mandatory restrictions would limit the amount of water I could draw from my well.

I wondered if Rafe's cash flow problems would be resolved in time for him to begin purchasing water from beyond the valley. I didn't ask him what was going on, but he was my friend, and I worried about him. As for myself, I was doing well for now. Once the restrictions were in effect, I wouldn't be making much beer.

I remembered Dad saying there was an old well on the property, and I wondered if finding it would allow me more water. The county might set a limit for my business regardless of the number of wells I had. I put in a call to the county supervisor to get an answer. He wasn't available, but the secretary said he'd call me. Why was I bothering to consider that well? I'd have to buy a new pump and piping, and I certainly didn't have the funds for that.

My cell rang.

"Thanks for getting back to me so soon. Here's my question."

"It's Jake."

"Oh, sorry. I thought it was the county supervisor." I told Jake about the old well.

"It's worth a try, anyway," he said. My, but he was being congenial, agreeing with my assessment of Claudia this morning and now being supportive of my attempts to keep my business going. I felt a twinge of guilt about what I was keeping from him. I shoved it to the back of my mind. It was so silly to keep these secrets and for what reason? Did I really think I could beat Jake at the game of cops and killers? Did I want to?

"Still looking for those letters?" he asked.

"Nope. I'm convinced they've been pilfered."

"What's your afternoon shaping up to be?"

"Quiet, just watching my brews ferment and doing a rain dance in the yard. Why?"

"Since we proved to be such a good pair in talking to Claudia this morning, I thought maybe you'd like to interview someone else. I'm revisiting everybody, especially if I think their stories might change or be altered with a little encouragement."

"Who?" I asked.

"Cory Andrews, Michael's girl."

"She doesn't like me much."

"That'll work."

I hesitated. "Is this some kind of test?"

"What?"

"You told Claudia this morning that alibis can be made and broken, and Cory's only connection to this case is her role as Michael's alibi. Obviously, you think she's lying, and you're asking me to help destroy my old friend's alibi. Right?"

"It's not a test. I want to gang up on her, and if that means Michael is left without an alibi, then he'd better start explaining himself. Interesting, if she denies being with him, and it may be important, but it doesn't necessarily mean he killed his father. It does mean he's a liar, but I think you already know that. This getting too tough for you? You want to back out of our deal?"

"Pick me up in ten minutes."

I thought Cory would live in one of the more upscale neighborhoods in town, but her house was a ranch-style home located in a subdivision built in the fifties. All the houses were small, most owned by retirees who kept the yards neatly trimmed and the houses in good repair. Cory's was the only one on the block in need of painting.

"Huh," I said. Jake turned off the engine and looked at me.

"What are you thinking?" he asked.

"It's not what I expected, but now that I see the house, I've got some ideas about the girl."

"Go ahead. I'd be interested in what you have to say."

"I'd say she's very interested in Michael's money."

When she came to the door and saw me on her porch with Jake, Cory put her hand on her hip and stood in that defiant posture with the door closed behind her.

"What's she doing here?" asked Cory.

"Her truck broke down nearby, and since I was on my way to see you, I thought I might as well give her a ride and talk to the two of you together. Saves me time," Jake said. And Cory bought the excuse. *Or was it an excuse? Jake could just as well play the two of us off one another and poke holes in both our stories. The sly dog.*

"How'd the golf game go the other day?" I asked.

"Great. I broke one hundred." I wondered if that was her score or the number of clubs she damaged.

She ushered us into a dim living room, furnished with overly large furniture in a Mediterranean style. Heavy brocade drapes hung on the front window, the swags held in place by curved bronze bars with marble balls at their ends. Cory gestured toward the red and gold gilt couch while she took a seat in an overstuffed chair upholstered in orange silk.

A window air conditioner roared at us. I sank into the couch and continued to descend until my knees were at eye level. The room made me feel small and insignificant, smothered by too much texture and pattern. She may have thought this was the height of luxury, but I thought it was the epitome of bad taste.

Jake, seated beside me on the sofa, attempted to extract his notebook from his back pocket, but he had to stand up to get at it. He remained standing.

"Let's go over the night Michael's father was killed. You and Michael were together here. Is that correct?"

"Right. I told you all this before. Nothing's changed."

"None of the neighbors remember seeing his car in your drive."

"We used my car."

"So then you had to drive him home. What time was that?"

"I don't remember."

Jake tapped his pencil against the notebook, then

flipped it shut and gave Cory a disappointed look. "When we talked before, you said he left around three in the morning. Now you say you drove him home."

"I mean, he drove my car home." Cory got out of the chair and walked to the window. She began to smooth out the drapes, flicking off invisible flecks of dust, her back turned to us as if her furnishings were more deserving of her attention than were her uninvited visitors.

"Your neighbors did say your car was here the next morning."

"They must be mistaken, then." She began braiding the large tassels that hung from the drapery pull-back.

"Don't you own a silver Mercedes convertible?"

"Yes."

"That's the car they saw here in the morning."

Cory dropped the tassel and spun around. "Look, unless you intend to arrest me or something, I'll have to ask you to leave. Now!"

"Just a few more questions," Jake said. He ignored her, opened the notebook again and flipped through it. He looked as firmly entrenched in her living room as a dandelion growing in the front lawn.

She stalked past him, picked up the phone in the kitchen and dialed. "Michael, that cop and your skinny blonde friend are here harassing me about the night of the murder. You've got to do something." She paused and listened, then hung up.

"He's calling the family lawyer, who will be here shortly." She sat back down in the chair with her arms across her admirable chest. "We'll just wait."

"Never mind. We're finished here. Sorry to inconvenience you."

"I can't believe she backed you down that way," I said. We were in the car headed out of town.

"She didn't. I just let her think she did. I've got a better idea, anyway." Jake pulled into the drive to the Ramford house.

"Claudia won't be happy to see us again today. There'll probably be no tea this time."

"I don't want to see Claudia. We're stopping by to chat with Michael."

"Michael? No way. I'll just walk the rest of the way home from here."

"You want to help on this case? I've seen the way Michael looks at you. He's embarrassed to parade Cory or Stanley or his other weaknesses in front of you. Maybe you'll shame him into telling the truth today." Jake grabbed my arm and propelled me along with him to the house. We didn't need to knock. Michael slammed through the front door and confronted us on the steps.

"What's the idea, treating Cory like that?" he asked.

Before Jake could speak, I interrupted. "She's a big girl. She was doing just fine until Jake tripped her up about the car on the night of the murder."

"What about the car?" Michael had that look on his face, the one from grade school days, when the teacher asked him a question he didn't know the answer to.

Again Jake seemed prepared to speak, but I put out my arm and raced on. "She said you drove your car to her place when Jake first questioned her, but when Jake told her none of the neighbors saw your car there, she said it wouldn't start in the morning, and you had to call a tow truck to take it into the garage. She then said she drove you home. So what towing company was that?"

Lies, but who cared, if they got me what I wanted. Jake kept quiet, gazing at me with something like astonishment and admiration on his face.

"She said that?" Michael shook his head and muttered something under his breath.

"What did you say?" Jake asked.

"We need to talk somewhere," he said.

Jake and I started up the steps.

"Not here. Stanley's in the office, and Mom's around someplace. Let's try the barn."

We followed him to the brew barn, and we all took up positions leaning against the racks in the gift shop.

"I know you don't like her," Michael looked at me when he said this, "but Cory is a great girl."

"Loyal," offered Jake.

"Yes, she's loyal, and that's more than you can say for me. She offered me an alibi for the night of my father's murder. I never asked her to lie for me, but I think the girl's in love."

The girl's in love with your money, was what I was thinking. Jake caught my eye.

"She may even think I killed my father, and she just doesn't care. She's crazy that way."

"I'm going to repeat what I asked you when I first questioned you. Where were you the night of your father's murder?" asked Jake.

"I can't tell you that," Michael said.

Sixteen

The next morning, I tuned into the weather channel but flipped it off in disgust. The forecast promised some rain on the weekend. *Yeah, right, like the piddling little bit we got last Saturday, just enough to keep the tourists away from the tasting, but not enough to raise the water table.*

The head of the county board had called back earlier in the day, saying he could not dictate how much water I used, nor how many wells I drew from, but from his tone of voice I could tell he was unhappy that I was considering opening up the other well.

"We're talking about the need for water conservation here," he said.

And I'm talking about whether I stay in business, I thought. I needed him as an ally, so I tried to reassure him that I shared his concerns about water usage.

"I appreciate that, and I certainly wouldn't consider taking this step if I thought I'd be directly affecting the water table here. The old well is on a long finger of property that extends east beyond the Butternut Valley. A water resources expert from the college in town told me it was more likely the well was tapping into the aquifer associated with the Chenango River. The population density is far less there, and they have fewer commercial interests needing water for their operations."

"That's not solving the water problem," he said.

"I'm well aware of that, but neither I nor any of my brewing colleagues can solve the problem." I was trying to keep the exasperation out of my voice. "All of us are behind your water conservation plan. We intend to do our part and not be greedy, but we have to stay in operation. We're a significant part of this county's economic health."

We danced around one another for a few more minutes. He agreed that I was more than considerate to contact the board about what I was contemplating with the old well. I emphasized that I understood his position and the seriousness of the drought.

"You do whatever you think best for now, Ms. Knightsbridge," he said.

"I'll keep you posted on my plans."

Just what were my plans? I had a vague recollection of my dad and me hiking out to that well when I was a kid, maybe age seven or so. I remembered it was beyond the ridge to the east, away from any of the breweries and in a small glen surrounded by pines and maples. An old hunting cabin stood at the edge of the trees, but that might be gone now, fallen down over the twenty-plus years since I had visited the spot.

My cell phone chirped at me while I considered the county map laid out on my kitchen table.

"Jake here. I thought we could get together and exchange notes on the case. Did you get a chance to talk with Sally and Francine yet?"

I hit myself on the forehead. *Damn.* I'd forgotten Jake gave me a sleuthing assignment last night after we left Michael. I was supposed to visit Sally and Francine. Jake assumed they might be more comfortable talking to me woman-to-woman. The casualness of the get-together might loosen up some memories or thoughts about the night of the murder, thoughts that had to do with Michael especially. I hadn't contacted either of them.

"The assignment too tough for you? Don't want to spy on your boyfriend?" Jake asked.

"It's not that. Michael's reluctance to provide information about his whereabouts that night got me curious. I assumed it was because he was cheating on Cory with some new woman."

"Or hiding something to do with his father's murder," Jake reminded me.

I didn't think that was the case. I knew Michael well, and he was too much like his father with respect to the fairer sex. He obviously liked Cory and wanted to keep her in his back pocket, but if there was anyone else, she'd be furious.

"I had more pressing things to do," I said to Jake. "There's the little matter of water, you know, the main ingredient in making beer."

"You've got water."

"For how long, though?"

"What are you going to do to change that?" he asked.

"I'm going to take a hike and ask Rafe to join me."

"When?"

"This afternoon, I guess, if he's free."

"I'm free. How about I accompany you two on this jaunt and see what you're up to. Rafe won't mind."

"I know the two of you were getting to know one another, but since Bernie came into the picture, he's been less than anxious to be around you. He knows you think it's odd he hired the guy, rounder that he is."

"You think it's odd, too. Don't you want to know

why?"

"Yes, I guess so." I thought about Rafe's odd behavior of late—hiring Bernie, contending suddenly that he had no money, and being secretive about his financial situation after he had been so forthright with me about his past.

But then, I owed Jake. I hadn't talked with Francine and Sally, and it wasn't because I was protecting Michael. I was a little miffed Jake thought I'd be willing to use my friendships to leverage information out of them, and I was feeling guilty about the secrets I was keeping from him, especially with respect to Ronald. I had tried to contact Ronald and got no response. Telling Jake what I knew or didn't know about Ronald's whereabouts wouldn't change anything, or so I told myself.

"Okay, you can come along. Be here around two, and wear hiking shoes." I snapped the phone shut and then flipped it open again to call Rafe. He said yes to looking for the well this afternoon. I didn't tell him Jake would be accompanying us. *That wasn't wrong, was it?*

Rafe looked at me with curiosity and concern on his face when Jake appeared at my barn in the afternoon, but he recovered his composure when he learned Jake would be joining us to look for the well and said he was glad to have the company. Jake merely nodded. The three of us were quiet on the hike up to the site.

I was right. The old cabin was merely a pile of rotten logs now. The only structure left standing was a stone fireplace, and many of the rocks making up the chimney had let go and were scattered around the hearth. I remembered once Dad and I hiked up here and spent an overnight. Part of the cabin was still standing at that time, but we had lain under the stars in our sleeping bags and stared into a clear, October sky. Dad pointed out the constellations and taught me their names.

Jake's hand on my shoulder brought me back to the present. "Is that the well over there?" he asked.

I nodded. It stood fifty yards to the east of the fallen timbers. It was an old-fashioned well, made from rocks also, probably taken from the same source as those used in the cabin's fireplace. Weeds had grown up, but by standing almost on top if it, you could see down into its depths. Was there water down there? I grabbed one of the smaller stones on the ground nearby and tossed it in. A second later it made a lovely splash.

"You'll have to sink a pipe down there and put in a pump, but it sounds like water to me," said Rafe. He seemed almost as excited by this find as I was.

"So why did you stop using it?" asked Jake.

"We never did use it. This property wasn't part of the original parcel purchased by my dad. He bought this one several years later. I think this well provided water for the cabin. Dad planned to renovate it and move in here when he retired. He never got to that," I said. I turned away from the men so that they couldn't see my eyes fill with tears.

"Any ideas about how you're going to get this water to your barn?" asked Jake, who looked skeptical about the project. "If you run a pipe out of here, you'll need to cross the glen, the ridge we hiked over, and then run it down the side of the hill to your barn. That's a lot of piping."

I felt depression settle in on my shoulders. *What was I thinking? I'd never find money for all that pipe.*

Rafe turned about in a circle, perusing the small valley we were in and the ridge the pipe would have to cross.

"She won't need pipe. I can get my water truck up here with little trouble, that is, if Michael will let me cross his property. Otherwise, I'd have to run around behind his place and mine and use the logging trail to the west."

A good plan, but I'd have to offer Michael some concession with respect to water, or he wouldn't go for it.

Rafe could read my thoughts. "We'll both talk to Michael. The three of us can work out something—your water, my trucks, Michael's property. We all have something to gain."

"Tell that to Stanley," I said.

"She'll have to get someone up here to do the work for her," said Jake.

"I have just the man for you. Bernie," replied Rafe.

"Bernie! Why him?" I asked. I remembered serving as his reluctant hostess the night he broke into my place, and I wasn't eager to have him on my property again.

"He can do all kinds of work. Handiest man I've ever met. With your permission, I'll have him come up here tomorrow and take a look at the project," Rafe said. I nodded my consent. I wasn't happy Bernie would be doing the work, but who else knew how to set the pipe and install a pump? Who else that I could afford, that is.

"Sounds like you know Bernie well," said Jake. Rafe looked uncomfortable for a moment, then let out a long sigh.

"I know you've been wondering about Bernie and me since I hired him after he broke into Hera's place, but he's not such a bad fellow. I knew him when I was working on the Continent, Germany, to be exact. He was one of the assistants in a small brewery where I was the brew master. It was located in Cuxhaven on the North Sea. A jack-of-all-trades, master of most, he was. Now he's a bit down on his luck, so I offered him a job until he can get on his feet again."

"I guess picking locks is one of his specialties," said Jake.

"I expect it is, but he's very contrite about that, you know. He was desperate. Came here knowing no one, recognized my name, and wanted to get in touch with me. I'm sorry he frightened you," Rafe said to me. "He's not big on manners."

"It wasn't bad manners that got him arrested," Jake reminded him. "It was breaking and entering. When he comes before the judge, and that'll be soon, he'll have to spend a few days in the county jail, unless ..."

I thought Jake was going to say "unless you vouch for his integrity," but instead, he said, "unless I find out he has a record, and I suspect he does. Then we're talking prison."

"Minor things back on the Continent and in England, only minor things." Rafe seemed eager to assure us that Bernie was a humble working man down on his luck, but I thought he was acting very uncomfortable with the idea of Jake looking too closely at Bernie Fisher's past.

Our hike back to my place was like the one up to the well, filled with silence.

I called Michael that evening, and he sounded as if I were the last person with whom he wanted to talk. When I told him Rafe and I had a proposition for him about water, he lightened his tone. Then, of course, he spoiled everything by suggesting that Stanley be in on the conversation. We arranged to meet later in the evening at his place.

Meanwhile I had my homework to do, finding Francine and Sally and having some girl talk with them.

First, I stopped at Francine's place. It was on my way into town, where I knew I would find Sally at her bakery. Marsh greeted me as I got out of my truck and told me Francine was out in the supply barn.

"Looks as if you're making real progress at fixing this place up," I said to Marsh. All of the outbuildings had been painted red with white trim, and a new weather vane sat on top of the cupola of the brew barn. "It's looking good. How's the set-up coming for the brewery?"

"Slow. We just got in our fermenter yesterday, and the mash tun is due to arrive this week sometime. We won't be up and operating until the beginning of July, if then. But we're getting there, unless another cow decides to visit the barn." He laughed, and I joined in.

"The winery is going strong, I guess. Having tours and tastings on Saturdays, then?"

"Yup. Francine isn't certain whether she wants to distribute or remain small and sell from here."

I wished them the best of luck, but I was still grateful that Francine had no use for that bottler, and she wasn't in the business of making beer yet. I didn't need the competition right now.

"Go on into the barn. I've got her slinging some sacks around. Do the woman good. She needs to understand just how much manual labor is involved in a place like this."

"Hera!" she called to me when I entered the barn. "Good, now I've got a chance to take a break." Sweat rolled down her face. She had rolled up the sleeves of her shirt, and perspiration caused sheen on her forearms. Her damp shirt clung to her ample breasts.

"I sure wish I had your build. You look like you could play catch with these bags." Francine plopped her rounded body onto a bag of malt and pushed damp strands of her thick auburn hair away from her face.

"I'm not an Amazon, you know."

"No, but your height and those stringy muscles of yours must make it easier to do this work than these short arms and legs of mine, to say nothing of the extra pounds I'm carrying."

Those extra pounds were pretty attractive on her, I thought. She was all curves with the redhead's complexion, pale and luminescent with peach cheeks, and coral lips.

"It's my own fault. I told Marsh when I hired him I wanted to learn the business from the ground up, and he's not holding back on me. Don't tell him, but I'm far less delicate than I look. When I lived at home, I helped out at my father's winery in Spain. Of course, that was years ago, but I'll get back into shape. Have a seat." She patted a sack of grain next to hers and looked at me with curiosity.

"What can I do for you? Not that I don't welcome a visit from my brewing friends, but I suspect you have something on your mind other than a friendly chat." Her brown eyes examined my face closely.

So this wasn't going to be a girly chat. She was too savvy for that. I might as well get to it.

"How well do you know Michael?" I asked. The smile faded from her lips.

"Who wants to know?" she asked.

"I do." Could she tell I was lying?

"I don't think so. You grew up with him. I think you're on a fishing expedition for your deputy friend."

Now why would she think that, and how did she know Jake was my friend? "Look, I'm in a real bind. You're right, I'm here running Jake's agenda, but I have to find out all I can about it. The bank won't loan me money so that I can stay in business, because Mr. Culler thinks I had something to do with the murder." Only part of that was a lie.

"You know Michael better than anyone around here. Do you think he had anything to do with his father's murder?"

"No, but ..."

"I don't either. Tell your cop pal to look under another rock for his suspect. If we're going to be friends, and I hope we will be friends, you can be up front with me. I know everyone around here, including Marsh, thinks I'm out of my element, just a rich, dumb, widow. I think you know better. I'd like to have you as a friend, Hera. I can use a woman to confide in. Just don't lie to me anymore."

She patted my shoulder, and I took another look at her bare forearms. They were more muscular than I first thought. She arose and picked up a grain sack and tossed it onto the pile next to me. It missed me by several inches.

"Pretty good, huh?" she said. She turned to pick up another one and prepared to send it my way. There was a smile on her face, but her eyes were alight with a fire that could as well have been anger as delight in demonstrating her strength. I had misjudged the woman. There was more to her than the wealthy widow she portrayed in social settings.

Seventeen

I've put this off long enough, I thought as I pulled my truck up in front of Sally's store, turned off the engine, and sat there, reluctant to go in and confront her with questions I didn't like asking.

I hadn't seen her since Saturday's tasting, when small storms moved in and out of the valley, ruining our sales. She had been grouchy early in the day and snapped at me when I began talking about the water shortage in the valley.

"It's just all about your problems, isn't it?" she said, her face shiny with sweat and her eyes flat with barely suppressed anger. Then suddenly, she changed and apologized, saying she was working long hours, and the shop wasn't doing well.

"It's okay, Honey. I am kind of into my own world lately," I replied. We both smiled, and that was that. She was her usual perky self the rest of the day.

Regardless of her mood today, I knew she would see right through me when I began to ask her questions. To Francine, whom I had known for only several months, I had appeared transparent. There was no chance I could slide into girl talk about the night of the murder without Sally calling me on it. Oh, God. I was no good at this sleuthing thing. I propped my arms on the steering wheel and put my head on them. A knock on the window made me jump.

"Are you coming in to say hello, or are you just out for an afternoon of parking in front of my shop?" Sally wore a blue-and-white-checked apron with an appliqué on the bib that read Sally's Tea Room and Bakery. Her face looked as welcoming as her homey costume.

"Oh, so the aprons came in. That's a nice, friendly look, the blue and the white."

"Don't sit out here in the heat. Come on in, and I'll treat you to some lavender scones I made earlier today. I've only got two left, so you're in luck." She opened the truck door and pulled me after her into the shop.

"Good day, then?" I mentally crossed my fingers for her.

"Great day. Everyone wants to get out of the heat. They take one look into my shop with its blue and white décor and think *cool*. See the sign?"

She pointed to a large chalkboard that sat to one side of her door. Passers-by could clearly see what it said: Sally's Way to Beat the Heat—your individual twenty-four ounce pitcher of iced tea and choice of a lavender or lemon scone.

"I ran out of lemon scones about two hours ago. Here, try this." She set a pastry on a willow-pattern plate, pushed me into a chair, and rushed out to the kitchen. When she returned, she carried a glass pitcher filled with an amber liquid in which pieces of ice floated. I bit into the scone as she poured me the tea. I took a sip. The liquid cooled my throat like breathing in on a cold winter's day, but it did nothing to make my task any easier.

She bounced into the chair opposite mine, like a kitten pouncing on its favorite ball, plopped her elbows on the table, and propped her head on them. Drops of perspiration on her forehead told me she'd had a busy day.

"It was a good day. No, a great day."

"You said that. Look, I don't mean to be a wet ..." I began but was cut off when she jumped up to wait on customers who entered the door.

"Back in a jiff." She danced over to the next table, flashing her inviting smile at the four ladies who were seating themselves. "I'm out of the scones, but how would you like to try one of my lemon tarts? They're wonderful with the iced tea, so light and fluffy. Just the kind of sweet delight for such a hot, hot day."

The girl was on a roll, bustling around with pitchers of iced tea and pastries balanced on her tray, recommending another confection when the women finished their lemon treat. The front door opened, and yet another set of customers, a family with two young children, entered the shop.

"Sorry, Hera." She sped by me with another full tray. "I'll be right back."

I sat at my table for a while, watching the ice cubes melt in the pitcher of tea, and I determined that this was not a good time to talk with Sally. Not only was she busy, but I was losing my nerve for prying information out of her. Michael was, after all, a prickly subject, so why bring him up just to ruin her good mood? What could she possibly know that would have any bearing on the night of his father's murder?

I turned at the sound of the door closing and looked around the shop. All the customers had left, and Sally was turning the sign in the window from Open to Closed.

"So what were you saying?" She picked a crumb of

scone off my plate and touched it to her tongue. "They are good, aren't they?" I nodded.

"Okay, let me be straight with you. I'm helping Jake on his investigation." I explained to her about the bank's unwillingness to loan me money because of their concern I might be involved in the murder.

"Okay. So how can I help you?"

"Is there anything I should know about Michael that I don't already know but you do?"

A cloud seemed to pass over her sunny features. "Well, you are notorious for sticking your head in the sand when it comes to Michael, but I'm not the one to ask. Try Francine."

"Francine? I just came from her place. She didn't seem to know anything."

"Maybe you didn't ask her the right questions." Sally dropped her eyes to the tabletop and drew her finger through the condensation left by the tea pitcher. I knew this would be hard for her. Finally, she lifted her eyes to meet mine.

"You haven't a clue, have you?"

"What?"

"Michael was sniffing around me at Christmas time, you know that. By Valentines' Day, he was giving Cory chocolates and champagne. Come Easter, his car found parking spaces in two locations, in front of Cory's house and in Francine's chicken coop."

Francine? That just couldn't be right. Francine was so much older than Michael and she was a widow. I mentally clapped myself on the forehead. Sally was right. I was so dumb.

"You mean they're, uh ... sleeping together?"

"That, I don't know for certain, but rumor says when he visits, he comes late at night, and he hides his car in one of the barns." All her former joyousness at the day seemed to have disappeared. She slumped in the chair and picked at the lace on her apron. I felt guilty for ruining her day, but my curiosity made me ignore my friend's mood, and I pressed on.

I was gnawing on an idea. Cory's alibi for Michael seemed to break down when Jake questioned her. She could have been lying to Jake and me. Perhaps Michael had been with Francine that night.

"When did this, uh, this relationship begin?" I asked.

"This is just town talk, you know. I think I began to hear of it around the time of the murder. If you want to know more, ask Michael, why don't you?" Her voice was beginning to take on a perturbed tone, and I knew I had pushed hard enough. She reached across the table for my plate and glass.

"I need to wash these and ready this place for tomorrow." She turned toward the back of the shop.

"Listen, I'm sorry about all of this. I know you must still have feelings yet for Michael."

"Oh, don't be such a ninny. It's not about my feelings for Michael. It's about me and what a jerk I was to have fallen for the guy in the first place, given what a satyr he is when it comes to women. I hate being reminded of how gullible I was. Why you continue to moon after that man, I'll never know. I'm your best friend, and you see what he's done to me. It's a matter of character, Hera, and he's got none."

"Cory must be furious," was all I could think of to say without showing my idiocy.

"She's playing dumb about the matter."

"Why would she do that?"

"Because she's recently acquired another admirer of her own, one she believes is more capable of making big money. Stanley Frost."

This was all so confusing and contorted. It was probably irrelevant to the murder anyway, but I had to know all the details, even at the cost of upsetting our already shaky relationship.

"Does Michael know about them?"

"I don't know. I'm just passing on what I hear when people come in here. You'd have to ask Michael. You see him more than I do." She giggled nervously. "Well, I guess I wouldn't recommend that, especially if he doesn't know, or it's just rumor." She flapped the dishcloth she held in her hand in the air with a snap. "But it would serve him right."

"It would," I agreed. *So who was Michael with the night of his father's murder? Cory, Francine, someone else?* I stared out the window as Sally rushed around clearing off glasses, plates, and pitchers and wiping down tables. She turned to me with a tray full of dishes.

"Where are you? You're off in another world." One hand supported the tray, the other rested on her hip.

"Just thinking about Michael and that night. Who do you think he was with?"

"He said he was with Cory." She turned her back on me. I began to wonder if my questions about Michael were making her face memories she didn't want to examine or something else was going on. She didn't want to meet my eyes. She was hiding something. No time like the present to turn a friend into an enemy, so I plunged ahead with a crazy idea.

"I don't think so. I think he was here with you."

Sally set down the tray on the counter and walked over to my table. Tears spilled from her eyes and rolled down her rosy cheeks, undeterred by the few freckles they encountered on their way toward her quivering chin.

"I'm such a fool. I still care for him, but I think he killed his father." She sank down into the chair across from me and buried her head in her apron. I got up and went around the table to her, leaning down and putting my arms around her shaking shoulders.

"How long have you been carrying around this crazy idea?"

"No, no, you don't understand. It's not a crazy idea. We talked that night." She wiped her eyes on the apron as I returned to my chair. I gripped her hands in mine.

"So he was here. Tell me. You'll feel better."

But I was wrong. When she was finished with her tale, neither she nor I felt better. Once I'd called Jake to ask him to come to the bakery, I knew things might get a lot worse for both of my friends.

"He stopped by here around what time?" Jake sat at the table, his notepad in hand, eyes fixed on Sally's face. He had arrived a mere ten minutes after I put in the call to him. By the time he walked through shop door, Sally had composed herself. I'd made her a quick cup of hot tea, and she was sipping it while she picked a bran muffin into a mountain of crumbles on the plate in front of her.

"Late evening, I guess. It was sometime after I closed up. It was my late night."

"Just a friendly visit?"

"No, I asked him to stop by some night that week whenever he found the time. I told him I wanted to talk to him, but you know," Sally shifted around in her chair, sat up straighter and met Jake's gaze, "I don't think he even remembered I'd asked him to come here. In fact, I got the feeling he was avoiding me, but that night, he stumbled in here as if by accident. I think he saw me in the store as he passed and just wanted someone to unload on. I was available."

"Go on." I hated it when Jake used that cold, interrogation tone of voice, but Sally seemed wound up now, ready to tell him everything about that night.

"He came in here like a tornado. I asked if he wanted to sit down, but he said no and began to pace around the front of the store, waving his arms and yelling that he hated his father. Went on and on about how he had given his life over to the man, but no more. Michael said he was finished with living under Michael Senior's boot. He was leaving just as his brother did and starting a new life somewhere else."

"That sounds more like a man at a crossroads, about to leave, not entertain murder." Jake didn't know how wrong he was, but he hadn't heard the rest of her story.

"I thought so, too, but then he said something else that worried me. 'I'm not going to let that man have the final word on this. He needs to listen to me. And he will listen this time. I'll make him.' He was angry. I've never seen him like that before. He ran out of here as if he had the devil on his tail."

"So you think he went to have it out with his father? Did he tell you what their earlier disagreement was about?"

"No. He wasn't making very much sense, just said he was determined to make his father hear his side of the story. No, no, wait. Not his side of the story. He said, 'her side of the story.'"

"Any idea who he was referring to?"

"No. Maybe Hera, maybe his mother, or Cory or …"

"Or any number of women in his life. I know, I know, butt out," I said. I sat back in my chair, determined to keep my observations to myself.

"Time to have a showdown with Michael." Jake got out of his chair, heisted jeans higher on his lean hips, and prepared to leave.

"Sit. She hasn't finished yet." Jake was jumping the gun, so despite my resolution to keep out of his interrogation of Sally, I put my hands on his chest and pushed him back into the chair.

We waited. I watched her swallow hard and take in a deep gulp of air.

"I followed him. That's how I know he killed his father."

"You saw him at the barn?"

"No, I followed him until his car hit the hill leading past Ramford Brewery. Then my old truck gave out and just stopped on me. It took me a few minutes before I could baby her into starting again. By then, his car had disappeared. I knew if I drove down the lane to the brewery, he would see I'd followed him. I didn't want to take that chance. I felt really stupid chasing him down country roads like that. Now I wish I'd just turned in the drive. I could have stopped a killing."

"More likely, you would have become another victim." It was Jake's observation, not mine. I couldn't quite wrap my mind around Michael as his father's murderer.

I sat next to Sally, rubbing her back as she talked. The backrub seemed to be calming her. I could feel her relax, and she moved into my massage as I worked her shoulder muscles in a circular motion. Suddenly, she tensed and shifted her weight forward.

"My baby's father is a killer," she said, "and I let him do it."

Eighteen

"I don't want to talk about it." Sally twirled one of her springy red locks around her index finger. The flour on her hands deposited a light dusting on the strand of hair, making it look as if she had suddenly gone gray in one spot.

I grabbed her hand. "Quit that. You're getting flour all over your hair. You can't just shut me out after dropping a bomb like that one. Does Michael know?"

"No, of course not. What did you think? I would tell him, and we'd get married and live happily every after?"

Her sarcasm signaled she was about to go into one of her stubborn moods, where nothing I could say would dissuade her from doing and thinking just as she pleased. I might as well go home and let her settle down, but thinking back on her abrupt mood swings over the past week, I reconsidered leaving.

"I'll just sit here until you're ready to talk." I tried to settle back in my seat to wait her out, but as authentic as these old metal-backed chairs were, they were not comfortable. I hoped her stubbornness would be short lived.

Jake seemed to be weighing his options. He could stay for an inevitable outpouring of hormone-driven female emotions or use his job as an excuse to leave. He chose the latter, the coward.

"Uh, I think I'll just mosey along and let you two ladies work this thing out for yourselves. I have a job to do here."

Sally jumped from her chair and grabbed Jake by his shirtfront. "If you're going to see Michael, don't you dare tell him about the baby, hear?"

"Yes, ma'am."

With Sally clinging to his shirtfront, the two of them reminded me of a veterinarian with an uncooperative cat climbing his lab coat. "I'll keep it to myself, but I do have to ask him about that night."

She wasn't finished with him. "That's all you ask him about. No questioning him about me." Her little freckled fist let go of his shirt, leaving a wrinkled pucker on the otherwise pressed material.

"Just calm down. As much of an insensitive jerk as he can be, Jake will honor your wishes on this one, right?"

As quickly as she had become a tigress with Jake, now Sally deflated like a Mylar balloon the day after a birthday party and sank back down into her chair.

"I think I'm going to be sick."

"I'll be right back." I rushed Sally off to the restroom in the back of the store. I closed the door on her, because I wanted to give her some privacy and because my stomach behaves sympathetically when others are sick. I retreated to Jake's side.

"I'm an insensitive jerk?"

"Sometimes. All men are, but I know you'll handle this one with respect for Sally's privacy." I patted him on the back and shoved him toward the door. "Go, get 'em, fella."

I locked the door after him and turned toward the bathroom. I could hear sounds of, well, I could hear sounds coming from there. Sally emerged, her face resembling a spaghetti squash greased with olive oil.

"Yuk. Is this the way it's going to be for the entire pregnancy?"

"You're keeping the baby?"

"Of course, I'm keeping the baby, and before you say anything, I know it won't get Michael back. I haven't even decided if I'll tell him about it."

I'm not the only one who has it bad for Michael, I thought to myself as I drove home after getting Sally settled on her couch in front of the television. She was eating lemon squares and drinking a cola, a combination that seemed downright normal given the stories I'd heard about the eating habits of pregnant women.

I opened the truck window to clear my mind. The woodsy smells of decaying logs and blooming dogwoods, lilacs, lily of the valley, and field grasses rushed at me through the evening air. Not a cloud in the sky to produce a sunset worthy of a painter's brush. The sun was there, and then it was gone. Darkness settled into the valley.

Much as I knew how difficult the months and years ahead would be for Sally, raising a child alone, I anticipated the joyous times in store for the new mother, and I hoped she would want me to share in them. Then there was the issue of Michael. She had to tell him about the baby, and she knew that, but what would his reaction be? Happiness? Anger? The old Michael would act in a responsible manner. Even if they didn't marry, Michael would help out financially and in any other way he could. The new Michael? Well, neither Sally nor I could predict.

I was running a nursery rhyme through my head. *Hickory, dickory, dock, the mouse ...*"

I steered past my driveway and took the next left into Michael's. My curious nature got the better of me. What tale was Michael spinning for Jake about that night? I was dying to know—oops, bad choice of words—I needed to know, even though I suspected neither Michael nor Jake would welcome my visit.

Either Claudia was happy to see me, or she anticipated that whoever was at the door would be far easier to confront than the possibility her son was a murderer.

"Your friend has some insane story about Michael and the night of the murder. Maybe you can set him straight." I noted that she was holding her usual beverage with a grip that would have given a boa constrictor a run for its money.

She led me through the great room, which was lit only by occasional flashes of heat lightning brightening the expanse through the skylights above.

"It better not rain tonight. Those skylights leak." She took a sip of her drink and beckoned me to follow her into the study. "Of course," she turned toward me as she held the door open, "rain would be good for business, our business." Her eyes, usually such a peaceful blue, now flashed with anger. "How long are you going to hold us hostage to your wells?"

I opened my mouth to reply, but the scene in front of me swept the words away. Jake and Michael were standing toe-to-toe. Jake held himself forward, his face expressionless. I could see the side of Michael's cheek twitch as if he were grinding away at some tough meat.

"Who said they saw me come back here that night? Someone's lying to you."

Both men ignored Claudia and me as we came into the

room, but I knew Jake was aware of my presence by the deepening of his frown.

"Someone sure is lying, and I think it's you," Jake said.

Claudia positioned herself between the two men. "You like to come here and accuse this family of murder. Don't you have any other suspects, or are you trying to make a name for yourself by taking on one of the most prominent families in this county? Don't you realize that we're still mourning the death of my husband and Michael's father.? Didn't that school teach you anything about respect for others?" *Quite an outburst from Claudia,* I thought. She should be making crazy quilts, considering her shifts in mood and behavior.

"I ... " Jake began.

Claudia reached back to steady herself on the chair behind her. I don't think any of us, including her, knew what she was about to say next. "I never offered anyone coffee, did I?"

I sucked in a quick breath and scrutinized her face. *What the ...?*

"Hera, could you see my mother to her room? I think she's not feeling well." Michael's concern for his mother didn't alter the focus of his attention on Jake, nor did Jake take his eyes off Michael's face.

"Never mind, Dear. I'll just finish up a little quilting I left earlier this evening." She made jerky progress toward the door and stopped. Then, seeming to gather her strength, she walked from the room with a familiar ladylike step.

"Go check on her, would you?" Before I could point out to Michael that I was not his mother's caretaker, Jake interrupted.

"I'd like her to stay. Since she was the one who found your father's body, and you seem to be the person who was in that brew barn, Hera might want to know whether you intended her harm also."

"What? I'd never harm Hera. Never."

"Guys, I hate to interrupt, but would you not talk about me as if I wasn't here?" My words penetrated the haze of male testosterone surrounding them, and the two men separated.

"Let's all sit down, shall we? There's got to be a way to settle all of this." Michael gestured toward the chairs. I caught him sneaking a peek at his watch as he settled himself behind the desk.

I was seething about Sally's pregnancy, but I felt honor-bound by my promise to keep her secret. Still, I couldn't resist goading Michael about his bacchanal-like evenings of lust. "So which woman gets the distinction of alibi for the night?"

"I've told both of you again and again that Cory and I spent the night together."

"She seems to be confused about the particulars of the evening," Jake said, "and I have someone who will testify that you drove home here around nine or so."

Michael remained silent for a moment, then seemed to reach some conclusion.

"Fine. Go talk to Francine Ortiz. We had a business meeting that night. She can tell you what time I arrived and what time I left."

"Why didn't you just say so? Why bring Cory into this?" I had to interrupt. I found it difficult to hear all of the ways Michael was using women.

Michael eyed me and for a moment, I thought I saw

sadness in his eyes, but he confronted Jake with a challenging look. "Is that the question you wanted to ask, Officer Ryan? Or did you have something more pressing on your mind, like why your witness lied to you about my being here? Maybe your witness isn't very reliable. Maybe she or he has something at stake they're not telling you."

Did Michael know Sally was following him that night?

"You're like walking through poison ivy, easygoing until you get home and start itching. Why did you show up when you knew I was questioning a prime suspect? You're not a cop, you know."

"No, but I am your unofficial partner, and my presence made Michael say a lot more than he would have if just you were there." We were standing in the Ramford drive beside our vehicles after Michael dismissed us from the house. It was after ten at night, and heat and humidity still saturated the air.

Jake stepped forward and reached his hand toward my face. I held my ground.

"You've got a bead of sweat that's going to drip off the end of your nose. Not very ladylike." His finger tapped my nose. Then, as if realizing how inappropriate his gesture was to our conversation, he dropped his hand and cleared his throat. "So how was our mother doing when you left?"

"Eating her way through the refrigerator."

"Do you think she'll tell Michael soon?"

"Drop it. Did you believe Michael when he said he didn't want to tell anyone about his meeting with Francine because of Marsh's jealousy? What's Marsh got to be jealous of, if the two of them were only having a business meeting? That doesn't sound like Michael, to be solicitous of another man's feelings."

Jake let out a bark of a laugh. "You finally seem to be coming around to seeing Michael for what he really is, a very self-absorbed man." He held up his arm as if to ward off the blow he expected from me.

"No, I get it now. He's not what I thought he was, but that's because of his father's death."

"Oh, lord, here we go again. Excuses for the suffering Michael. You ought to ask Sally how much latitude she's willing to give Michael just now."

I was ignoring Jake's comments and thinking instead of Sally's assertion that Michael returned to the house after he met with her. She seemed so certain of that, and I was sure she wasn't lying.

"Let's try something, okay?" I jumped in my truck and signaled Jake to join me. "Leave your car here. We'll be back in a jiff."

I drove out of the drive, up the road toward town, and down the hill just before Michael's driveway. I executed a quick U-turn, taking Jake by surprise. He slid across the seat toward me, and when I stomped on the brake, he pitched forward.

"Should have put on your seat belt. It's the law."

Jake scowled at me.

I looked down the road, then got out. "Don't you see it?"

"No. What?" We stood in front of my truck, its headlights casting our shadows ahead of us into the light streaming down the road.

"From both inside the truck and outside, you can't see whether a vehicle turns into the Ramford driveway or continues down the road. There's a dip beyond the drive so that any car proceeding on would be hidden from anyone looking for it from here."

Jake got back into the truck, stared at the distance for a time, and got back out again.

"You're right."

"Oh, goody. This is great. Sally was mistaken. She merely thought Michael turned into the drive. You know what lies beyond the drive and down that road?" I was about to answer my own question, but Jake interrupted me.

"Francine Ortiz's place."

"Both Michael and Sally were telling the truth, then. I knew it."

"Time for me to visit Mrs. Ortiz."

"I want to come along, too."

Jake walked around the truck to face me and put his hands on my shoulders, leaning his head toward mine. I thought he was going to kiss me. Instead he touched his finger to my nose again. "Damn hot, isn't it?"

Waves of heat lifted off the asphalt and enveloped me, but they couldn't match the warmth I felt with his body so close.

"So, let's take my truck home, and I can ride to Francine's with you."

He didn't argue. I pulled into my drive and had to slam on the brakes in order not to hit the sixties VW van sitting there. My headlights reflected off a California plate, and I thought I had been transported back to the days of Woodstock, way before my time. The illusion was reinforced by the appearance of a head adorned with long auburn hair and a full beard. The man wearing the growth smiled at me, a grin I had seen far too seldom in our childhood, because he had little reason to use it then.

"Ronald?" I saw Jake's headlights hit the base of the drive. "Quick. Pull the van around behind the barn. The cops'll be here in a second," I said.

Nineteen

"I don't run from the cops now, Hera. I'm not a rebellious teenager getting into trouble anymore." His upstate New York accent was gone, his speech softened by the warmth of the west coast.

"Ronnie." I stepped forward. He enveloped me in deeply tanned arms and kissed me. Jake's headlights as he came up the drive illuminated our embrace.

He was wearing his cop look when he approached us, and his words said his visit had become official.

"Let me guess. This must be the prodigal son, come home to claim his share of the estate." *Good heavens. Not another wave of testosterone tonight.* Jake's mouth was set in a tight line that would surely snap if he stretched it any more tautly.

Ronald ignored Jake's comment, his arms still around me, his eyes as brown as chocolate jellybeans. "You've filled out a bit, I see. Bet the guys don't call you Skinny Minnie now."

I wanted to tell him he was right. *Nobody except for Michael.* He liked tall blondes, but he preferred them to look more like a Playboy centerfold. My physique ran more to a center for a women's basketball team. No, I guess I wasn't over him yet.

He reached around me for Jake's hand. "I'm Ronald Ramford." He nodded toward the sheriff's car. "What did she do? Speeding? Shoplifting? Your sticky fingers in junior high got you in some trouble, didn't they, Harry?"

Puzzlement joined Jake's frown. "Harry?"

"She was a real tomboy. We thought she needed a name that wasn't so wimpy, so we called her Harry."

Jake ignored Ronald's good-natured ribbing of me as well as the looks of pure joy on both our faces. His police presence said he didn't have the patience for jokes or a review of old times. "Do you know that the authorities have been looking for you for the past several weeks?"

Ronald and I weren't in the mood to have our get-together ruined by Jake's sour attitude.

"You read my ad in the Albany paper then?" I asked.

He nodded. A woman emerged from the passenger side of the van. She, too, appeared to have walked right out of a how-to-be-a-hippy manual. Long black dreadlocks swung in the moonlight, and delicate silver bells sewed onto the hem of her skirt tinkled as she stepped around the van to take my hand.

"Ronald has told me about you and your family. You saved his life, you know. If you hadn't showed him such kindness when he was here, he would have killed himself. Surely he would have." Her accent said she might have been from Jamaica. Listening to her with the jingle of the tiny bells in the background was like an island song set to the sound of the waves.

I gave Ronald another hug and reached out for Deni's hand. "Good. You're here, and that's all that counts. How about a cup of coffee or a beer?" I put my arms around their waists and began steering them toward the house.

"Oh, hell, I give up. I'll be back in the morning to ask you some questions." Jake stalked off to his car and sped out of the drive, spraying gravel and dirt in his wake.

"Don't visit Francine without me." I yelled loud enough for my voice to carry into the next county, but I feared Jake might have decided not to hear me.

"Did we interrupt something important?" Ronald asked.

"I don't think so. Let's go into the house, and I'll make some coffee and dig up a few stale cookies. Where are you staying? You can stay with me, if you like. Or you can have beer. You might want to try one of my new brews, or I think I've got a little wine." I was so excited at Ronald's appearance that I was running on and on, and I couldn't help myself. Neither of my guests seemed to mind my chatter.

"I almost came back here five years ago when I heard about your father. He meant a lot to me, you know." Ronald and Deni sampled Knightsbridge Ginseng Rush in my living room. "Great brew." Ronald lifted his beer glass to the light and studied the amber glow of the liquid.

"This could make a beer drinker out of me." Deni stuck out her tongue to lick away the foam that settled on her top lip.

"About Jake, he's not such a bad guy. He's just a little tense about this case. It's his first in the county, and he wants to make a good impression on his boss and the people in the area."

"You don't need to explain. We understand." Ronald spoke, but both heads wagged up and down in agreement. "I'm kind of glad you're over Michael. I never thought the two of you were a good match anyway."

Oh, no. They thought Jake was my boyfriend.

"Let me give you the whole story." Deni and Ronald sat close on my battered maroon couch. She leaned her head on his shoulder, and the two sets of brown eyes focused on me. I rocked back and forth in my mother's chair and told them about Michael Senior's death and how I found the body, then updated them on the investigation so far and included Jake's suspicion that my father's death wasn't suicide. I left out two things, Sally's pregnancy and most of what they really wanted to know about Jake and me, but they seemed to respect my omissions and never pressed me for more about him.

"We'll take you up on your offer to let us stay here. I'll visit the family tomorrow, and I think I'd better go alone. From what you told me about Mother and Michael, I can't trust how they might treat Deni, and I don't want her hurt by their unkind words."

Deni lifted her head off his shoulder, straightened up, and looked him in the eye. "I can take care of myself. Besides, when did you want to spring me on them?"

"She's always right. Reminds me of you, Hera."

Kind words, but nothing felt right in my life now, not my business or my personal life. Deni tried to hide a yawn behind her hand.

"We can talk more in the morning. I'm not being a very good hostess. I don't even have anything substantial to offer you to eat. Everything's in the freezer. I'll give you my bedroom, and I'll take Dad's old room."

"No, you won't. We'll sleep in your father's room." I squeezed Ronald's arm in gratitude as I passed by him to run upstairs and make the bed. I hadn't spent any time in Dad's room since he died, and Ronald seemed to sense how difficult it would be for me to spend the night there.

As I showed the two of them into the room, Deni hugged me goodnight. "I don't care what you say about Jake's trying to impress the good citizens of this county. I think he's trying to impress someone else." She kissed my cheek. "May your dreams reveal the path of truth to you."
I slept well, and if I dreamed, I didn't remember the content. I awoke with a sense that the sound of bells accompanied whatever gifts came to me that night.

Jake caught me in the barn the following morning. I'd dumped the malt in the mash tun and was adding the hot water. Not only was the temperature in the vessel producing enough heat to melt my face, the temperature on the outside thermometer had read above eighty when I entered the barn.

I ignored his arrival by feigning concentrated interest in the water filling the vessel.

"I just talked with Ronald. He arrived from California before his father's murder, not after, so he's been stretching the truth a little about why he's here."

I tried not to let my surprise show by plunging my head further into the kettle with the hot liquor in the bottom.

"Did you hear me?" he asked.

I decided not to reply.

"He dropped Deni off to visit her family two days before the murder and said he spent time alone in the Adirondacks camping, but he's very vague about where he was."

I banged the lid shut on the vat and turned toward him.

"So now you're saying Ronald is your suspect? Who is

it, Ronald or Michael, or do you think they're in this together?" I took the metal steps down off the platform two at a time and landed in front of him.

"I thought you might like to know, since you're my unofficial snoop on this case."

I walked around him and entered the cooler to check my yeast supply.

"What do you want from me? You interrogated Ronald. Don't you have someone else to annoy?" Why did this man aggravate me half the time and turn my limbs to spaghetti the other half? I could have thought about that if he hadn't been standing so close.

"Why are you so mad at me this morning? Last night we seemed to be getting along so well, and I thought ..."

"This is my property, and Ronald is my guest. Could you not use my house as your office?"

"You'd prefer I hauled him down to headquarters and put him in one of our rooms with the metal chair, light bulb hanging from the ceiling and peeling paper falling off the walls?"

"You'd better take a closer look at your facilities. I attended the open house last spring, and it didn't look anything like that." I closed the cooler door, wishing I could shut out the conflicting feelings I had about Jake and the case with as much ease.

I turned to face him. "I'm sorry. Let's begin again. I am a little peeved that you just came in here and questioned Ronald. Considering what he will be facing at home, I wanted this to be a kind of sanctuary for him."

"And the rest of your mad?"

I couldn't admit it had to do with the arrival of Ronald interrupting Jake and me, so I shrugged. "The weather's getting to me. When it's hot outside, and I'm in this stage of brewing, it's an inferno in here."

"How's the water holding up?" *Nice of him to ask.*

"Rafe's man connected a new pump on that old well and laid some pipe to the road leading to Ramford property. I'm supplying Rafe and Michael with water, but for how long, I can't predict."

I climbed the steps to the platform again and looked in my tank, adjusted the temperature gauge on the water heater, and leaned against the railing.

"I'm like an aerial act in the circus. So far I've been lucky to have Rafe and Michael catch me with an infusion of just enough money, but tomorrow, I may lose my partners and fall without a net underneath me. Then what?" A loud clanking sound came from underneath the boiler, and hot water began to pour out onto the floor.
"There goes my net. I've got a leak in my boiler. Shit."

By late afternoon, Jeremiah had determined that the boiler was not leaking. A hose from my water holding tank to the boiler had broken, rotted, Jeremiah thought, because of its age. I wasn't so certain. I thought I remembered replacing that hose a year ago.

"Good as new." Jeremiah got up from the cement floor after installing a new line and brushed himself off.

"Where'd you put that old section with the leak in it?" I held out my hand for the hose, and Jeremiah slapped it into my palm.

"You know, that doesn't look like old hose." He pulled his glasses down his nose and looked over the tops of them.

I bent the hose in half, and the rupture revealed itself.

Instead of disintegrating rubber, I saw a clean cut lengthwise on the tube. "It's been cut." A lot of good changing those locks was. Someone was still invading the barn. I'd tell Jake about this when he stopped by tonight to pick me up.

I heard a car rumble up the drive. That might be Ronald and Deni back from their visit to his family.

"I'll let you take over now. I don't know what I'd ever do without you, Jeremiah. Is Brian coming in soon? We could use him on cleaning out those kegs that arrived yesterday."

Jeremiah assured me that Brian was due to arrive within the hour. Then he acted as if he had more to say.

"I know this isn't the time to drop this on you, but I've had an offer for a job at higher pay. I guess I'll be giving you my two weeks notice."

I felt another rope on my safety net let go.

Twenty

"Have you seen Mom much lately? She seems a little, uh, a little on edge," Ronald said.

I didn't know how to answer his question, so I merely shook my head and continued with the tour I was giving him and Deni of my operation. Ronald seemed to be remembering most of the process from his childhood.

I pointed to the floor as we approached the boiler. "Watch the hoses and that wet area. We had a bit of a water leak this morning."

"Michael told me about the drought here. I'm happy to hear that you, Rafe, and he worked out a deal on water."

"Rafe was responsible for that. One of his men did the work on the well, and the rest just fell into place."

"Nice that you can see it that way, but from what I observed of Michael's new hire, I doubt things fell into place. I'll bet Stanley was maneuvering behind the scenes."

I stopped walking and leaned against the barn wall. "What do you think of his skill as a brew master?"

"It's been years since I had any contact with the brewing business, but he seems to have some fresh and innovative ideas. It's getting beyond his personality that's difficult." Ronald gave me a look, I nodded in agreement, and he let forth a bark of a laugh. "Right, then. You've seen that in him, have you?"

"We don't get along. He's too entrepreneurial and

pecuniary for my taste. Thinks bottom line first, then quality, and he's talked Michael out of the Ramford recipes." I clapped my hand over my mouth. What a jerk I was being. Stanley worked for the Ramford brewery, not just for Michael. That meant Ronald was his employer also. "Me and my big mouth. It's not my place to pass judgment on the guy."

Ronald's eyes narrowed. "Please go on. I'm especially interested in the Ramford brewing recipes. You say Michael sold those to him? This is the first I've heard that."

"Maybe I got it wrong, then. You'd better ask Michael."

"You can bet I will. I'm sure Michael's not thrilled to have my hand in the running of the brewery, but Dad's will specified that it went to the three of us, Michael, me, and Mom, to run. So he's stuck with me."

Deni said not a word up to this point. Then with a swirl of her musical skirts, she turned away from the bottling line and faced Ronald.

"I thought you were going to sign over your share to your mother and Michael, that you wanted nothing to do with your father's inheritance. Something's different now. What?"

"I don't like what's going on, Mom's erratic behavior, Michael's lack of interest in brewing, and the circumstances of Dad's death. I thought the murderer would be behind bars by now, but Jake tells me everyone has an alibi, and the physical evidence is minimal. I can't leave until I know who killed my father."

Deni's expression said she wasn't pleased with his decision, but she understood. "I think you should take me back to the city. I'll just be a distraction here."

"Not a distraction at all. You're my center, my rock. I need you here." Ronald pulled her to him and held her close to his heart.

Later, over the pizza I'd thrown together, I worked up the courage to ask Ronald the question on my mind. If my summons in the paper hadn't called him home, and he returned east before his father's murder, what brought him back here?

"I was looking for something, and I could only find it here, I guess." He took a swallow of his beer and wiped away a dab of sauce at the corner of his mouth. I waited for him to continue. Deni's head nodded up and down as if she knew just what he was going to say.

"It was time for me to talk to my father, to tell him how much he had hurt me, to ask him why he treated me as he did, and to try to forgive him. I also ..." A knock at the door interrupted Ronald.

"That's probably Jake. He's stopping by to pick me up. We're going to visit Francine tonight and ask her a few more questions." I stopped there. I shouldn't reveal the particulars of the proposed conversation with Francine, especially the part about Michael's alibi.

"Come on in." I scurried up the stairs as Jake entered. "I'll be down in a second." I peered at my face in the bathroom mirror, pulled my hair back into a ponytail, and slathered a little moisturizer on my cheeks where the steam from the mash tun had dried them out.

"Ready." There was no talking among the threesome in the kitchen, and Jake's eyes wouldn't meet mine. He mumbled a good night to Deni and Ronald and pulled me out the kitchen door.

"What's with you tonight? Why so unfriendly?"

"Ronald's appearance only makes one more suspect in this murder. I'm supposed to be pleased the list just got longer?"

We rode to Francine's in silence.

Francine answered the door and invited us into the house. She led us to the central living area, sunken two steps below the rest of the rooms. Marsh sat in front of the fireplace. He stood to greet us, then walked over to Francine and stood close at her side like a rooster guarding his hen from the fox. From the papers scattered over the coffee table, it was obvious we had interrupted a business discussion and perhaps something more.

I took in the room as Francine gestured toward the butter yellow couch Marsh had abandoned. Mediterranean-style rugs warmed up the saltillo tile floor, and planters in shades of cobalt blue, azure, and sun-drenched orange gave the place a friendly feel. The room said welcome, but the people in it spoke another language.

Francine held her hands clasped tightly in front of her, the knuckles white. She appeared wary of the purpose of Jake's visit. "Just a few quick questions," reassured her not at all. If she was wondering why I was here, Jake handled that well, claiming that he and I were having dinner in town reminiscing about our years in law school.

"I was driving Hera home, saw your light, and thought I should drop in while I was in the neighborhood to save myself a trip here tomorrow." *Right.* It was a pretty lame excuse, but Jake followed it up by taking the offensive. "Or you could stop by the office tomorrow, if this isn't a good time."

Francine nodded her agreement, seated herself on the couch, and gestured to several other chairs. I sat. Jake remained standing. He turned his attention to Marsh.

"I don't mean to take up your time, Marsh."

Marsh shook his head. "The work can wait."

"I'm fine. Go ahead and check on our inventory for next week." Was it my imagination, or was Francine trying to get him to leave?

"I'll stay here. No problem."

Jake opened the usual little notebook and flipped through several pages.

"Ah, here we go. I understand the night of the murder, you and Michael Ramford had a business meeting. I'm wondering why you never mentioned it when we talked before."

Marsh's face blanched then began to turn red. "That's not correct. Who told you that?"

Jake ignored Marsh's outburst and continued to look at Francine.

"Francine?"

"I'm sorry I didn't tell you, but Michael and I met several times, both before and after I hired you." Her tone was reassuring, and Marsh dropped his shoulders and relaxed. She turned her attention to Jake. "We were discussing a merger of our enterprises. It didn't work out. That's all. I can't see how that meeting is important."

"The time it took place is important. We know the meeting began late, but when did it end?"

"Oh, I see. You think he was here when his father was being killed? But he was with Cory. She told you that, didn't she?"

"That's what she said at first, but now she's having difficulty remembering the details of that evening."

Francine looked at Marsh and made some kind of a

decision. He didn't notice her glance. His focus was on the floor and not on her any longer.

"I'm afraid I can't help you." She got up from her chair, signaling the end to our visit.

Back in Jake's cruiser, he expressed his disgust at the conversation by slamming his fists on the steering column. "That was pretty useless. I thought maybe keeping it casual would take her off guard."

"Let me give you a tip for future use. You don't put anybody at ease when you remain standing and check in your little black notebook. It smacks of cop and interrogation. As for taking Francine off guard, that woman is too self-assured to be taken unawares. I also think she wanted to say more but couldn't."

"Because of Marsh."

"Because of Marsh."

"I need to separate the two of them without making it obvious that's what I'm doing."

I placed my hand on his as he reached out to start the engine. "I took care of that. Hold on a minute."

The front door opened, and Francine appeared, holding an object in her hand.

"Hera, wait. You left your purse." Francine handed the bag to me through the open car window.

"What really happened between you and Michael that night? Don't spare my feelings," I said.

She leaned in the window. "You see how protective Marsh is of me. I think he's in love with me, and he's jealous."

"Jealous of a business meeting between you and Michael? I don't ..." Jake began.

"Oh, shut up, Jake. It wasn't just business, was it?"

"No, it was, I mean, it is more than that. If Cory changed her story, it's because Michael is giving her plenty of reason to think twice about her feelings for him." *Or maybe Cory found other reasons to wriggle out of that tale.* I didn't say that to Francine. I encouraged her to go on with her version of why Cory might be backtracking.

"So, when Cory found out Michael was with you the night of the murder, she …" I paused, but Francine wasn't biting.

"Michael is a foolish young man. He's trying to protect me, my reputation. Such gallantry. I don't need it or expect it, but I must be truthful. Michael was with me that night, the entire night. I'll be happy to come down to the station tomorrow and provide you with more information. Now I have to go." She walked up the steps and back into the house. Marsh stood in the open doorway, waiting for her.

Jake and I rode back to my place in silence. I couldn't stand it anymore.

"You think I horned in too much tonight? Are you mad I told you to shut up when Francine came out to the car, or didn't you like the ploy I used to get her out there? What? Something's wrong, and it's not the weather." My voice got louder, and the pitch was reaching the dog whistle range.

"You did fine, just fine. I've got a lot on my mind sorting through all these stories. Every time I track down the truth of one of them, something else pops up, and I have to run off and examine that."

I took a good look at him. Maybe it was the dimness in the car, but I thought he looked bone tired.

"Sorry. I didn't mean to go all ballistic on you. I'm not

used to your moods any more. In law school, silence from you usually meant you were working on some legal issue and didn't want me to disturb you."

"Now, it means the same thing. I'm working on some legal issue, like I told you, all these pieces and how they fit together." His tone was sharp. It told me he'd like me to drop the subject, so I couldn't.

"Maybe if you laid out all the pieces, the two of us could put them together. Another head might help."

"Hera. I'm tired. I just don't want to deal with this now. Not now." He clamped his mouth shut, and his lips stretched across his teeth in a tight line that said he was about to explode. I'd made him mad.

"Okay." A sniffle escaped.

"Oh, for God's sake, don't cry."

"I'm not crying. It's my allergies." Now we were even. We both were lying.

The next morning I found out Jake wasn't lying. He was withholding information, information I would have found unsettling, information he knew I would resent him for unearthing.

His cruiser pulled into my drive around seven followed by two other sheriffs' cars. I heard the vehicles as I finished making my coffee after a night sleeping in the barn to be certain no one broke in to do any more damage to my equipment. The night was uneventful with respect to prowlers, but I hadn't slept well. I looked out my kitchen window to see Jake and four men dressed in county sheriff's department uniforms heading toward my door. I beat them to it.

"I see you brought the posse this morning." I was in a

testy mood, and it came through in my voice. If Jake noticed, he ignored my lack of good humor and selected his official voice to address me.

"Is Ronald Ramford here? I don't see his van."

I stood in the doorway while Jake and his men gathered at the bottom of my steps, hands on their holsters.

"Ronald and Deni left early this morning. Since I'm not their babysitter, they didn't tell me where they were going, but you might check at the Ramford place. Or Deni might have decided she wanted to go back to the city."

"Can we come in?" Jake stepped onto the first riser, and I held out my hand to stop his progress.

"You might tell me what this is all about."

"Official sheriff's business."

I thought about delivering the line about having to get a search warrant, but remembering the fatigue on Jake's face last night, I reconsidered.

I held open the door, stepped to one side, and gestured the crew into the room. "Oh, crap, Jake. What's going on?"

"We need to search the house."

"Fine, go ahead, but could you please tell me what's happening?"

"I'm bringing Ronald in for questioning. We have reason to believe he killed his father."

Stunned, I lowered myself into a chair at the table, dropped my head into my hands, and worked my fingers through my hair. Jake signaled his men to search the other rooms. They returned in a matter of minutes.

"No one, Sir."

The officers left, and Jake sat down beside me at the table. "I'm sorry I couldn't tell you last night, but in canvassing the hardware stores in this area, we found one which recently sold a shovel similar to that used to kill Mr. Ramford. I took a picture of Ronald to the owner early this morning, and he identified him as the person making the purchase several days before Ramford's murder."

"So what? So Ronald bought a shovel like the one found in my shed."

"Mr. Ramford's blood was on that shovel, as were Ronald's prints. I know he lied about being in this area before his father's murder. Now I want to know why."

Twenty-One

After Jake left, I called the Ramford residence, but there was no answer. Everybody must be out in the barn. I climbed the stairs to Dad's room. At least the officers hadn't left it in a mess when they looked for Ronald. It was tidy, too tidy. None of Ronald's or Deni's clothes and other possessions were in the room. Well, maybe they decided to move to the Ramford house. *Why didn't he leave me a note?*

Ronald's unscheduled departure plagued me throughout the morning as I checked the supplies of beer for the Saturday tasting and took a peek at the fermenting tun in which my newest ale was developing. I still had time during the summer to get it out to my customers, as well as the space to consider brewing other product to satisfy the Saturday crowds, and I was hoping for crowds, large crowds.

I checked my hoses while I waited for Jeremiah to arrive. I had learned my lesson. Don't trust locks. Until Jake arrested the person who vandalized my equipment, I'd be sleeping in the barn. Then I remembered. Jake's unfriendly and official visit this morning put the slit hose right out of my mind. I hadn't gotten the opportunity to tell him about it.

The barn was stifling, so I headed out the door to wait under the maple on the lawn. Instead of Jeremiah, Brian rode up on his bicycle.

"Hey, Brian. I thought Jeremiah was going to work today, and your days were Tuesday and Thursday afternoons." We walked to the barn together.

"That's right." He leaned his bicycle against the side of the building. "But Jeremiah got into an accident on his bike yesterday when he left here. The tire came off on the way down the hill into town, and he went over the bars and hit his head. The doctor said he should take it easy for a few days. A concussion, he thinks." *Good heavens. What an awful accident.*

"He could have been killed. Why didn't he call me?"

"He said you already had too much on your mind and didn't want to add to your worry. I heard he's quitting. I could increase my hours, if you'd like."

Brian had only been with me for a short time, and he didn't know most of the operation, but he was an eager worker. So far he'd picked up on things fast.

"Okay, you're on. You'll have a lot more to learn, long hours to put in, and not all of them are going to show up in a paycheck, you know."

"I know, and that's cool. I'd really like to learn to make beer." He paused. "An uncle of mine is a home brewer of sorts, so I guess it runs in my family."

"That's settled. You understand this is probationary, to see how you work out." He nodded and appeared happy with my proposition. With Jeremiah out now and his eventual departure, I'd be trapped in my own brewery, if I didn't have Brian. Then I chastised myself for being selfish, thinking only of my needs when it was Jeremiah's head that took the hit.

I left Brian in charge of the barn and decided to take the long way into town past the Ramford place. At the foot of the drive to the brewery, I hesitated. What excuse could I give for my impromptu visit other than poking my nose into what happened to Ronald? *Oh, the hell with it,* I thought as I cranked my wheel left and headed up the drive. Ronald was my friend, and that's all the excuse I needed.

The only car in the driveway was Stanley's. The trunk was open, and he stepped out of the front door of the house carrying a suitcase and some clothes on hangers. He glanced up, saw me, and returned his attention to throwing the items into the car. Glee bubbled up in my chest. Stanley was leaving? How perfect. I tried to suppress a smile as I rolled down the window of my truck and greeted him.

"Taking a trip, Stan?"

"Mind your own business." He slammed the lid closed and headed back into the house.

A car pulled up the drive and parked behind me. Michael's.

"Come to gloat?"

"I don't know what you mean. I just came by to see if Ronald was around. Jake was looking for him earlier this morning."

"That's the only good thing that's happened since my wayward brother arrived home. The cops are after his ass, and I hope they find him."

This was all so confusing. I knew Michael wasn't happy Ronald was here. Ronald had said that, but why so angry?

I got out of the truck, rushed after Michael, and caught him as he was opening the front door.

"What's going on around here?"

He turned to me, hesitated, then spoke. "You mean you really don't know?" I shook my head. "Ronald got some big shot lawyer in here, and the court declared all the moves I made since Dad's death null and void or whatever legal term was used. Anyway, it seems Mother and I had no right to make those decisions unless Ronald was consulted. Now, how the hell could he participate? We didn't know where he was."

I seemed to recall that neither mother nor son was eager to locate him until their lawyer insisted. Stanley came back through the door with his briefcase in his hand.

"You'll be hearing from my lawyer. You can't just weasel out of the contract we have. I'll sue you for every last grain of malt." He pushed past Michael, got into his car, and roared out of the driveway.

"Shit." Michael sat down on the top step with his head in his hands. "When Ronnie appeared two days ago, I was convinced that we could work things out, but he'd already gotten the wheels in motion with his own lawyer."

"You can't blame him, can you? You turned the brewery upside down once your father was dead."

"I screwed things up, didn't I?"

I sat down beside him. "Not well thought out or business-like."

"Don't you start on me, too. I count on you to be my friend. I couldn't stand it if you were angry at me." He reached out and took my hand in his. That's how Jake found us when he pulled up to the house.

"Any word on Ronald?" Jake asked.

Michael shook his head no. Jake looked at me.

"Hera?"

"As I told you before, he and Deni stayed with me last

night but left before I got up this morning."

"I'm certain the two of you will be sure to let me know if you hear anything."

The two of us? There was no two of us, and I was tired of being Michael's friend every time he did something stupid. I pulled my hand free.

"Michael, you're a real jerk." Michael's mouth dropped open, and Jake stopped mid-stride in his walk back to his car.

"What?" Michael's face was awash with disbelief at my words.

"You want to be my friend, but only when it's convenient for you, and always when you need something. You've known for years I had a crush on you, and you used that to keep me dangling just in case your well of women ran dry. That's all over now. I'm glad Ronald's back, and he's giving you what you deserve. I hope your ass lands in jail. It might teach you some humility."

"You know I have always loved you, Hera. Now that Cory's left me, we could be together."

"Cory left you? I feel so stupid. She dumped you after only several months while I needed all my life to find out what a jerk you are. Goodbye, Michael."

I stalked past Jake, whose hand was in front of his face trying to hide a smile. I turned and walked back to him.

"You're only marginally better." His eyebrow jumped a half inch, and he dropped the grin.

I left the two of them standing there with expressions of confusion on their faces as I drove out the drive. My heart was racing, but I was calm and serene in my own mind. I hadn't found Ronald as I thought I might, but I had found my backbone.

"You said what to him?" Sally giggled with amazement at my gumption.

"Oh, sorry. I shouldn't have unloaded all this on you, with the baby and all."

"Don't be silly. I feel fine, really I do. I've made up my mind I'll tell Michael about my pregnancy and insist that a lawyer set up child support."

"No regrets over Michael?" I was surprised. I always thought of Sally as having a tender heart, but she also had more determination than I gave her credit for. It was a trait I ought to emulate.

"No regrets. I know Michael would like to believe I loved him, and so would I, given my ideal version of myself, but I think it was a little more on the side of lust than love. I hate to admit this, but I was jealous of you."

"What?"

"Michael was so desirable, the best catch in town, and you always had him. I mean, he always seemed to come back to you. You're so tall, and blonde, and sexy, and I'm so short and chubby, and just kind of cute."

"Dumb, too."

She grabbed a red curl, twisted it between her fingers, lifted her blue and white pinafore with the other hand and curtsied. "Right, but now I'm smarter."

"I'll be right back. Wait here."

"Where would I go? I have to keep the shop open."

When I returned, I held a bottle of sparkling cider in my hands.

"This should be champagne, but given your condition, it will have to do. A celebration."

"Okay, but just what are we celebrating?"

"The loss of our old wimpy selves and the location of female determination."

We drank the cider, made plans for tomorrow's tasting, and talked about baby names. Sally was certain it would be a boy, while I wished for a girl. Somewhere in our conversation, as customers poured in and out of the shop, Sally asked the one question I wished she hadn't.

"What about Jake?"

"I gave him the old heave-ho, too."

"Oh, I don't think you should have done that."

"Well, I left the door open a bit." After all, we were sleuthing partners, weren't we? Oops. I was having so much fun shedding my dependence on old habits, I forgot I should stop by and let Jake know about the slit hose, but first I needed to visit Jeremiah.

I rang Jeremiah's doorbell with my free hand. In the other, I held a box filled with half a dozen of Sally's apple fritters, which I knew Jeremiah loved. His sister answered the door.

"He's much better, and if you have in that box what I think you have, he'll be in tip-top shape in a jiffy."

"Fritters? Yum." He was lying on the couch but raised himself to a sitting position, the better to grab a pastry.

I asked him what happened to his bike.

"I don't know. It was fine when I rode out to your place, but the tire just kind of peeled off the rim when I hit that bump coming down Carver Hill. It's getting old, and I guess I should have paid closer attention to my rubber."

"Brian's out at the barn now, so I'd better get going. Take what time you need. Rest and get better. You get out of bed too soon, and there'll be no more pastries for you."

"I'm sorry about leaving you."

"I understand. If I got a better paying job, I'd be out of here, too." I thought joking about his pay at my place might encourage Jeremiah to reveal where his other job would be, but he kept that to himself, and I decided not to pry. At the door, I asked his sister where his bike was.

"In my truck. I picked it up off the road taking him back here from the hospital. I thought about just throwing it out, but he assured me it could be fixed." Good old Jeremiah. He could fix anything. I would miss him.

"Mind if I take a look at it? Maybe I can get the spare parts for it while he's recuperating." She pointed toward her truck in the back of the house.

I leveraged my body onto the tailgate. The bike was in better shape than I hoped. A few of the spokes were broken on the front wheel, and the handlebars were twisted, but the frame looked undamaged. When I examined the front tire, looking for a replacement size, I saw the rubber that gave him the trouble. A five inch slit appeared along the tire, not all the way through the rubber, but deep enough that a bumpy road blew the damaged area open. It reminded me of my slit boiler hose. It was past time for me to let Jake know about these so-called accidents.

I called Jake on his cell but got no answer. It was now around midnight. No word from Jake or from Ronald and Deni. I was lying on the cot I set up in the tasting room of the barn, trying to keep my eyes open. An hour earlier, I had turned off the old gooseneck lamp, which I had bungee-corded to a chair back next to the cot. It gave me light by which I could read my book, but the story was boring, and I kept nodding off. I gulped down a cup of coffee while I was reading and another as I lay in the dark. Usually caffeine keeps me awake, but tonight, for some reason, it wasn't working.

I sat up, pulled on my sweatshirt, and was considering a walk around the outside of the building when I heard a noise from the other end of the barn. It sounded as if someone stumbled into the stack of kegs Brian cleaned the other day and left in the middle of the floor near the fermentation vessels. I grabbed my flashlight. I was familiar enough with the layout of the floor that I wouldn't need the light, but it would make a fine weapon.

A wave of dizziness forced me back onto the cot. *What the hell?* I grabbed the chair to rise and managed to pick my way toward the brewing area. My head continued to spin, and I feared I would fall, alerting whoever was there to my presence. I gripped the side of one of the tanks to remain upright.

"Crap," I heard a voice say as I struggled to stay on my feet behind my cover. I tried to let my eyes adjust to the dark, but that did little good as the images in the dim light spun around me. I intended to nab whoever was breaking into my operation and sabotaging it. This time, surprise was on my side, and I meant to take advantage of it if only everything would stand still.

I could just make out a figure near the stack of kegs. Using the tanks as support, I moved toward it but stopped when another person emerged from behind the first. They outnumbered me. As courageous as I wanted to be, tonight I was a dizzy blonde and no match for two of them. I stepped behind my mash tun and waited.

"You told me someone would be here."

"She's here. She's in the tasting room, probably asleep. I put something in her coffee to make her drowsy."

"Hadn't you better check to see if she's out?

It's now or never, I thought and flipped on my flashlight. It caught both figures in its beam. I slipped to the floor in a faint.

Twenty-Two

"Wake up. Wake up." I was at the bottom of a deep well, and Jake was shouting at me from the surface. Then I felt something cold on my face. It wasn't icy water.

"Good lord, you're pouring cold beer on me. You could drown me." I grabbed the bottle out of his hand and looked at it. "It's a bottle of Ginseng Rush. That's no way to treat my lager."

"It was the only thing cold enough to revive you. I tried tap water, but you weren't coming round."

"What happened?" I took in my surroundings as I sat up. I was in my own living room on the couch. "How'd I get here? Last I knew, I was in the barn about to catch two prowlers. Did you get them?"

"Sorry. I heard someone run out through the gift shop when I entered your barn door. I thought it was kind of funny you'd leave it open, after Rafe and I took the time to install new locks and all."

My head felt as if it were about to explode, and there was a funny taste in my mouth. "I think someone drugged me. I heard them say they put something in my thermos."

"Where's the thermos now?"

"In the tasting room." Jake started toward the door. "No, don't leave me. You can look at it later."

"Who had access to it?"

I thought over yesterday's events. I filled the thermos here right before I left for Sally's shop, stopped by the barn to check on how Brian was doing. It was in my truck at Sally's and when I visited Jeremiah. I took it out of the truck when I got home and put it on the bar in the tasting room. I told Jake what transpired.

"I drank several cups of coffee from it while I was reading last night. I wondered why I kept falling asleep. That book was supposed to be a thriller."

"Did you get a good look at them?"

"Uh, not really. I dropped my flashlight on the floor." Jake got out of the chair he was sitting in and walked toward the kitchen. "Now where are you going?"

"Just to get you a glass of water." He brought it back, and I drank it down in several gulps. It took the vile taste out of my mouth and quenched the parched feeling in my throat.

"What were you doing here? Isn't it kind of late for official business, although I know you like to take people off guard?" I asked.

"Looking for you. I couldn't sleep thinking about what you'd said earlier today, well, yesterday. I thought we should talk."

"Talk?" I swung my legs to the floor and sat up. My head spun only slightly.

"Yes, but first, would you mind telling me why you were sleeping in the barn?"

I told Jake about the cut hose and Jeremiah's bike.

"Did you keep the old hose? I'd like to see it."

"Sure, I'll get it for you, but about that talk."

"Yeah?"

"I'm not interested in talking." I reached out, grabbed

him around the neck, pulled him down onto the couch, and let him figure out the rest.

Later, we were reacquainting ourselves for the second time tonight with each other's bodies, now a little older than when we were in law school, but perhaps a little less rushed in our passion. Oh, yeah, there was a lot of passion there, but we both seemed more interested in taking our time, letting the lust ooze out of our pores rather than racing to a finish line. I think we began to understand better the reason why the tortoise won that race. As we neared the end again, an explosion rocked the night air.

"Wow," we said in unison, then realized the blast came from outside the house and not from the bed we were thrashing around in. Through the bedroom window, we watched a red ball of light and flame shoot toward the heavens.

"It's up there beyond the ridge. It's got to be the old well." I grabbed my jeans and shirt as Jake searched around the room for his clothes.

"Here." I handed a pair of jeans to him.

"No, these are yours."

"Sorry." I stripped off the too-large jeans I was zipping up and threw them in his direction.

"Shirt. Where's my shirt?"

"Downstairs. You took it off while we were on the couch."

In the distance, I could hear the wail of a siren. Jake's cell phone began to ring. I dove back into the rumpled bedcovers and extracted the cell from the other side of the bed. I tossed it to him. He flipped it open and began making official sounding grunts into it. I leaned over his shoulder, trying to hear what was being said, but he fended me off with his arm. He closed the phone and ran for the stairs, taking them two at a time. I was right behind him, matching him step for step, the advantage of being a tall woman.

At the bottom of the stairs, he turned to me. "Bad news. Your well blew up." *I already figured that out.*

"Wells don't just blow up. How the hell could it?"

"I'm going to find out." Jake strode toward the door and threw it open.

"I'm coming with you," I said.

"No, you don't. You're staying here and locking yourself in." He slammed the door. I could hear the cruiser speed out of my drive.

That's no way to treat your partner, an old friend, and a new and old lover, I thought. *The hell with staying here.* I grabbed my keys, locked the house, checked the doors on the barn to make certain they were secured, and set out for the well. I might make it there on foot faster than Jake could in his car.

As I topped the rise that led into the small valley where the well was situated, I could see emergency vehicles wending their way over the rutted fire trail leading to the area. It had to be slow going. There was nothing much else to see, just the sun coming up over the pine trees on the eastern hill and illuminating a large, blackened hole in the earth at the well's location. Once I got close enough, I recognized the lone figure standing there, his shoulders slumped forward and a beat-up leather hat in his hand.

"Rafe? What are you doing here?"

He turned to me with eyes that looked as dark and deep as the well that used to occupy this site.

"It's my fault. It's all my fault. I shouldn't have refused his demands."

A few twisted lines of pipe littered the area, blown into the air and then tossed like matchsticks onto the ground. I turned my attention back on Rafe.

"You're not making any sense. Who?"

Jake pulled up in one of the sheriff's department's four-wheel-drive vehicles, followed closely by two fire trucks. He jumped out and strode up to where we were. "Better stand back. It's still pretty hot around here." Like a good sheepdog on duty, he herded Rafe and me back from the depression in the ground. Then he turned to me. His face no longer held the look of a man glad to see his woman. More like a parent about to scold a child.

"It's my well. Or it was. I've a right to be here."

"I'm surprised to see you, Rafe," Jake said.

"Makes it a lot easier to arrest me, I guess. I'm the one responsible for this mess."

Jake's face showed no expression.

"No better time than now to tell me what's going on."

The three of us retreated farther from the hole while several fire trucks pulled up. There was little flame and smoke now, because there was nothing left to burn.

"Lucky there were no trees close by, or with this drought, we'd have quite a fire on our hands." The fire chief directed his men to put out the small clumps of burning grass and spray the area with water to make sure nothing caught again. Then he called in his arson crew, and they began sorting through the tangled pipes.

Rafe, Jake and I walked to the tree line and sat on a downed log, watching as the men traversed the area, picking up objects from the ground. "Parts of a pump, looks like," one of them said. "Wow, that blew over fifty feet at least."

"How'd you know it was my well so soon? Was someone up here when the call came through to your cell?" I asked Jake.

"Someone placed a call to the dispatcher's number a few seconds after the explosion just in case anybody in the county was still sleeping after that roar." Jake turned to Rafe. "That wouldn't have been you, would it?"

"No, not me. It had to have been Bernie."

"Bernie, as in Bernie Fisher, your employee? The man you were so keen to get out of jail and hire. You never did tell me what that was all about. I guess now it's a little too late to explain your motives, but give it a try anyway." Jake worried the muscle in his cheek. He was working up a big mad, and I was grateful it was directed at Rafe and not me.

Rafe appeared eager, even relieved to tell his story. "I know Bernie from England. We got pretty drunk together one night, and I got in a fight with another man, some stranger in the bar where we were drinking. The three of us left the place, and the fellow and I began to argue over some silly thing. I can't even remember what it was now. Anyway, I landed a good one on his jaw, and he went down, hit his head on the pavement. Bernie tried to rouse him, but he was dead. I killed a man that night, and I never paid for it."

"That's an interesting story, but I can't see how it relates to Hera's well being blown up."

"Bernie did it. He's a master with explosives." Rafe dropped his head into his hands.

"And you were the one who had him do this?" Jake

seemed puzzled. I was, too.

"I might as well have. You see, I stopped paying him to keep his mouth shut about the murder. He decided to get back at me through Hera."

"Where's Bernie now? I'd better have a talk with him. Meantime, one of my men will take you back to headquarters, where we'll get your statement about tonight's events."

Rafe nodded and got up off the log, rising with the stiffness of a man twenty years his senior.

"I'm sorry, Hera," he said. He reached out his hand to me, but I ignored the gesture.

"I don't know what to say. I thought you were my friend. You knew he was a scoundrel, yet you hired him and let him work on my well. You had to know what he was capable of. I just don't understand at all." I shook my head, turned my back on him, and started home.

"No, you don't. You wait right there," Jake called to me. He walked with Rafe to a sheriff's car and exchanged a few words with one of his men, who held the back car door open for Rafe. Jake returned to my side, grabbed my arm, and walked me back to his vehicle.

"Ouch, you're hurting my arm."

"Sorry, but it seems I'd better get a firm grip on you, or you'll be off to who knows where. I'm taking you back home, and this time I'm warning you. You stay put. Whoever drugged you and broke into your barn is still roaming around free." He shoved me into the passenger's seat of his SUV.

"Fasten your seat belt," was the only thing he said to me as we drove back to my place, except for a romantic "Get out and lock your doors. I'll be back," when he dropped me off.

I sat at my kitchen table and thought about everything that had happened so far this summer. My business life was like an old carnival. Most of the rides were broken down, and the ones that worked had pieces falling off them. As for the games of chance? Well, I'd run out of quarters to toss on the plates, and the ones that did stick only returned a paper fan. *Shit!*

My personal life had looked good at around four in the morning. I glanced at the kitchen clock. On the other hand, now that it was seven in the morning, I wondered if I'd just dreamed last night. Of course, I was about to do something to jeopardize any hope of that dream repeating itself.

A vehicle pulled into the drive. *Great. Reinforcements.* Ronald jumped out of his van and rushed up to my kitchen door.

"The cops are looking for you. Did you know that?" I swung the door open, looked around the back yard as if I expected Jake to materialize from under the lilac bush, and pulled Ronald into the house.

"Why are they looking for me?" He raised his eyebrows in astonishment.

"Sit down. I made some coffee. We need to have a long talk. Then I'll need your help, assuming you give me the straight story on why you came back here and what was going on between you and your father." He opened his mouth to interrupt me. "Don't even try to sell me some stupid half truths. I've had a bad morning, and I'm in no mood for fantasy. Bring your cup. I need to check on the barn."

Ronald sat on some barley sacks while I climbed the

steps to the fermenter.

"Deni got a call from her mother. Her younger brother went into the hospital with some abdominal pains and was rushed into surgery for a burst appendix. We were in a hurry when we left, and I didn't think of leaving a note. I'm sorry if I worried you."

"How's her brother doing?"

"Fine. I wanted to stay, but she knew I was worried about what was going on here, so she encouraged me to come back."

"Hmmm." I checked the temperature gauge on my fermenter. I was cold conditioning the beer. I had dropped the temperature in the cone-shaped vessel. Soon I would know how good an ale I had produced, but before that happened, I wanted Ronald's story about why he returned to his father's house when he did. I could be patient with cold conditioning my beers, but I'd be damned if I was in any mood to wait long for his tale, so I may have jumped the gun a little with my next question.

"The shovel. Why did you need that shovel?"

"What's so important about a shovel? I needed it to dig up some stuff, things I'd buried a long time ago when I was a kid."

"You weren't going to use it to do in your father?"

"What?"

"The shovel you bought. It was the murder weapon, and it has your fingerprints on it. That's why Jake is looking for you."

Ronald began laughing.

"It's not funny. Your shovel killed your father."

He extracted a handkerchief from his pocket and wiped away his tears of laughter.

"No, it's not funny, but it is ironic that only here at home do I get in any trouble. I'm sure your cop friend told you I have no record of any kind. Away from these parts, I seem to have no difficulty leading an exemplary life."

"The shovel."

"Right." He dug into his other jeans pocket and extracted something which he held out to me in his closed fist. "Take a look. My reason for the shovel." He opened his hand and in it I spied several pieces of pointed stone. Arrowheads.

"You dug up these arrowheads?"

"Yep. I buried them just before I ran off and didn't have the time to dig them up then, but I vowed to come back and get them someday. I know it seems like an adolescent dream, but they meant something to me. Your dad and I found them up near that old well."

The old well, now wiped off the land. I wondered if Ronald knew about it, but I had other questions for him.

"You met with your dad the night you dug up those arrowheads, didn't you? And you had a fight."

Ronald remained silent, as if he considered lying about the meeting, but then he decided otherwise.

"He caught me digging up my treasures on the other side of the brew barn. He didn't recognize me at first. The sun was going down, and it was almost dark. When I told him who I was, he ordered me off his property. Told me I was no son of his and that he was changing his will to cut me out of the inheritance."

"He disowned you?"

"You know, it was kind of funny. Not like he disowned me, but like he believed I really wasn't his. I know he would have preferred I didn't exist, but the whole encounter was odd."

Not so odd. Claudia could have lied to Jake and me. Perhaps she and my father did have an affair, and Ronald was his son. That meant he was my half-brother.

I examined the man perched on the malt sack for similarities to my father or to me. There were none, but that didn't mean a thing. I looked nothing like my father, aside from inheriting his height. My fair complexion and blonde hair, I got from my mother. Ronald appeared to have inherited no features from either parent. Not tall and dark like his father or mine, nor was he short and fair-haired like his mother.

"Why are you looking at me that way?"

I was tempted to tell Ronald about my suspicions, but I couldn't see how that would help anyone.

"What night was it the two of you saw each other?"

"It wasn't the night he was killed. It was a few days before that. I know what you're thinking. I could have come back here with my shovel and bashed in his head, right?"

"Don't get all defensive on me. I'm on your side and always have been."

"That's why you've always been so entangled with my brother." It was the truth, but I never suspected Ronald saw my closeness to Michael as a betrayal of him. He got up off the sack and held out his hand to me. "I'm sorry. I shouldn't have said that." I hesitated a moment, then took his outstretched hand.

"No, it's okay. You're just saying what needs to be said to clear the air between us. Michael always did come first with me. It wasn't that I took Michael's side against you."

"You just kind of ignored me, forgot I existed."

We were alone in my barn, no one knew we were here, and I didn't expect visitors. I should have been on guard before. Ronald had plenty of reason to kill his father, and now I knew about his visit with him before the murder. I listened for any note of threat or anger in his voice. There was none, but he seemed to tune into my wariness.

"I'll leave. Better for you anyway. I'll go visit your sheriff friend and let him know I'm back."

"He's kind of busy right now." I told him about the well.

"Good God, Hera. Your life is in more turmoil than mine. How can I help?"

Just the offer I needed.

Twenty-Three

The Saturday tasting opened at eleven to a crowd of almost fifty people. Many of them turned out to be parents dropping off their children at nearby summer soccer or baseball camps. Product flew out of my barn, a blessing and a curse. Jeremiah's sister agreed to help me. I led tours, then followed them with samples while she worked the gift shop. I spelled her when I wasn't busy.

Customers jockeyed for position at the counter while others bought sausages, bread, and herbs outside. I swiped credit cards like a winner at a craps table raking in chips. On the other hand, the diminishing number of six-packs and liter bottles of beer reminded me that I couldn't replenish my inventory without an infusion of real money and soon. I tried to forget about the disaster with the well. I had no funds for repairs, and I'd lost the income made from selling the water.

Jake stopped by to say hello in the early afternoon. I think he was astonished to see me where he had told me I ought to be. With the crush of people wanting to make purchases, Jake and I couldn't find time to talk about Rafe or Bernie and their involvement in blowing my well. I invited him over later in the evening for after-dinner coffee. I hoped I would have a surprise for him then.

The last group of people left the grounds around three in the afternoon. My vendors reported more than a usual number of sales, too. Several more Saturdays selling this volume of beer, assuming I could produce more product, and I might hold off the wolf at the door until late September, when the other brewers and I would put together an Octoberfest, but that meant I'd be working day and night.

At four in the afternoon, I pulled my truck into a lane downhill from the brewery and waited for Ronald to show. He and I had agreed to present a united front to the culprits who drugged me, but after fifteen minutes of waiting for him, I decided to go it alone. He would show up soon.

I hiked up the hill, circled the buildings, and approached the operation from behind. This place was so different from mine. It shouted state-of-the-art brewing, whereas mine cried for paint and repairs. His buildings were painted white and trimmed with blue. A split rail fence enclosed the property. Gold-lettered signage provided visitors with information about hours of operation and the location of brewery, gift shop, and tasting cellar. I spied my target's wheels parked at the end of the driveway. I used the door at the rear of the barn to enter the building.

The person I was seeking stood alone beside the bottling line, his back to me as I entered. I wondered where his buddy was. I fantasized about putting him in one of the vats and fermenting him along with a hearty stout. It would do the stout no good, but it would give me some satisfaction. He whirled around as my footsteps echoed on the concrete floor.

"You."

"Where's your partner?" His face looked pale in the

afternoon light. Not so brave now without back-up, but then, I was without my back-up, too.

"So, is this what you meant by a relative that did some home brewing? Just how are you and Teddy related anyway?"

I watched as he swallowed, his large Adam's apple working its way up his throat and back down. He picked up something from the floor and moved toward me. It looked like a short length of hose.

"Here I thought you were such a quick learner. I never suspected you knew it all before you came to me," I said. I began to circle away from him, keeping my eyes on his hand holding the hose. *Reinforcements. Where was my back-up?*

Before he could answer, the door linking the bottling area to storage opened, and another man appeared in the doorway, his figure backlit by the sunlight coming through the opening. It was too short to be Ronald. With that height and rotund belly, it could only be Teddy.

"What's going on, Hera? What are you doing here?"

"I found her snooping around. She looked like she was up to something, Uncle Teddy."

I saw Teddy take in the piece of hose in his nephew's hand. "I don't think so. Put down that hose, you idiot. Tell me what's happening, and don't lie to me."

Brian dropped the hose to the floor, then hung his head and muttered something under his breath.

"Speak up." Teddy pulled back his hand as if to hit him.

"Let him alone, Teddy. I think he's too scared to say a word. I'll tell you what I know."

I quickly told Teddy about the slashed hose, the cut tire

on Jeremiah's bike, and the attack on me by Brian and an accomplice.

"You saw Brian before you passed out, but did you see the other fellow's face?"

"There was something familiar about it, but I didn't recognize him."

Brian's head came up, and he let out a snort of a laugh.

"You're not so smart. It wasn't a fella at all. It was a girl."

I put the call in to Jake, knowing he would be furious that I had gone on a snooping expedition when he'd ordered me to stay put. He arrived at Teddy's place only minutes after my call. Another sheriff's car followed. The officer took away Brian. Teddy, Jake, and I talked in the tasting cellar.

"My sister's kid. He was always a problem, but recently I thought he'd straightened himself out a bit. I guess I was wrong. Then the little bastard tries to blame the whole thing on me, saying it was my idea to make trouble at your place." Teddy's face got redder and fuller as he spoke. I worried that he was going to have a stroke.

"It's okay. I know you wouldn't have your hand in such a thing." Jake's face said he didn't agree with my assessment.

"Let me tell you a story about Teddy." I looked at Teddy for his permission. He knew what I was going to say. After a moment's hesitation, he nodded.

"Teddy loves beer. You can visit here any time of the day or night and find him wandering his brew house, taking in its smells and sounds. But what I didn't know until one evening, as I was walking the hills between his place and mine, was that Teddy is a true romantic about the history of brewing in this area. I found him sitting next to the old hop house now burned to the ground. Can I tell him what you said, Teddy?" He stood with his hands in his pockets, looking at the floor. All I could see of his face was the top of his bald head. He gave an almost imperceptible nod.

"He said, 'Too bad mold got the hops and wiped them out as a crop around here. Wouldn't it be great to make a brew like the old days using local hops?' Then he added in true Teddy fashion, 'Oh, not that you could make any money doing it. Too risky. Mold might hit again, but it would be great. Those were the days.' So you see, our Teddy might be a bull of a business competitor, but he's honorable."

Teddy's face got red again, but this time I thought it was from blushing. He cleared his throat and spoke.

"Find out who was behind what Brian did. I know he wasn't in this alone. He's not that smart. He's a follower. Someone must have been paying him."

"I'm following Hera home, then I'll be visiting Brian's accomplice."

"I want to come with you," I said.

"This is official police business. I can't have you with me when I make an arrest." Jake walked with me to the lane where I parked my truck.

"I want to see the expression on her face and hear her try to wiggle out of this one."

"She'll clam up around you. I'll apply some pressure."

"Be careful what kind of pressure you apply."

"Jealous?" He placed his hand on my chin and pulled my face nearer his. "Go home. I'll arrest Cory and tell you all about her exploits when I stop by. It might be a little later than we planned." His lips touched mine, and we drew closer together. Soon, not even one of the gnats buzzing around our heads could have fit between us.

"So you're not mad at me anymore?"

"No, but I'm sure, given your propensity for not doing what you're told, I will be again, probably sooner than later."

He twisted me around to face my truck, patted my ass, and walked off into the fading light. I watched him go, admiring the way his uniform pants cupped the muscles of his buttocks. Then I remembered.

"What about Rafe?"

"Later."

What about Ronald? He'd failed me, hadn't showed when he agreed to help. Everything turned out fine, but what if Teddy hadn't appeared when he did? Would Brian have used that hose on me?

As darkness set in, the breeze from the north picked up. It felt like a storm was brewing. This time, I thought I could smell rain in the air, but I'd imagined that before, and the winds tossed us nothing but dust. I paced my living room, waiting for Jake to appear. When I heard a vehicle in the drive, I rushed to the window. Mammoth raindrops hit the panes with enough force to rattle the glass. I could just make out Jake's SUV through a sheet of water driven almost horizontally against the house. Jake banged on the door, then opened and closed it quickly to keep out the storm.

"This looks real bad. Maybe we should be waiting it out in your basement," he said, but just as soon as the words left his mouth, all was quiet. The storm retreated with as little warning as when it arrived. A light rain continued to fall, but the wind subsided. Just another false alarm. I poured coffee, and we sat down together on the couch.

"Cory admitted she and Brian tried to scare you last night, but she said it was only a prank. She said Stanley recommended it. I guess he doesn't like you." He looked at me, and we both laughed.

"When I asked her about the slashed hose and the bicycle tire, she looked genuinely puzzled. Brian may have accomplished those deeds on his own or maybe under Stanley's supervision." He relaxed into the couch and slipped his arm around my shoulder.

"Stanley, that impotent jerk, playing adolescent games with me. What did I ever do to him?"

Jake let go a short laugh. "Let's see. Maybe your influence over Michael. Neither Cory nor Stanley was happy Michael held you in such regard. Although he's out of the picture now, Stanley carries a grudge. I think he wanted to leave his calling card in your brewery. I'll find him, and then we'll have a little talk. As for Brian, Teddy bailed him out minutes after we slapped him in jail."

"I feel kind of sorry for him. I'd rather spend my time in a cell than be in debt to my Uncle Teddy, who'll probably keep Brian busy in the brewery for no pay. Then there'll be Teddy's nagging at him all day. And Cory?"

"Jail also, but I think she's trying to get someone to bail her out. She couldn't locate Stanley. Isn't that a big surprise? So she was considering calling Michael."

I paused and thought about what I was going to say next with caution.

"You still think Ronald is guilty of his father's

murder?"

He withdrew his arm from around me and sat up, his eyes darkened with suspicion.

"What do you know?"

I told him about Ronald's trip to the city with Deni and his return here after Jake left last night.

"Where is he now? You'd better tell me, Hera."

Instead, I told him Ronald's story about the shovel, the strange words his father uttered when they met, and my suspicions about Ronald's parentage. Jake wasn't happy that I had kept the story from him, but he relaxed again as I recited my tale.

"It's about time you leveled with me. You have such loyalty to the Ramford family, I find it hard to trust you. Now that everything is out in the open, I can deal with the situation."

I smiled and mentally crossed my fingers. Of course, I hadn't told him about how Ronald failed to show up at Teddy's after he promised to help me.

I was quick to add, "Anyone could have gotten hold of that shovel. Ronald left it behind, so it was there when the murderer met Mr. Ramford that night."

Jake's cell phone rang. He answered and listened while playing with one of the curls that escaped my ponytail.

"What?" There was a note of disbelief and anger in his voice. He got off the couch and moved to the window. He flipped the cell shut, turned and looked at me with disappointment in his eyes.

"Ronald's van ran off the thruway heading north out of the city."

I clapped my hands across my mouth in shock. "Oh, no. Is he all right?"

"He's in a Kingston hospital with a broken clavicle. Deni wasn't with him. He sent a message to you."

"Oh."

"He said to tell you he's sorry he didn't show up today at Teddy's. What the hell is going on?"

I told him. When I finished, he stood at the window, a bolt of lightening ripping apart the night sky. I waited for another flash to follow, but the storm rode away beyond the western hills.

"I've got suspects to question." He walked to the door and paused with his hand on the knob, then turned and looked at me.

"Just so you won't worry, your friend Rafe never killed anybody. Bernie admitted he made up the story and gave the victim a cut of the blackmail money to keep his mouth shut. Then, when Rafe left for the United States, it took Bernie a while to track him down and begin hitting him up for cash again. Rafe got tired of the charade, decided to stop paying and to come clean with the authorities in England on the murder. I contacted them, and there was no report of a murder. All these years, he's been paying for a crime he didn't commit."

He settled his hat on his head, straightened it, and looked at me with hard eyes. "You've lied to me all along about one thing and another, Hera. All your lies were to protect the Ramford family, and that hurt me, but I think it's hurt you more."

He touched the brim of his hat. "I'll be going now. 'Night."

I gulped and dug my nails into the palms of my hands. I thought I'd never see him again.

But I did see him, and sooner than I expected. I couldn't sleep Tuesday morning, so I was in my brew barn, my steps weaving in and out of the barley sacks, vats, and fermenter, calculating how much longer I could stay in business. Supplying water to Rafe and to Michael out of the old well was no longer an option for me, and the other well couldn't handle the demand from all three operations. I was back to where I started before I opened the additional well. I sang the same refrain—water, now more limited than before, and still no money. I was counting on Saturday tastings to both sell my product and create public demand for my beers.

Rafe no longer paid blackmail to Bernie, but that didn't mean I could hit him up for a loan. The last time I saw him, I turned my back on him, damning him for his relationship with Bernie and what it had done to me. Wasn't I in the same situation with my connections to the Ramford family? I couldn't blame Jake for how he felt about my defense of them, especially when I shaved the truth so many times on their behalf.

I heard the fire whistle blow, then waited for the warning sounds of the fire engines to see what direction they would take out of town. The sirens got louder, so I ran out of the barn, shaded my eyes against the sun, and saw black smoke and flames rising from behind the ridge separating Ramford's place from mine.

I started up the path to the crest of the hill. When I got to the highest part, I could see the barn and outbuildings of the Ramford brewery in flames. The house, which stood some distance from the other structures, was not yet affected, but it soon could be, depending upon the direction of the wind. Suddenly, an explosion rocked the air, and the house roof lifted off the walls, shingles and splintered wood flying skyward and then cascading to the ground in flaming waves of debris.

The fire engines rumbled up the drive. The men on them jumped off and began their dangerous work. By the time I ran down the hill and arrived at the scene, the heat from the burning buildings was so intense, I couldn't approach the area but could only watch flames consume the place while firefighters struggled to contain the blaze.

A car pulled into the drive, but the crew kept the person from getting too close. I avoided the heat by running to the road and approaching the car from behind. Thank God. It was Michael, but where was everybody else? I touched his arm, and he turned to look at me.

"I spent the night out and was just coming home when I heard the sirens."

"It's all gone," I said. I searched the inferno, trying to make out the shape of the barns. Michael's eyes registered only anguish.

"No, no. It's more than gone. My mother brought Ronald home from the hospital yesterday. Both of them were in that house. You don't think Ronald could have set this fire, do you? He wouldn't return to his old ways, would he?"

His words jarred a memory. He said the same thing to me when the hop house burned. I remembered the day well. Michael and I had met on the hill above the place and were making ourselves comfortable on an old log when we saw Ronald run from the broken-down shack. A few minutes later, we spotted flames jumping out of the windows. In little more than a half an hour, the only things left at the site were blackened timbers.

Michael turned to me that day and said what I was thinking also, that Ronald must have set that fire. Soon after, Ronald, accused by his father and with the threat of arrest for arson in his future, left his home as a teen and returned less than a week ago.

"What did you say?"

"I said Mother and Ronald were in there."

"No, the other." He turned his face toward me.

"What? Oh, that Ronald must have set the fire. You know, like that hop house fire." He looked back at the flames, and I saw something on his face I remembered from that other day, as well. It was a look of ecstasy.

That look pierced my being, and everything I had felt about Michael fell like burning embers, dying black in the dust at our feet. Without thinking, the words tumbled from my mouth.

"Ronald never burned down that hop house. It was you, Michael. Somehow you set that fire, and Ronald saw you. He went in there to try to put out the fire. I was your witness, wasn't I? We both framed poor Ronald, but this is different. This fire took two lives. You're a monster. Those two lives mean you are sole proprietor of Ramford Brewery."

He grabbed my arm. "Don't be stupid. This fire makes me sole proprietor of nothing. There's nothing left. You said it yourself." He said these words like a man overburdened by his life, but I couldn't tell if the expression on his face was anguish or anger.

I turned my attention back to the buildings in front of me. Little remained to remind me this once was one of the most successful small breweries in the Northeast. Now it was charcoal, burned timbers, and twisted steel with the smell of burned malt in the air.

He was right. There remained nothing of his father's work, not the barns or the house.

"You'll have to rebuild." Once the words slipped out of my mouth, I realized that was just what Michael wanted. Not a brewery, but something else. He could now do whatever he desired and not have to run his decisions by anyone.

I wanted to scream at him, but I held my tongue when I heard a car approaching from the road. A county sheriff's vehicle slid to a stop behind us. I saw Jake's face through the windshield.

"Where have you been, Ramford?"

"If you must know, I was at Francine's again."

The back doors of Jake's cruiser opened. Claudia and Ronald got out. I thought Michael paused just a second too long before he said, "Thank God," and ran to embrace his mother. I wasn't being fair. His nanosecond of silence could just as well have been relief at finding his family safe.

Twenty-Four

My phone rang several hours later, and Michael was on the line. I expected to hear from him, and I wasn't surprised he wanted to talk to me.

"Let's make a picnic of it. We'll meet by the old burned hop house and talk."

"I don't think a picnic is really appropriate, do you? Your family lost everything in that fire, and the arson investigation team's initial analysis is that it was set. Doesn't that worry you any? All of you could have been killed."

"Well, we weren't. We're just fine. Besides, we were heavily insured." His voice took on a note of impatience. "Look, I don't want to talk over the phone. Meet me around six. Guess you'll have to bring both the beer and the sandwiches, since I don't have either." He rang off with a chuckle.

I knew Jake still held me in contempt for the lies I told him, but I also knew better than to leave him out of this meeting. Once I called and told him what I was thinking, he seemed to let go of his mad at me.

"I'll be right over."

"Meet me in the barn."

I was opening the fifty-five pound sacks of barley and pouring the grain into the hopper that fed the mash lauder tun. Tomorrow I would add the hot water and begin making my last batch of beer until I got the money to buy more barley.

"Need any help with that?" Jake entered the brew barn just as I was jockeying the last sack of grain across the haymow floor to dump into the hopper.

"Nope. I'm almost finished."

He looked around the barn and seemed to catch the implications of my statement.

"Sorry about that. How long can you hang on?"

"Maybe another month." I slit open the sack and wrestled it into position. "I don't want to talk about that now." I finished the job, threw the sack on the floor, and descended to the metal platform.

Jake joined me there and took a look down into the kettle.

"Hard work."

"Yes, it is, and maybe that's why Michael has no more stomach for the brewing business. Even with all the bells and whistles you can buy, it's still difficult work. Challenging, a science that can go wrong if you're not vigilant." I hesitated. What I wanted to say next wasn't easy, and Jake's nearness made it more difficult.

"I think Michael killed his father." He didn't look shocked. The only reaction he gave was a slight dilation of his pupils.

"I think so, too, but I can't prove it. He's got an ironclad alibi, the most respectable woman in the area, Francine."

I moved away from him on the tiny platform and leaned against the railing. "Oh, she didn't lie about Michael being with her. She just didn't know how easy it was for him to sneak away that night. He drugged her wine or something like that, I suspect. Then he walked from her place over the hills to his own, met his father at the barn, and hit him with the shovel."

"You seem pretty sure of this."

"When I was walking back from the fire this morning, I was thinking how closely knit a group of brewers we were, yet how there were so many secrets among us. We've shared good and bad times, like now with the water shortage. And we are close, geographically close, near enough to make it a short hike from one of our places to another. That's what Michael did. I think he also did that other thing this morning. I think he set the fire." I told Jake about watching Michael the night of the old hop house fire and how his face this morning held that same expression.

"I can't arrest a man on the basis of how his eyes look."

"I know, but Michael is worried. He thinks I know something, and he wants us to meet."

Jake moved forward and grabbed my arms, pulling me toward him. "God, you're a pain, Hera. You're not going to meet him. If what you believe is true, you're a danger to him. I can't let you do this."

I pushed him away from me. "I've let my feelings for Michael get in the way of reason for too long. I don't want that to happen with another man. Let's leave aside the you and me thing until we sort out tonight."

We sorted it out. I would take the direct route to the hop house, arriving there around six, while Jake would take the path that led through the woods, wound around the old mill pond, and came up behind the burned ruins of the barn. He'd be in place, waiting for Michael to arrive, then listen in on our conversation. He asked me to wear a voice-activated recorder, and I agreed.

At five thirty, the recorder was taped to my waist, and I carried a picnic basket with sandwiches and four bottles of my lager in it. It seemed macabre, but fitting, to use picnic items and my brews to entrap a murderer.

I looked at the sky when I left my house. Another ersatz storm was rolling in. I knew not to get my hopes up. Mother Nature was playing one of her tricks, getting us to anticipate rain when all she intended to produce was wind, thunder, and some lightning.

Jake and I walked together for several yards, then he cut off for the pond, while I headed over the ridge toward the hop house. The tape holding the wire in place itched, and I scratched at my waist, then reminded myself I should quit it, or Michael might get suspicious.

I put the picnic basket on the ground and sat on the hill overlooking the charred timbers of the small barn. I recalled the days when Ronald, Michael and I played in the old place. We pretended we were storing and drying hops, all of us determined to become the best beer brewers when we grew up. That didn't happen as we planned, and now I wondered if any of the three of us would be brewing beer this time next year.

The sun worked its way down the sky and hovered near the ridgeline to the west. I checked my watch. Michael was a half-hour late. I inserted my finger into my waistband and tried to move the tape a bit. A hand touched my shoulder.

"Poison oak, poison ivy? Might want to try calamine lotion for that." Michael looked as if he'd run all the way from his place. His face was dripping sweat, and his shirt was soaked under the arms. "Sorry I'm late. Something came up."

I said nothing. My mouth was suddenly too dry to speak. When I glanced up into his face, his eyes appeared black, not their usual twilight blue color, and his words came from lips narrowed in a grimace.

"You have something to tell me, Hera? Is there something you know that you shouldn't?" I screwed up my courage. I had to tell him what I suspected in order to get him to talk.

"You set that fire today, just like you burned that old hop house down years ago. Then you used me to help you frame Ronald for setting the fire. And you killed your father. I don't know why you did, but you killed him, planned it out and drugged Francine so she would sleep through the night. You took the shovel and bashed in your own father's head."

His hand on my shoulder tightened, sending a shot of pain down my arm.

"He wasn't my father."

His words didn't surprise me. He spoke out loud what I had feared since I read Claudia's letters to my father.

"You don't really think I'm a murderer, do you, Hera?" His grip on my shoulder lessened. I turned to look him in the face. Perhaps the light show presented by the storm deceived me, but his face had the gentle look of an innocent man on it.

"I wanted to kill him when he told me I was your half-brother, but when I got to the brew barn, someone had already done the job for me."

"Who, then?" Lightning flashed around us, and raindrops began to fall.

"Any number of people who hated him. Who cares? He got what he deserved. Mother wouldn't have sought comfort elsewhere if he had been a better husband, and Ronald, well, Ronald had his own demons when he was younger." The raindrops came down with greater ferocity, driven now by gusts of wind.

My head buzzed in confusion. None of this made sense. Mr. Ramford told Ronald that he wasn't his son just days before the murder. Or had Ronald lied to me?

"We need to get inside." Michael pulled me toward the broken-down hop house. I didn't want to go with him, but the raindrops hit with such force that they raised welts on my face and arms. He shoved me under a fallen beam and led me to the part of the roof that remained over a corner of the building.

A rustling noise came from behind one of the broken timbers.

I figured Jake's cover was blown so I yelled, "Come on out, Jake." But Jake did not appear. I tried again, "Jake." Michael let out a laugh.

"Just some woodland creature seeking shelter from the storm like we are. I don't think you can expect Jake to arrive here tonight. He had an unfortunate fall, and I think he's lying at the edge of the mill pond as we speak. Did you think after the things you said to me this morning I wouldn't keep an eye on you? I saw the two of you heading out together, and I figured you would set some kind of a trap for me." He twisted my arm, and I cried out in agony.

"Michael, you're hurting me."

As quickly as his voice had protested his innocence just a moment ago, it now turned ugly. He pulled me close to him. "It's a pity, but I think I'm going to have to do more than hurt you. What you suspect about the murder and the fire could get me in a lot of trouble. Better to just remove you from the picture and eliminate a messy investigation of the family."

"Not yet, Dear." The voice was not that of a woodland creature, but rather that of Claudia, who emerged from a darkened corner of the dilapidated structure. The storm made the light dim enough to obscure the expression on her face, but her tone of voice carried authority. Tonight she appeared to be sober, functioning without the crutch of alcohol but with another kind of back-up, a pistol, which she pointed at us. The coolness of her tone frightened me more than Michael's grip on my arm or his threats.

"Don't think I can't use this. Years ago, when I bought that pistol for protection, Michael Senior insisted upon my going to the firing range in town. I'm a pretty good shot yet today."

"Mother, what are you doing here? I told you I'd take care of Hera." Michael pulled me in front of him so that I stood between him and the pistol.

"Can I trust you, Dear? Just like your father, you sometimes lie to me and don't follow through when I tell you to do something. I told you to get rid of that shovel, didn't I? What did you do? You put it in Hera's shed, and it was traced back to Ronald. That got your brother in a lot of trouble."

"I'm not like him, and he's not my father. He told me he wasn't my father, and you told me he wasn't." Michael shouted the words at his mother, but the pistol didn't waver. I didn't understand any of this. My heart banged in my chest, my hands trembled. Despite my fear, I knew my life was forfeit unless I did something. I had to play on whatever tension existed between the two of them to take their focus off me.

I wanted to say something to confuse or annoy one or both of them. I used what I knew about Claudia's propensity for lying, hoping that she hadn't shared the truth or the lie about Ronald's parentage with Michael.

"Wait a minute. I don't get it. When Ronald talked with his father several days before the murder, Mr. Ramford told him that Ronald wasn't his son. Neither one of your boys is a Ramford? You told Jake and me that you didn't have an affair with my father. So who's the father or fathers?" Claudia narrowed her eyes at me for a moment, then dismissed the issue.

"That's not important now. Michael worried that he gave away more than he should have this morning at the fire and that you would try to entrap him into saying something incriminating and convince your police friend to pursue him. An accident. Your death has to look like an accident."

Desperate, I tried another approach. "You know Michael set the fire this morning, don't you? You and Ronald were meant to die when the house burned down."

Claudia's chin came up, and she took her eyes off me and stared at her son. The roar of the wind caught her next words and carried them out through the mangled walls of the hop house. "... you told me ... Ronald ..." She gestured with her pistol at the broken-down remains of the barn.

"Don't listen to Hera, Mother. I'd never burn down my own house. It had to have been Ronald. Ronald always liked fires. He did it, set it somehow before you left for the sheriff's office and timed it to go off when both of you were gone."

The wind drove the rain through the large gaps in the walls, drenching the two of us. Only Claudia, snug in a corner of the barn, remained dry.

"Is that true, Dear, or have you lied to me yet again? Did you set that fire and try to kill Mummy? Lying again. Just like your father."

"I'm not like him!" Michael yelled. Something heavy, probably a tree limb, hit the side wall, startling all of us. I took the opportunity to throw myself toward an opening in the back wall and take my chances in the howling storm. The ping of a pistol shot rang out behind me, splintering a wood beam as I ducked underneath. Then I was caught in the maelstrom of rain, wind, and lightning strikes. I ran for the woods ahead.

Once in the cover of the pines, I looked behind me, but it was impossible to see if anyone followed. I headed toward the only place where I knew I could hide, as well as find refuge in this storm, the old mill where Michael, Ronald, and I had played as children. I hoped Michael didn't remember it. I wanted him to assume that I headed for home or went to find Jake. *Jake.* Once I got to the mill, I could find help for Jake, but for now, I had to be certain I wasn't being pursued.

Twenty-Five

Water continued to flood down on me, but the wind had let up. I could pick my path through the woods toward my destination in the light breaking through the whirling clouds. The mill loomed out of the downfall up ahead, giving me the incentive to make a final dash for it.

The metal roof was intact, but the wooden walls were rotted, and sections on the second floor had fallen onto the first. As I approached the building from downstream, I could see the rain had swollen the creek. Brown, churning water buffeted the broken wheel, but it remained steady, its paddles covered with moss and wet decaying leaves. I threw myself through the door and banged it shut behind me. If anyone entered the building, I was certain to hear them when they tried to open the door on its rusted hinges, but I hadn't counted on how clever and fast Michael could be. He stood in front of me and to one side of the window through which I could see the wheel rock back and forth as the water tried to entice it into action.

"Where's Claudia?"

He smiled and opened his mouth, but if he said anything, I couldn't hear it because of the noise of the driving rain on the roof. I made a dash for the open window. Michael moved as quickly as I, reached out and grabbed my leg as I ran by him. His fingers dug into my calf for several seconds. Then, because my leg was slick with water and his hand was wet, his hold on me slipped. I dove through the window and landed on the top paddle of the wheel, thinking that I could climb down the wheel. Then what? Throw myself into the swollen, turbulent stream?

Before I could think through my next move, Michael leaped onto the wheel, claiming the paddle below mine. But he didn't count on his extra weight, the rotten boards, and the slippery surface of the paddles. The wheel broke beneath him, and he plunged toward the churning water. For a moment, his hand got hold of another paddle, and I thought he was safe. Without thinking of my own danger, I reached down to help him back up and into the mill. A puzzled look crossed his face, then his features were obliterated by a curtain of rain. I thought I saw him shake his head no before he plummeted into the roiling caldron below him. I wiped the rain from my eyes and blinked When I looked again, I could no longer see his head above the water. I pulled myself onto the ledge by the wheel and continued to scan the stream below, but I knew I'd never see him again.

I could do nothing more here, and my cold, wet clothing clung to my skin, making me shiver. I couldn't think about that now. I needed to search for Jake and hope that I found him alive and could get help for him.

I backed through the window of the mill, almost too fatigued to get on my feet. There was a lull in the rain's clattering on the roof, and I thought I heard breathing behind me. I whirled around, expecting to find that my nerves were playing tricks on me. I was mistaken.

"Where's my son? Where is he?" Claudia stood inside the door to the mill, her clothes soaked through, her silvery, shining helmet of hair now hanging like limp seaweed around her face. She still carried the pistol in her hand, but it hung limply at her side.

I said nothing. With a shaking hand, I pointed out the window to the stream below. She approached the window and looked down.

"You killed him."

"No, I tried to save him, but the paddle broke. He slipped and fell into the water." Claudia turned toward me and leveled the pistol in my direction.

"No, you killed him, and now I'm going to kill you, just like I did your father." With her free hand, she smoothed back the wet tendrils of hair from her face, then flipped her head in a gesture of carefree sexuality. "He rejected my advances when I needed him most. I wasn't as young as when we had our fling, but I was still attractive, and Michael Senior was ignoring me, as he usually did. I went to your father for comfort. He said he didn't want me."

"So you shot him?"

"No, you fool, I got Michael Senior to do it for me. I told him the two of us were having an affair, that I wanted to end it, but that your father wouldn't let me go. He took my gun and shot him, made it look like suicide."

She came closer. I considered my options. Jumping into the stream wasn't one of them. I saw what the water did to Michael, pulling him under and burying him. She seemed intent upon telling me her story, so I let her talk, hoping some opportunity would present itself soon.

"We had a few good years then, Michael Senior and I. Then he began to wander again. So I told him some more stories about your father. I told him Ronald was your father's son. Then I told him Michael was your father's son. The night he died, I told him I lied about everything. He didn't know what to believe, and that was fine with me. As he lay dying on the barn floor, his last words to me were, 'Tell me the truth.' I just laughed."

She was close enough that I could have reached out and touched the pistol with my fingertip.

"I always liked you, Hera. You had real gumption, and I thought you would have made Michael a good wife, shared his interests and put some backbone in the boy."

I was shocked. "But that would have been …"

"Incest? Well, maybe, but who was to know, unless Michael Senior blabbed it all over? He told Ronald when they met days before the murder, and he told Michael. Michael was a funny one. He wanted to be his father's son, yet he didn't, and he hated the way his father treated him this last year. Senior was going to tell you he suspected his sons weren't his, and I couldn't have that. There was my reputation to consider. So I stopped him, with Michael's help, of course."

I didn't want to believe Michael was responsible for killing his father. I shook my head no. I didn't want to hear what Claudia was saying, but she rushed on with her story.

"Senior told me he was meeting you in the brew barn to tell you about Michael. That would have ruined my plan for you and Michael, and I couldn't have that, so I sneaked into the barn and hit him from behind with the shovel. Hit him several times, you know. Michael saw me put him down, and he got me out of there and back to the house. Made me a nice cup of tea, too. Michael was a good boy. I'll miss him."

I held out my hand to her. "What's the truth about the boys' father?" I had to ask, not only for my sake but for that of Sally's child.

"The truth isn't important. It often isn't, I've found. Sometimes you have to create the truth and then live with that. But you're lucky, Hera. You won't have to worry anymore about your father and me and whether Michael and Ronald might be your half-brothers. The truth is, I don't need you anymore. You're irrelevant now."

The woman had to be demented. She didn't seem to be able to discern lies from truth, nor seem to care. Right now, neither did I. I made one last feeble try at saving myself.

"I'm wired. Everything since we met in the old hop house has been recorded." I pulled up my shirt and ripped the recorder off my waist. "It's a remote feedback to the sheriff's department. They heard everything, and they've got it all on tape. It won't even do you any good to destroy it, but here." I tossed the wire toward her. She wasn't stupid enough to try and catch it, but when she ducked to one side, I kicked out and connected with her ankle. She went down but managed to keep hold of the pistol. Her shot went wide, and I was on the run again.

Twenty-Six

I was taking a chance not making a break for someplace safe, but Jake needed my help. I headed upstream to the millpond and around the south shore. Although the rain slowed, it continued to fall as if it intended to make up for its absence all spring and summer. Gusts of wind whipped my wet clothes against my body, and I was far colder than I had been in the shelter of the old mill.

The pond's swampy and reedy southern edge provided good cover for someone lying on the ground. I assumed Michael wanted to make the assault look like an accident and had used his hands or a tree limb to attack Jake. There was hope he was still alive. I hoped I would find Jake in a dry spot where a blow wouldn't have put him face down in the water. I searched the cattails and reeds, but it was slow going because the water and mud sucked at my shoes with every step I took. Rain continued to drip into my eyes, and I wiped it away with my damp sleeve, a useless endeavor.

I knew Jake had to have come this way to circle around behind the hop house. Now I was losing the light. Something in the reeds ahead caught my eye, and I waded out to it. A shoe. I picked it up to examine it, but it was old and slimy from months in the water. As I straightened up, something cold pressed against my neck. *Claudia's gun barrel at my head.* But the object was removed, and I heard a familiar and welcome voice.

"What the hell are you doing here, caressing an old boot?"

"Jake." I turned and threw my arms around him. "Are you all right?"

"It took me a minute to tell it was you. I'm fine, unless you count this knot on my head as a problem. I'm alive, and that's something. Where the hell have you been? I tried to call your cell, and I got no answer."

My cell. I'd forgotten all about it. I patted my jeans pockets and then remembered. I'd placed it in the picnic basket, which I'd left on the hill when Michael pulled me into the hop house.

"I've got my men combing this area looking for you. Someone, probably Michael, ambushed me. I guess he didn't have the heart to kill me, so he just hit me on the head."

"He could have killed you. Are you sure you're okay?" I reached out to touch the back of his head, but he ducked away.

"Fine, fine, but what about you? What happened? I heard some of the conversation between you and Claudia when I came to, but I didn't know where you were. Where's Michael?"

"Probably dead." I explained to him about the incident at the hop house and then what happened in the mill.

"You were still wearing the wire, right? We got this on tape. Great."

"Not quite. I threw the recorder at Claudia, and I don't know where it landed. She may have picked it up and left the mill by now."

Jake shook his head and rolled his eyes at me as if my intelligence equaled that of a one-celled organism. He flipped open his phone and told two of his men to meet us at the mill.

A search there produced no Claudia and no recorder. I pointed out the broken paddle boards to Jake. The fresh breaks of the old wood showed the only use of the mill house within the last several years.

"You believe me, don't you? Claudia was here."

"I believe you, but that means now I've got a killer on the loose, and she doesn't have anywhere to run. Her house is gone. Think, Hera. Where would Claudia go?"

"Where's Ronald?"

"At the Pines Motel in town. Okay. It's worth a try."

I turned to leave, but Jake held up his hand to stop me for a moment while he called for additional officers to check the motel and determine whether Ronald was safe.

"Thanks for having your officers check on him."

"What do you think? Would she kill him?"

"I don't know. She seems demented to me. I don't know if she's told the truth or nothing but lies. Maybe she doesn't either."

I wrapped my arms around myself. My teeth hit against one another, and my body began a shaking that I couldn't stop.

"Let's get you home before you go into shock." Jake draped his jacket over my shoulders. "Think you can make it back on foot?"

"I'll be fine. I just need to get into a hot bath." I turned to look back at the old mill as we headed down the path toward my place.

"It was our playhouse, a place of such romance and

adventure when we were kids. No one else thought about it much, so we had it to ourselves to act out our fantasies. We had fun. Now, all I can think about is the look of despair on Michael's face when he let go of my hand."

"I'm coming with you to look for Claudia. I just need a quick shower and some dry clothes." The negative look on Jake's face said he didn't want me along. "Okay, I'll forget the shower."

At the house I ran for the stairs before he could say no or leave. On the way to my bedroom, I heard Jake speak into his phone, although I couldn't catch his words. I grabbed a dry pair of jeans, a long-sleeved shirt, and my rain poncho.

"We found her. If you're coming, get down here." I was at his side before he could draw another breath.

"Where? At the motel with Ronald? He's okay, isn't he?"

"He's fine. No, one of my men spotted her car in front of the Carriage Day Spa."

I snapped my fingers. "Of course. Claudia was a mess when she left the mill. She had to know you'd be looking for her."

"So she's getting a massage? If I were in her shoes, I'd be in the next state."

"Not if you're Claudia Ramford, perfect wife and hostess. She knows this is the end. C'mon." I was out the door and headed for the SUV.

"I guess the only way I'd get you out of the car would be to drag you out." Jake started the engine, and we slammed down the drive.

A few minutes later, he conferred with one of his men

who stood watch at the entrance to the Day Spa.

"I checked at the desk, and the woman there said Mrs. Ramford arrived about an hour ago. Tina had a cancellation and took her right in for a shampoo and blow dry, and now she's in the back room having her nails done." The young officer read these facts out of his notebook in a shaking voice. "You think she might be holding someone hostage in there, sir?"

I butted in. "No, I think Mrs. Ramford is more concerned with selecting the right color of polish."

Jake shoved me behind him and entered the salon with his pistol drawn. The young woman at the desk pointed toward a hallway leading to the private rooms in the back, but the manager appeared at that moment.

"You can't come in here with a gun. This is a spa, not a firing range."

"One of your customers already came in here armed. Step out of the way, please." She did as Jake ordered.

We proceeded down the hallway. Three doors opened off to the right. Only one was closed. Jake looked around the corner of the other two and proceeded on to the last door. I was right behind him as he moved on. At the closed door, he hesitated with his pistol held at face level in front of him.

"Police. Open the door."

A dark-haired woman pulled the door open. Jake grabbed her and spun her around and out of the room, then entered with his weapon raised. I moved in behind him.

Claudia Ramford sat in an armchair. Her perfect fingertips shone red in the room's light, and her feet rested in a bath of sudsy water. She was wrapped in a terry robe, and she looked nothing like the dripping wet killer I tangled with in the old mill. Her face had recently been made up, and her light hair had the finish of fine silver.

"Oh, dear, I wish you hadn't arrived so soon. Now I'll have to go to jail without my French pedicure. I don't suppose you might wait another fifteen minutes?"

"Where's the weapon?" Jake still held his pistol at the ready in front of him. If Claudia felt any threat from him, her face didn't show it. It remained as implacable as the surface of a frozen lake.

"I checked it along with my wet clothes. My locker key is in the pocket of my robe, but I don't want to ruin my nails. Could you get it for me, Hera, dear?"

Jake shook his head at me when I stepped forward. He nodded at the officer who had come back to the room with us. He removed the key from Claudia's pocket and left to find the locker area.

In several seconds, he came back into the room. "It's there."

Jake lowered his weapon, and I sighed, my body suddenly freed of the tension it had held for several hours. Every muscle now ached with the release.

"Take over here," Jake directed his man, then collapsed into my arms.

Twenty-Seven

"He's got a concussion. He was hit on the head and lost consciousness. He'll be lucky he doesn't have permanent damage." The doctor spoke to me as if I were Jake's mother and should have known better than to let him play with his criminal friends. "He needs rest, and we'll be monitoring him closely. You can stay for a few moments, then out you go." The doctor left the hospital room, white coat flapping behind him.

Jake smiled at me and gave a little wave from his bed.

"I'm fine."

"That's what you said when I found you at the pond. You lied to me. You were not and are not fine." I took the chair beside the bed.

"I lied then, but now I am fine."

"How do I know when to believe you?"

He looked at me with both eyebrows raised and delivered a zinger. "Now you know how I felt."

"Don't get cheeky with me, or I won't bring you your bedpan."

The door swung open, and Rafe entered.

"Rafe. I've been wanting to see you." I arose from the chair and approached him. I reached out and touched his arm.

"And me, you." Rafe took both my hands in his and squeezed them gently.

"Would you like me to leave so the two of you can work out everything?" Jake flipped the sheet to one side and made as if he were going to get out of bed.

"Sorry, old man. I just wanted to stop by and see how you're doing."

"I'd be okay, if I had more sympathetic visitors."

"Aha. On that note, I'd better leave, but before I do, I just want to apologize for not taking you into my confidence about Bernie. I guess he's going to spend some years in prison for blowing up the well."

"And for breaking into your brewery and locking poor Henry in the fermenting room, planting the yeast in my place, and slitting Francine's malt bags open. He's a real whiz at picking locks, isn't he?" Rafe didn't reply to my question, just shook his head and had the good manners to look embarrassed.

"I don't quite get why he did all that. He couldn't have had anything against me or Francine. He didn't know us," I said. One of my hands rested on Jake's arm, the other was still captured in Rafe's.

Jake pulled the pillows higher behind his head. "Why don't you tell her, Rafe?"

Rafe looked down at the floor, then back up at me. He cleared his throat. Before he could offer an explanation, the doctor stuck his head into the room, gestured with his thumb toward the hallway, and mouthed the word, "Out."

Rafe shook Jake's hand, and I kissed his mouth, fussed with his pillows, and then followed Rafe out into the corridor.

"Well?" I stood with my hands on my hips, awaiting Rafe's explanation for Bernie's shenanigans.

"Bernie knew I'd get the message. Once he made

himself known, I put it all together, as he knew I would. He didn't have to threaten me for more money. His activities made it clear to me what he was capable of. All of my friends were in danger unless I came through, and I did. Then I stopped paying him, and he blew your well, another demonstration of his seriousness about being paid. By then, I knew the only way to handle him was to get Jake to put him behind bars. So I came out with the truth, knowing it might put me in prison, too."

"Let's get a cup of coffee in the cafeteria," I said. As we walked toward the elevators, I tucked my hand into the crook of his arm. "It must have been awful living in fear of Bernie appearing in your life."

"To be honest, the guilt over what I had done, taken a man's life, was often overpowering, but Bernie had my number. He knew I was a weakling, that I hadn't the integrity to turn myself in. He counted on my cowardice."

"In the end, you weren't a coward. You did tell him no."

"And look what he did. Blew up your well."

We paused in front of a window.

"Will you look at that? It's still raining. So you see, I really don't need that well after all."

He reached out and touched my cheek, a gesture my father often used when we were making up after a fight. "You're being terribly nice about that, you know."

"I know, so I guess you owe me a favor."

"Anything."

"Be a reference for me when I go to the bank for a loan, will you?" I held up my hand as he tried to speak. "Uh, uh, no loan from you. I want to do this on my own."

Ronald demonstrated his gentle and giving nature by using the land and the insurance on the brewery house to post bond for Claudia. We never discussed whether he believed his mother murdered his father or his father's story that he wasn't Michael Senior's son. All he said to me about the situation was that he'd lived all his life believing he knew his family, and he owed his mother his allegiance now. How ironic that all these years, the community thought this sensitive individual was the black sheep of the family, the pyromaniac, the son who ran off and left his mother and brother to cope with a controlling and philandering father.

The judge set bail, because the case against Claudia revolved around her confession, which she altered in every interview with the police. We never found the recorder I'd thrown at her. Perhaps she took it, threw it away, hid it, or didn't remember where it was. I would have to testify against her, an act I approached with great confusion. I believed the part of her story where she claimed she killed Michael Senior. The rest of it puzzled both Jake and me. When I used the word *crazy* to describe her behavior, we both knew how the lawyer would present her case.

The only constant part of her story was her denial that anyone helped her dispose of the shovel, a statement contradicting what she had told me about Michael's involvement. At times, she seemed lucid, and in some of those moments, she claimed that her husband fathered both, one, or neither of her sons. We never found the letters she wrote to my father. In fact, she never mentioned him in any of her dialogue with the authorities.

Claudia moved into one of the newly constructed condominiums in town. I thought she would fill the spare bedroom with her quilting work and take up stitching together her works of art while she awaited the trial. Against Jake's wishes, I visited her several weeks after our struggle in the old mill to ask about the recorder. I hoped to catch her in a mood for truth telling. She swept me into the spare bedroom to show me a new project. Piles of yarn, along with stacks of baby clothes, toys, a crib, stroller, and playpen, filled the room. She had gotten wind of Sally's pregnancy and put two and two together.

"I'm going to be a grandmother."

"Does that mean I'm about to become an aunt?" She gave me a sharp look and ignored my question.

"It's going to be such fun." She wandered around the pastel yellow bedroom touching the tiny clothes and moving baby objects from one location to another and then back again.

"Does Sally know you're doing this?"

A ripple broke through her calm. "Get out. Get out! You're here to ruin everything for me," she yelled. I ran for the door, fearing the reappearance of the Claudia from the old mill.

I hoped it wasn't my question about Sally that sent Claudia down to the café the next day, where she threatened to try and take the baby away from Sally. Sally called me on my cell.

"Get over here quick. Claudia's in the front of the shop and spinning out of control. She just swept an entire shelf of teacups onto the floor."

"Call the police. I'll be right there."

By the time I arrived, Sally was out in front of her shop, and we heard the police sirens heading toward the store. When the police stormed the bakery, they didn't find

Claudia inside but at the back door, a gasoline can in one hand and a Bic lighter in the other.

"A passion for fires must run in the family." I tried to joke with Sally after the local cops took Claudia off to jail. Then I realized I was also talking about the baby's father. "I'm sorry."

"It's okay. I know you're trying to make me feel better. Sometimes I wonder if having this baby is such a good thing, but then I think there are my great genes and maybe some from your family, too." I hugged her for that. I felt like an aunt whether the biology said I was or not.

I left Sally up to her elbows in flour just as Jake arrived at the bakery. "Work makes me feel better. How's the head today?"

Jake touched the spot above his neck where Michael had hit him.

"Not there anymore and no permanent damage, unless you count occasional waves of passion for a local brewer an issue."

I punched him in the arm. "You think Sally's safe here, or should she come home with me?"

"Bet on it. The judge will revoke Claudia's bond any minute now, and I think she'll be sent off for observation and kept someplace away from society for a long time."

Sally gave us both a floury hug and continued with her kneading as we left the shop.

Jake and I stood in front of my truck.

"DNA would tell us something," Jake said.

"I thought about that, but Ronald says he's just not interested in knowing who his biological father is. He asked me if I was okay with that. I don't know if I am, but it's up to Ronald." I hesitated, knowing I didn't want to ask the next question, but I knew I had to find out. "No body yet?"

Jake shook his head no.

"When you do find, uh, him, is there any legal reason why you need to know Michael's parentage?"

"Not unless the lawyers think it's relevant. With Claudia's latest escapade, I don't think the case is likely to be tried anytime soon. No, I was thinking of something else, your DNA and the baby's."

I took in a quick breath. Yes, that was possible, but ... "But that's Sally's call not mine."

"Talk to her."

On the way home, I passed Jeremiah on his bike. I stopped the truck and pulled over to the side of the road. We hadn't spoken since I visited him after his bicycle accident.

"I see you got your bike fixed. Where are you heading?"

"Out to your place. I got fired from my position at Teddy's. He said I was too particular and slow in my work, so I was wondering if you'd consider hiring me back?" He said this with his head down, not allowing his eyes to meet mine.

"That's Teddy. Are you surprised? I was teaching you to be a brewer, not a hired hand at a brewery."

"Teddy also said he had all the help he needed right now with Brian working for him." That got a laugh out of me.

"You could have told me where you were going when you left me, you know. I would have understood the need for more money."

He kept his eyes cast downward and gave a tiny nod of

his head.

"I can't pay you as much as Teddy, but I will give you an increase in pay now that I've got my bank loan."

He raised his head and pumped his arm in the air. "Yes. What's first on the agenda?"

"Cleaning out the mash tun."

"No."

Claudia was assigned to the psychiatric wing of the Women's Correctional Institution in Payack. I heard she took up her quilt work again, stitching together blocks of fabric with the skill of a five-year-old. She acted more and more disturbed as the days went by, making up nonsensical tunes and only talking to the people her imagination created.

Jake said she seemed happy enough, but out of touch with any world but her own. It looked as if she would never leave the ward nor stand trial for the murder of her husband. Who was the true Claudia? This crazy woman, the cold, rational killer, or the perfect wife? Did anyone know? Did she?

Ronald and Deni planned to build on the Ramford property, but until Michael's body was found, the court wouldn't let them proceed.

It rained almost every day in the month since the incident at the hop house and mill. Early one morning, when the downpour threatened to wash away the road in front of my place, Jake's car pulled into the river which once was my drive. His face was grim when he entered my kitchen.

"All this water finally washed Michael's body down to the Susquehanna, where it caught on a pile of limbs and brush down near Chenango Forks."

"That's fifty miles from here. Could he have made it that far ...? "

"He was dead in minutes after he went in at the mill. He didn't suffer, Hera."

"I'll have to tell Sally."

"I already did. She's fine. Her mother came to visit yesterday, so she's got someone with her."

"Oh." I turned my back to him and stared out the kitchen window. Through the pouring rain, I could just make out the new addition I was adding to my barn. Only the frame was up, progress hampered by the wet weather.

Jake came to the window and put his arms around me.

"What are you thinking?"

"I've got to increase my production, but this rain is preventing me from getting the addition finished. There are September and October tastings yet, and I need more product. Don't worry about me. I'm okay about Michael. I knew he was dead."

He nuzzled my neck.

"I've got the day off. How about we spend a quiet morning and afternoon here?"

"Maybe you've got the day off, but I don't."

But Jake could be so persuasive.

Early afternoon hunger pangs drove us out of my bedroom and down into the kitchen. The rain had stopped an hour before, and the sun shone in a blue sky devoid of any remaining clouds. Jake and I sat at the table devouring salami and cheese sandwiches accompanied by my newest ale, Summer Serendipity, when we heard a car turn into my lane, then another, and another. Soon the drive filled with vehicles I recognized, and people poured out of them and into the yard. Everyone seemed to be equipped with a tool of some sort, hammers, saws, both hand and electric, and other building paraphernalia such as tape measures, saw horses, and ladders.

"Barn raising, barn raising," they chanted as they made their way toward my brew house. Jake and I ran out after them.

"Did we disturb something?" Rafe was brandishing a hammer and a smile saying he knew damn well what they disturbed but didn't think we minded. Teddy leaned a ladder against the two-by-fours forming the walls and began to pull his ample frame upward. I held my breath, hoping the rungs would support him.

"This is great. We can do the same for you when you're ready to start rebuilding your brew barn." Jake addressed his remarks to Ronald and Deni who dragged sawhorses into place for the lumber needing to be cut.

"Not a brew barn. We're going to set up a winery. We're from California, and we're more familiar with wine." Deni and Ronald smiled into each other's faces.

"Where do you want me to put these?" asked Francine. She jockeyed several two-by-fours toward the structure.

"No Marsh?" I asked.

"No Marsh. He moved on. Went back to the restaurant business. I'm looking for another brew master. Got any ideas?"

"Well, you can't have him now, but in another year or so, Jeremiah might be your man."

I was helping lift a rafter into place when I heard another car pull up. It was Sally and her mother. If pregnant women glow, then Sally would win the prize for illumination.

"The results of the amnio came back, and it's a girl." She set a basket of bread, pastries and muffins on one of the picnic tables we used for tastings. "You're going to be an aunt."

"We don't know that."

"I know it, and what difference does it make whether you're the biological aunt or not? As far as I'm concerned, you'll be babysitting a niece when I want to get out."

Jake, bare-chested and looking very yummy, came up to me.

"Everything's perfect, huh?" He threw his arms around me and hugged me, then followed the hug with a kiss.

I looked back toward the house and up at the bedroom window.

"Just about. But I think we could use more rain."

Meet Author Lesley A. Diehl

Lesley retired from her life as a professor of psychology and reclaimed her country roots by moving to a small cottage in the Butternut River Valley in Upstate New York. In the winter she migrates to old Florida —cowboys, scrub palmetto, and open fields of grazing cattle, a place where spurs still jingle in the post office. Back north, she devotes her afternoons to writing and, when the sun sets, relaxing on the bank of her trout stream, sipping tea or a local microbrew.

Lesley was the winner of the Sleuthfest 2009 short story contest. You can visit her on her website: www.lesleydiehl.com. She loves to hear from her readers at LesDieh60@aol.com.

Breinigsville, PA USA
30 August 2010
244554BV00001B/1/P